JULIETTE MILLER

HIGHLANDER
Mine

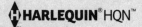
HARLEQUIN® HQN™

Recycling programs
for this product may
not exist in your area.

ISBN-13: 978-0-373-77833-1

HIGHLANDER MINE

Copyright © 2014 by Juliette Miller

Once again,
For M

CHAPTER ONE

THE DANGER OF the journey ahead was equal to the perils we had left behind, this I knew. My knowledge of the Highlands was practically nonexistent. I might as well have been embarking on an escapade to the jungles of Africa, or captaining my own pirate ship to the newly discovered Americas.

Yet I was glad to be free of stuffy, seedy Edinburgh. I had never been past its borders and I was sure we had entered another world entirely, one that was as free as it was possible to be. As we hitched rides farther and farther up into the rolling peaks of the high country, it seemed impossible that such a place could harbor threats of any kind, so peaceful and serene its landscape appeared. We could hide ourselves in these picturesque hills and protected valleys, I was sure. No more murderous ganglords to contend with. No cardsharks or knife fights. No bawdy dens full of loose women and predatory men. Just wide-open countryside, glistening expanses of sparkling, sun-shimmered water and an endless azure sky.

Of course, there *were* dangers. I was a young woman traveling alone, after all, aside from my small nephew, who fancied himself a mighty warrior but was in fact a nine-year-old waif with a toy wooden sword that he clutched even now, in his sleep, as we rode along on the back of a hay wagon. Its driver was unaware of our quiet presence—we had become surprisingly adept at keeping ourselves hidden, with all the practice we'd had over days past. As soon as the wagon slowed, we'd jump and take our chances with the next mode of transport.

I wasn't sure of our exact destination. The Highlands had seemed a good place to hide from our pursuers. Indeed it was a perfect choice. Was there a more expansive place on earth? I doubted as much, though I'd only read books on the subject of travel. I had spent my entire life cooped up in two city residences only streets apart. And, while the social divide of my homes' geography might as well have seen oceans between them, this was a detail that hardly mattered now. My past was well and truly behind me.

At least for now.

We'd been on the road for five days, climbing ever higher into the undulating green mountains. We'd seen very few people. Farmers, mostly. A lone fisherman. Shepherds and goatherds, who seemed as mild and docile as the flocks they tended.

Aye, this world was new to me, but I wasn't *that* naive. Men were men, after all, and I knew of their tendencies far too well. Everyone had heard of the Highlands clans and their armies, their fearsome

warriors and their bloody battles. Watching the glowing orb of the yellow sun hover ever lower over the
horizon, I wondered now if those stories were merely
folklore. I'd seen no sign of war or aggression in
these lovely heather-peppered hills. Only honest en-
deavor and peaceful coexistence.

It might have been a sixth sense or the slide of
a silver-edged cloud over the low-hanging sun, but
some instinctive flutter warned me that safety was
only a temporary illusion. Despite this, I felt wary but
not afraid. Even sword-wielding warriors were pref-
erable to the threats we'd left behind. At least skilled
soldiers loyal to their cause and their kin might have
some sense of honor and integrity, not like the law-
less, malevolent beast who would be scouring Edinburgh at this very moment to find our trail.

I only wished we could travel faster. I would go
to the very ends of the earth to hide and protect
Hamish. As I looked around at the countryside, it
occurred to me that we might have actually reached
a place where that might be possible.

The wagon driver slowed his horses to a walk.
I peered around the back of the wagon to see we
were approaching a large tavern. We'd reached some
oasis of community within this vast green desert of
solitude.

I shook my nephew. "Hamish," I whispered.
"Wake up."

Hamish was instantly alert, his dark eyes bright,
his sword held in his small fist. He understood the

danger, even if he didn't grasp the severity of our current predicament. It helped that his lifelong dream was to travel to the Highlands, a desire that seemed almost innate. He'd yearned for an adventure for as long as I could recall.

And now, despite the gravity of our situation, I almost smiled at his sparked excitement. He loved the open majesty of this place, so different from the enclosed, squalid streets of the city. "You've taken ridiculously well to this life on the run," I told him quietly.

He perched at the edge of the wagon's deck, his sandy brown hair tousled and flecked with hay. He looked back at me, a smile on his beatific face. "So have you, Ami," he whispered, pronouncing the address with all the flair of its French meaning: friend. He was the only person who used this shortened form of my full name, Amelia. Once, a short lifetime ago, I had attended one of the most exclusive schools in Edinburgh. Hamish had never had such a privilege. So I'd taken it upon myself to teach him everything I knew. It was one of the few things I had to be proud of: my nephew, at the age of nine, could read, write, do sums and speak basic French better than many of the fully grown men who frequented my family's establishment. I was slightly less proud of Hamish's uncanny knack not only for counting cards but also for dealing them. *I'm only taking after you, Ami,* he'd said to me. *You're the best dealer in Edinburgh.* Whether or not it was an accurate accusation was no longer relevant. I'd only done what I needed to do to survive, as I would again, in whatever way this new life required.

I held his arm, taking in the details of our surroundings. It was dusk now and the dimming daylight would give us an advantage. A thick copse stood behind the tavern: a place to take cover until we could fully assess the clientele of the inn. Wagons of many descriptions were parked along the road, and upward of twelve horses had been tied to a hitching rail. They were slow, sturdy farm horses. None were coated with sweat as though they'd been ridden at pace all the way from Edinburgh. I felt confident that there was nothing to fear here, that our pursuers were a long way from tracing our trail to this unlikely hideout.

"Now," I whispered.

The slow pace of the wagon made the disembarkment easy enough. Our only belongings were Hamish's sword and a small bag I carried, which contained two woolen blankets, a single spare, fine dress of my sister's, a wineskin full of water and a few coins I'd managed to take from the cashbox as we'd made our escape. I had also brought the small red book that was my most sentimental possession; in it, I had recorded dreams, scribbled poems and wishes, and drawn pictures of trees and stars and fanciful yearnings. An impractical possession, aye, but symbolically precious to me nonetheless and light enough to carry. Holding on to Hamish's hand, I led him past the entrance of the tavern and into the woods. We needed to check our appearances and get our story straight.

Tonight, it seemed, we might need to put all our skills of deceit and persuasion to good use. We were both, it had to be said, somewhat gifted in the ways of trickery, since we'd had a regular need to fabricate tales to various people and on a daily basis, like debt collectors, upset wives or the law, to name a few. These were skills we had honed over many years: an unfortunate necessity of our lifestyle, but one I was now glad we had some practice with.

"I'm hungry," Hamish said. "I want some meat and potatoes with gravy, some stew with bread fresh from the oven and melted butter and some—"

"Aye," I said. "But first, what's it to be? This tavern is sure to be full of local farmers and traders. They'll likely know each other, and they'll know that we're not from around here. We'll need a convincing story. I could get work here possibly, as a cleaner or a cook. We need money."

"A *cook?* You don't know how to cook, Ami. They'll probably want you to perform other services. Why don't we just offer up a card game and *win* some money?" Regrettably, my nephew was far too worldly for his own good.

"We're not playing cards anymore," I said. "We're starting a new life. An honest one. One that doesn't involve cheating, stealing, smuggling or gambling."

"But gambling is so much easier than working. And besides, it's the only thing we know how to do."

This riled me. But it would hardly do to get upset with him. It was my responsibility to be not only his guardian but also his role model. I would have to show him that honesty was more effective than the life we were used to. I hoped I could. I wasn't sure whether my new philosophy was even true, nor did I have any idea how to employ it. "It *seems* easier, Hamish. But it isn't. Look how it's turned out for all of us. Hiding, separated, on the run. Gambling is like stealing, when you use the kinds of tricks we do. Stealing makes people angry. You know it as well as I do. 'Tis up to us to find a better way for ourselves."

My nephew looked up at me, unconvinced.

"Or at least *try* to," I said, a suggestion that was met with at least a degree of acquiescence. His eyebrows furrowed in the middle as he mulled this over. And I continued to formulate our plan. "I propose that we are well-bred travelers from Edinburgh who have fallen on hard times, whose carriage was—"

"Taken over by bandits!"

I considered this. It wasn't a completely unreasonable suggestion. How else might we have parted ways with our transport? Were there bandits in these parts?

"Mr. Fawkes told me he once got robbed by bandits as he traveled the Highlands, years ago," Hamish said.

The very mention of my nemesis was enough to

see my blood run cold. My voice sounded frayed when I quickly changed the subject. I hated the sound of that vulnerability, that fear. "Or maybe a wheel broke off and we had to make way on foot."

"But why wouldn't we have an escort or a driver with us, in that case?" Hamish said.

A good point. "Maybe he stayed behind to fix the carriage, and promised to come for us as soon as—"

"Why can we lie but not play cards?" my nephew asked.

I paused. This was a difficult question and one that I wanted to answer with careful consideration. "We're only making up these stories to keep ourselves out of harm's way. As soon as we've secured a safe situation for ourselves, then we won't have need to lie anymore."

He appeared drawn to the novelty of this approach. "Let's try not to lie, then, as much as we can—except the part about the bandits," he said. "We'll say our father was a doctor—yours *was,* after all—and our parents have died, and we were forced to flee to escape our creditors."

My heart thudded in a grief-stricken beat. This lie was upsettingly close to the truth. It was then that I felt the first twinge of brittleness since we'd left Edinburgh. Making a concerted effort to be as fearless and resilient as I needed to be, I hadn't allowed myself to think about any of it, or any of them, for my nephew's sake. Hamish's words were shards of truth in the smashed pane of our history, with too many broken pieces to ever mend. It was true that my parents had died, years ago. The thought of Hamish's own parents and their precarious situation almost brought me to tears. But I held them back, concentrating instead on the task at hand. My father had been a doctor, aye. And we had fled to escape, although "creditors" was a generous allowance to what our pursuers actually were. "That makes us sound like criminals."

Hamish thought about this, and then his small face lit up with his idea. "Let's say we were en route to visit relatives, but were attacked by bandits who took all our money, and so we're now in need of work to pay for our return to Edinburgh—or to our relatives, if we can find them."

"They'll ask who our relatives are."

"*Mysterious* relatives," Hamish said. "We don't know their names. But we know we have Highlands relations, and since we're orphans, we were curious. Since we have no other family left, we came to search them out."

Not bad. Not bad at all. This would give us a reason to ask about the local people, the Highlands clans and the work opportunities. "I'm not sure if I should be happy about or rather alarmed by your ability to spin lies with such ease, nephew."

He grinned. "I learned everything I know from you, Ami."

I ignored that, and began picking the hay out of his hair. I only wished I could have taught him even more. When my education had come to a very abrupt and final end at the age of eleven, I'd vowed to read every book in Edinburgh, or at least those I could get my hands on. Since that very day, when I wasn't working, I was studying, teaching myself the ways and means of every damn subject I could get my hands on. My sister, Cecelia, had once said I was probably the most qualified astronomer, botanist, linguist, zoologist and everything else, if only anyone had bothered to test me. You just never knew when an opportunity might present itself, or a random morsel of knowledge might be your saving grace. My tenacious study habits were of little consequence now. Survival was, and always had been, the order of the day.

With our plan decided, we turned to our appearances. After removing all the straw from Hamish's hair, I used some water to smooth it into place. There was little that could be done about the state of my nephew's clothing, which was dirty but not yet showing signs of too much wear and tear. In our haste, Hamish hadn't thought to bring a change of clothes and I had not had the chance to retrieve anything for him. I'd only just managed to grab a spare dress for myself, from my sister's cupboard. Her clothes were finer than mine, since her husband refused to allow his wife and son to appear outwardly as though his business was in financial distress, which it most certainly had been. In hindsight, it seemed a strange detail for him to be so particular about, with all the other worries he'd had to contend with. But now I was glad of his pride. My brother-in-law's insistence that appearances be kept up meant that I now had a dark blue gown to wear that was not only clean but also of the finest quality, enough to support the story we were about to spin. It mattered little that the dress was in fact a size too small. My sister wasn't quite as curvy as I was. I ordered Hamish to turn his back and, after a brief struggle, managed—just—to pour myself into the garment. It was of a lower cut than I was used to and, with the sizing issue, was in fact quite revealing. I was glad I had my light blue shawl, which I wrapped around my shoulders and secured in the front with a silver kilt pin that had once belonged to my father.

"That will have to do," I said, attempting to tame my hair into place. My braid was still coiled, but some of the shorter strands at the front had come loose

"No one will expect you to be perfectly groomed," Hamish commented, turning to watch me. "We've been attacked by bandits, remember, and forced to walk for miles after our driver was killed and our carriage stolen."

"Killed? Now we've witnessed a murder *and* been robbed?"

"If he was still alive they'd look for him."

This was becoming increasingly macabre by the minute. Either way, he was right. I'd be more convincing if my hair was in some state of disarray. I left the escaped tendrils loose to frame my face. My hair was long, wavy and a light shade of red that was almost blond. Strawberry-blond, my sister called it. My sister Cecelia's hair was the exact same shade as her son's: light brown with streaks of honey and gold.

Hamish was looking at me and there were glistening tears in his eyes. My nephew, despite his tender age, rarely cried. The sight of his tears now sent an awful stab of woe through my chest. I knew I was reminding him of his mother, and it saddened me that she might be lost to him for quite some time, leaving him with only me for companionship and protection.

"Tell me again why they couldn't come with us," he said.

"You know why," I said. "They have business to attend to. When we find a safe place to stay, I'll send word to them, and they'll join us." I wiped his tears, knowing only too well that it would be too dangerous to send word; interception was too risky. "In the meantime, I'll take good care of you."

"And I'll take good care of you," he countered, recovering a shred of his earlier enthusiasm for this adventure.

"Now," I said, "let's go get that meal. Meat with potatoes and gravy. Stew and fresh bread. As much as you can eat."

This cheered him further and he wiped his eyes with the back of his hand.

"Holster your weapon, soldier," I told him. "We don't want to frighten anyone."

He slung the wooden blade so it hung from his belt.

So it was, and we headed for the tavern door.

It was a lively scene. Clearly a popular local gathering place. There was a large contingent of farmers and tradesmen who appeared to know each other and were already well into their evening's allotment of ale. They sat at long, central tables that had been laid with platters of food. Several of them watched as we entered, but their conversation remained on more important matters: the planting of crops and the shearing of sheep. In the quieter corners sat smaller groups of travelers. Several sat alone. I spied an empty table near the back of the tavern and led Hamish to it.

A serving woman came to us. "Is it a meal you're after?" She was perhaps thirty-five years of age, or maybe younger, with tired brown eyes and lank hair she'd tied back. Her clothing was plain and well worn, but neat. In her voice were inflections of boredom, resignedness, a clear note of I'd-rather-be-anywhere-but-here. Maybe she needed another server to help her, to ease her workload. I could earn money, to pay for food and accommodation. *It would take a long time to earn enough not only to survive on but also to save for the return journey and the stay in Edinburgh. Gambling would be quicker, and easier.* I refused the direction of my thoughts. But I couldn't help picturing myself, a year from now, wearing a similar coarse brown dress, taking yet another order, still hiding and waiting. I couldn't afford to be overly choosy, I reminded myself. I would make do as best I could and accept the lot I was given gracefully.

Or would I?

"A meal, for two, please," I said. "A large one. And a pot of strong tea. With sugar." I almost asked her right then if there was work available. Something stopped me. I could at least enjoy a meal first—the last I would be able to afford—before I resigned myself to my fate. *A fate. There were always choices.* I warred with myself as the serving woman walked off. Serving was gainful, honest employment. *But so dull.* There would be plenty to eat, a warm place to sleep. Hamish might get hired by a local farmer, out of sight of passersby, as I cooked and cleaned. *So isolated and monotonous.*

I thought of my mother, who had worried constantly about my impetuous nature. *You've a little devil that sits on your left shoulder, Amelia, who whispers willful ideas into your ear. Listen to the angel on your right shoulder. Let that be the voice that guides you.* But the devil's advice had always seemed so much more intriguing. To ease my mother's concerns I'd tried my best—and mostly succeeded—to do as she said, to tune that little devil out, to learn discipline and control. Tragedy, however, had all but silenced the voice of reason. My parents died when I was eleven years old. And once my sister, who was seven years older than me, had been forced to marry a struggling gaming club owner to keep us off the streets after the death of our parents, I'd had much more to worry about than conscience and etiquette.

Our meal was served. The food was plain but hearty. I hadn't felt so hungry for a very long time. Ever, in fact.

Before we could finish eating, there was a commotion at the door.

I reached for Hamish in an instinctive movement. *Could it be that Fawkes and his men had tracked us? So soon?* I grabbed Hamish's sleeve as terror flooded me, and I could taste my fear as a metallic, bitter tang.

Before we could make a move to flee, an imposing man walked into the tavern, followed by several more. These weren't city people: that was glaringly obvious at the very first glimpse of their brawny, unfamiliar-looking silhouettes as they entered the dining room, which seemed to shrink in their presence.

They wore tartan clan kilts and weapons belts equipped with plentiful supplies of swords and knives. They were enormous, not only tall but big and wide-shouldered, muscular and lethal-looking. I heard Hamish's quick intake of breath. These were the clan warriors we'd read stories of, with their weaponry and their battle scars. They looked every bit as savage as one might have expected. Their hair was worn long, to the shoulders, with small braids at their temples. Each one of them looked as though he could kill a man with his bare hands, if so inclined. They gave off an aura of confidence and contained ferocity. Yet I couldn't help noticing they were exceptionally good-looking men, for all their subdued aggression, with strong features and glowing vitality.

The farmers and tradesmen did not appear to be frightened by these men, but rather respectful. It occurred to me that warriors such as these would be not only the protectors of any given district, but also the lawmakers.

I noticed then that the men were followed by three women.

These women looked somewhat out of place, their fashionable clothing and petite, refined countenance offering a sharp contrast to the men's size and overt ruggedness. Groomed and glamorous, the women were well dressed in gowns and capes of unusual design. My sister and I had always had an interest in fashion, even if we'd only occasionally had the opportunity to indulge it, and it was easy to see that these women had access to quality seamstresses. It seemed clear enough, too, that these were Highlands clan women, and I was surprised at their elegance. I was reminded that the clans' ruling families were not heathens or barbarians, as I might have imagined, but were instead composed of nobility. This was something I'd had little cause to give much thought to, but now there was something highly fascinating about these very-masculine men and the trio of petite, stylish women they were clearly assigned to accompany on their travels, to guard with their swords and their lives.

Hamish had recovered from his initial fear and now, his mute fascination. "Do you think those swords are as long as the scabbards that hold them?" Hamish whispered.

I eyed one of the leather sheaths in question. "It seems impossible that anyone could lift one, if they are," I said in hushed tones, "but then, look at the size of those men's *arms*. And the scabbards look well made. I would expect that they would fit the swords like a glove."

"Aye," Hamish agreed, agog and wide-eyed. These men before us embodied everything his childhood fantasies had promised, and more. He'd modeled himself on the stories of the Highlander warriors I'd read him as a small boy, on their strength and their bravery, having never seen anyone like that on the backstreets of Edinburgh. And here they were: real and fierce. Hamish had been carrying his toy swords around since he was barely old enough to walk, but he'd never seen anything like *this*. I couldn't help thinking he'd found his element here in these Highlands, and we'd barely just arrived. I wasn't sure why this realization, though hardly surprising, caused a ripple of unease in me. I realized in that moment that I was entering new territory that would very likely change not only my outlook but the entire course of my future.

Then again, that's exactly what I'd intended all along, by fleeing the city. A new life, for him, at least. And here, in this very place, I could feel that new life beginning to unfold, reaching and affecting us both.

The women took a seat at the table next to ours and the men sat at a large round table near them. The server attended to them immediately.

One of the women noticed our interest and she caught my eye. She appeared to be the youngest of the three, and she was, even from this small distance, quite strikingly beautiful. Her eyes were a brilliant shade of cerulean blue that matched her dress, and her hair was a shiny, rich dark brown. She appeared equally interested in my own appearance, taking in the snug fit of my dress and my slightly windblown dishevelment. She smiled, and behind a thin veil of shyness, I could detect genuine interest, and a light note of concern. Clearly I was unaccompanied by any escort aside from a small boy whose eyes were glued to her guards even as he continued to wolf down his food as though he hadn't eaten in weeks.

My position, as a woman traveling without protection, was clearly not only inappropriate, but dangerous. Especially from the vantage point of such privilege. I guessed that these women were returning to their Highlands clan after a short trip to Edinburgh on business of one sort or another—which had more than likely involved copious amounts of shopping. They were practically sparkling with fresh grooming and the newness of their garments.

I felt a million miles removed from such splendor. My dress was fine enough, aye, if somewhat constricting, but I had in fact been on the run for upward of five days, had eaten little, slept on hay wagons or in open fields and, now for the first time, felt the accumulating effects of all the tumult of recent weeks to my very bones.

In fact, I should have been counting my blessings. I was alive, and so was Hamish. And I held on to hope that Cecelia, too, was holed up in some safe haven, being fed a meal as fortifying as ours. For her sake, and her son's, I resolved to somehow beat Sebastian Fawkes at his own game, to get my revenge by saving her, and saving myself.

I noticed then that Hamish had left the table. Curiosity had overcome him. He was circling the soldiers, keeping a not-so-subtle distance from them, and arousing the interest of the young woman in blue, as well as the other two.

They watched my nephew for a moment, taking in his outfit, and his beauty; it was true he had been exceptionally blessed in this way.

"Would you like to touch one of the swords?" the young woman in blue asked him.

Hamish, alas, lacked any hint of bashfulness. He was a straightforward boy who was quite aware of his angelic face, his sun-touched hair and his long, graceful limbs. He had used his looks to his own advantage upon many occasions, a practice I had not only encouraged but taught him. "Aye, milady. I'm the son of a doctor, not a warrior. I've seen plenty of scalpels but never a sword."

Ah. I felt an equal amount of pride and dismay at his quick response. He was already spinning our tale.

"Lachlan, would you mind terribly?" the young woman addressed one of the guards. "The lad is so sweet."

The guard named Lachlan eyed Hamish for a moment, and I detected his mild annoyance, as though he was lamenting the fact that he wasn't out-of-doors spearing things, instead finding himself relegated to guard duty and the unappealing assignment of entertaining a vagrant boy. Even so, it was clear enough that Lachlan would not refuse whatever request the young woman made of him. He obliged, unsheathing his colossal weapon in one easy swipe, holding it up in front of Hamish's rounded eyes.

I'd never seen Hamish so awestruck. He reached up tentatively to touch his fingers to the flat side of the blade.

"Don't touch the blade, lad, or you'll be picking your neatly sliced fingers up off the floor," Lachlan said with persuasive eloquence.

"I wasn't going to touch the blade," Hamish replied, miffed that the soldier would think him so dim-witted. "I know it's sharp. It wouldn't be much use if it wasn't."

Several of the other soldiers chuckled at this and I felt a ripple of shame that Hamish would respond with such impertinence. Lachlan, however, appeared more impressed by Hamish's answer than angered. Strength and bravery were their currency, I supposed. Hamish understood this and had just bought himself a hint of this soldier's respect. Clearly, despite his small size in the face of these enormous, armed men, my nephew was not intimidated. And there was a shiny-eyed eagerness to him that Lachlan could not help but respond to.

"I'd offer to let you hold it," Lachlan said, "but the sword outweighs you."

More laughter from the men.

"Here," Lachlan continued, retrieving a large knife from its holster at his belt. "You can hold this one."

Now that Hamish was well and truly engaged, the young woman in blue took the opportunity to make light conversation. She was clearly somewhat overcome with curiosity about my obvious predicament. Her blue eyes gleamed with bright interest, and her shiny brown hair waved prettily around a pale face that was highlighted by the subtle paint of pink on her cheeks.

"I'm Christie Mackenzie," she said. "This is my sister, Ailie." She motioned to the woman on her right, whose beauty was equal to her sister's but somehow more reserved. Christie's beauty had a fresh, mischievous appeal while Ailie's conveyed composure and sophistication. Ailie smiled politely. Her hair was darker than Christie's and her eyes were a deep shade of indigo blue. "And this is our friend Katriona," Christie continued.

Katriona was perhaps as many as ten years older

than the two sisters, and her manner was markedly less friendly. Her smile was so forced that if taken out of context, it might have been mistaken for a grimace, perhaps from a mild case of indigestion. She was not as beautiful as the sisters, but it could be said that she was exceptionally well presented. Any beauty she might have possessed was eclipsed by the pinched, rigid impatience that set her face, and by the youthful radiance of the two women she traveled with. The ill fit of my dress did not escape her notice, nor did she appear particularly pleased by Hamish's precocious joy as he held Lachlan's glinting knife.

"I'm Amelia Taylor," I said. "And this is Hamish." I stopped myself from giving Hamish's correct surname just in time. We were pretending to be siblings, I remembered. "My brother."

Christie asked the question she must have been dying to ask all along. "And you travel alone?"

"We *had* an escort, of course," Hamish answered, with such sincerity I suffered a pang of guilt that overshadowed any pride that might have accompanied it. The lad was gifted. I should, as his guardian, be grooming him for a career in stage acting and if he hadn't been so staunchly adamant about his decision to become a soldier, I might have considered setting our sights for the theaters of London as a hideout, rather than the remote expanses of the Highlands. My guilt only compounded as I recalled telling him that it was likely that we would be reunited with his parents more quickly if we were particularly convincing in our storytelling. "But he met an untimely end at the hands of the dastardly bandits that stole our carriage and all our belongings."

This news was met with the collective dismay of his now-rapt audience. "Bandits?" said Lachlan, bristling, his eyes surveying the room as though they might be among us. "What bandits?"

"Aye," replied Hamish. "Five of them. They wore black masks and capes and they rode black horses. Ruthless, they were. Killed our escort right in front of our eyes. Speared him through the heart with a silver-hilted sword."

A twinge of pain brought me to the realization that I had bitten my own lip. I hoped Hamish's imaginative yarn wasn't *too* creative. I didn't like the thought of what these war-hardened men might do to us if they suspected we were deceiving them. But there was no point correcting my nephew; it would only make them more inclined to doubt us. Strangely, I felt an uncharacteristic sense of regret that we were in fact deceiving them, these beautiful sisters with their kind eyes and their enviable lot in life. I would never have thought to wish for such a thing, but I couldn't help feeling a sense of wonder at their fortune. Their manly band of escorts, all rugged good looks and masculine protectiveness against any and every potential threat these sisters might face; their dark beauty; their innate sense of style that was only enhanced tenfold by the wealth that so flatteringly showcased it.

Ah, well. Overblown luck was not something I sought out, or even valued especially, having experienced so little of it. Which was why I had made a point of learning the tricks and mathematics that ensured something akin to luck. My kind of manufactured luck, however, was only useful at the gaming tables. It didn't translate further afield than that. And even my skills at trickery in the gambling den hadn't been enough to keep my brother-in-law's broken, corrupt business afloat. Or my sister safe. It was best to carry on and appreciate the smaller fortunes in life, like this hearty meal we were almost finished with. And this fine brew of sweet tea.

"We've been forced to make our way on foot," I said, before Hamish could elaborate further. "We were fortunate to get a ride part of the way on a farmer's wagon, which explains our somewhat ragged appearance. And then we saw this tavern."

"We've come from Edinburgh," continued Hamish. "To search for some long-lost relatives whose names we don't even know."

"You have relatives in the Highlands?" Christie asked, intrigued.

Hamish answered before I could. "We do, but we know nothing about their identity. Our father's final words to us, as he lay pale and choking for breath on his deathbed, his life seeping away from the disease that tragically stole him from us, were these— 'Go to the Highlands and seek out my cousin. He's a good man and he will take you in. He'll care for you as if you were his own.' Of course, we were asking him, 'Who, Father? Who is this cousin you speak of? Why have you never told us of him before? What's his name?' But it was too late. Father's eyes had gone dull and lifeless. His final breath rasped from his body in a weak sigh. And then he was gone." Hamish's eyes, the little puck, were shiny with emotion. And he was still clutching the lethal-looking knife with both hands, which somehow only added to the performance. "We buried him next to our mother."

"Oh, you poor child," exclaimed Christie.

"I have Amelia to take care of me," Hamish told her, with what I knew to be genuine relief tinting his words. "And I take care of her. We're not alone." I'd practically raised Hamish, since his parents had been so busy running the club, and I'd loved him madly from the moment he was born. In the nine years between then and now, my role in his life as aunt and guide had offered me as many moments of joy as any relationship I'd ever had. His complete trust in me—a trust that shone now from his seraphic face—strengthened my resolve to keep him safe and to give him every chance in life, despite our significant hardships. If I had to stoop to servitude or to spinning a few harmless lies to do it, then so be it. "And so," Hamish continued solemnly, "with no living relatives left in Edinburgh, we've come to seek out this cousin. But then, out of nowhere, a band of renegades surrounded us, attacking as one! Ours was a fine enough carriage, filled with all our belongings. They took everything. James tried to protect our family heirlooms. We told him to let them have it, that it wasn't worth his life, but he wouldn't listen. He was loyal to his bones."

James. His father's name. An odd choice for our fictional driver. But then, I knew Hamish's bond with his father had never been a strong one.

"I've never heard of such a thing," Katriona said, her mild empathy laced with more pronounced vestiges of disbelief. "Who are these bandits in black? I had no idea such people even existed."

Unfortunately, Katriona's skepticism aggravated the little devil in me, the whispering contrariness that resided persistently within my character no matter how hard I tried to banish it. That she would so immediately question Hamish's sincerity irked me, even if she had good reason to do so. I found myself yearning to bolster my nephew's story to support him, and to silence her. "Oh, I'd never heard of such a thing, either," I said. "At first we thought them an apparition, a wayward fear that might have stepped out of the fathomless pages of medieval history, traveling as we were through such unfamiliar territory. It was why our escort was so unwilling to cooperate with them. We simply couldn't believe we were being robbed so aggressively, and in such an idyllic setting. And when they demanded we step free of the carriage, I was relieved, at least, that they intended to let us go. I willingly bargained with them, giving them all our possessions, my jewelry—most of which belonged to our dearly departed mother—our horses and the carriage itself in exchange for our freedom, even if it meant we might wander for days on end without any sign of shelter or assistance. But James was worried about our safety under such conditions. He argued. He refused to relent." I faltered here, almost getting swept away in the emotional momentum of my tale. "'Twas a brutal end," I finally said. "But thankfully, Hamish and I were allowed to flee. We hid behind the incline of a small hill until they were gone."

"If I'd had *this* knife," Hamish added, "I'd have run after them."

Christie's eyes sparked with concern as she pictured our harrowing ordeal. Lachlan, however, sported a completely different expression as his gaze flicked back and forth between Hamish and me. If I wasn't mistaken, he appeared faintly amused, more relaxed than a soldier should have been when confronted with news of this kind: that evildoers were loose in his near vicinity, that his noble charges might be under dire threat. I had no way of knowing if he was reading our lie with ease. I suspected it. Maybe, as a seasoned soldier born of these lands, he knew that there were no black-clad bandits wreaking havoc; he'd know of them if such people existed. Maybe he'd banished those that once prowled these lands himself. Or he'd listened at the knee of his warrior father, who'd killed them off one by one.

If Lachlan did detect our dishonesty, he made

no effort to expose it. His concentration returned to his ale, from which he took a long drink. For this I was profoundly grateful. I decided I liked him, and if there was ever a way I could ever reciprocate the favor, I would.

I realized that Hamish was now holding something in his right hand, the hand that was not currently occupied with the glinting, oversize weapon. A bag, small and blue. Exactly the same fabric, in fact, as the dress that Christie wore. A matching accessory.

My heart thumped with a clenching realization. *Nay,* I thought. *He hasn't. He's pickpocketed her!* I knew only too well how deftly skilled he was. One might have argued that our predicament was severe enough to warrant theft, or worse. But it was exactly what had put us in this position of vagrancy in the first place, and I wanted nothing more to do with it. *This* lady, given her hefty bodyguards and their abundant weaponry, was quite possibly the worst choice of target ever in the entire history of thievery.

Hamish spoke, with the utmost politeness. "Milady. Your bag. You dropped it. I wouldn't want you to leave it behind mistakenly."

Christie looked confused. Her hand ghosted to the now-empty pocket of her coat, where her bag had been. Then she reached to take the small purse that Hamish held out to her. "Thank you. What a kind-hearted lad you are."

With that, as my heart rioted in my chest, Christie looked at Ailie somewhat beseechingly. "Knox would want to hear about their plight," she said to her sister. "And he'd want to learn more about these bandits from the witnesses themselves."

Ailie appeared to contemplate this for a moment, and she looked at me thoughtfully, weighing her decision.

"Aye," Ailie finally said, to my surprise. "You must come with us." It was the first time she had spoken. Her voice was soft yet ingrained with a sure, quiet strength, as though she was used to being listened to with interest and obedience. It made me wonder what kind of rank these women held. They were clearly noble; their obvious wealth and their brawny entourage were evidence enough of that.

"I don't think that's a good idea—" Katriona began.

"Aye, you must," Christie agreed quickly. "You can't stay here at this tavern, and you've nowhere else to go. You'll come with us and we'll help you find your family. Knox will probably know of them. He knows everyone."

"Who's Knox?" asked Hamish.

"Our brother," said Christie.

"*Laird* Knox Mackenzie," Katriona stated with emphasis, as though everyone on the planet, from the tribesmen deep in the jungles of Africa to the painted plainspeople of the faraway Americas, had heard of Laird Knox Mackenzie. Except us.

Not only Katriona's tone but also her reveren-

tial mention of this Laird Knox Mackenzie made
me question whether accompanying these women
would be in our best interest, as appealing as such
an offer might seem. The last thing we needed was
to be under the thumb of a lordish, controlling overseer. It was the very situation we were fleeing from.
And while I could easily recognize that the brother
of these charming sisters might be a far more appealing overseer than the one we had left behind,
my pride would not allow us to be charity cases, no
matter how desperate we might have been.

I shook my head. "Nay. We wouldn't dream of
imposing on you like that," I said. Hamish gave me
a look of startled irritation. I already knew he would
follow Lachlan around like a loyal puppy wherever
the beefed-up warrior happened to go if given half
the opportunity. "I had already decided to search for
gainful employment, to pay our way to our father's
cousin's lands, wherever they may be."

"Perhaps we could help you find some work,"
offered Ailie, "once you have spoken with Knox."

"Aye," said Christie, turning to me. "Our brother,
laird of lairds, is very thorough when it comes to the
details of any threat to peace within a fifty-mile ra-
dius of Kinloch's walls. It's been quite some time
since we've seen bandits in these parts and I know
he'd be very interested to hear of them. I'd say you'll
be well occupied for some time to come."

Her playful respect intrigued me, but I didn't
like the thought of being interrogated by some all-

powerful, self-important laird, to spin further, deeper lies that might be as transparent to him as they had been to Lachlan.

"I'm not sure if—" I began.

"We can't possibly leave you *here*—" Christie interrupted, glancing around the crowded bustle of the tavern somewhat critically "—unchaperoned and vulnerable to any number of perils, as you are. We're very close to Kinloch's borders and it's therefore our duty to harbor you. I'm sure Knox would agree."

"I suppose he would," Katriona tentatively agreed, as though not entirely persuaded.

"We should be on our way as it is," Ailie commented. "We'll ride through the night and reach Kinloch by morning."

"It's settled, then?" Christie asked. I suspected that these sisters were acting not only out of kindness and benevolence, but also in the interest of their own clan, as it made sense that they would. We were unknown wanderers, after all, with a somewhat outlandish past. We must be investigated as well as protected. And their guards were on hand to ensure not only our safety but their own. Even though we could hardly be considered threatening, it was possible that our story had not fooled either Lachlan or the women, and that Hamish and I might be seen as a riddle that needed to be solved, just in case our riddle presented threats this close to their home.

"You'll accompany us to Kinloch—our clan's keep," Ailie continued. "'Tis very comfortable there,

I can assure you. You and your brother will be well cared for."

The way the sisters said the name of this place made it sound like some mythical Eden.

I should have refused. But the absolute elation on Hamish's face as he realized that we would travel with these soldiers swayed me. Knowing that he'd be safe for a time, and well fed, clinched my decision. He wouldn't have to stay here in this tavern, or another like it, helping me clean or cook—an occupation that, it occurred to me only now, would be very *visible,* and unprotected, if our pursuers happened to, in time, track us this far north. We would be far safer inside the walls of a well-armed keep. Practically untouchable.

Despite my apprehensions at putting myself at the mercy of this Laird Knox Mackenzie and all his noble authority, it was these details concerning my foremost priority—my nephew's safety—that found me agreeing.

"All right, then," I heard myself saying, and my voice sounded uncertain even to my own ears. "We will accompany you to Kinloch."

Wherever *that* might be.

CHAPTER TWO

I SUPPOSE I shouldn't have been overly surprised that Hamish and I were subjected to a careful—and quite thorough—search, not only of our bag but also our clothing before we were allowed into the carriage. This inspection was carried out by several of the guards, at Lachlan's command. He appeared to be the highest-ranking of these men, and they obeyed his directive without question. "A routine exercise," was Lachlan's gruff comment on the subject, although I couldn't help wondering how regularly they came across wandering, unchaperoned young women in these parts. Maybe it happened all the time.

"I'll exercise *you*," I muttered inaudibly, as Lachlan's men patted the shape of my legs through my dress, to ensure that I carried no weapons, presumably.

"Pardon, milady?" Lachlan said. "Did you say something?"

"Nay," I replied innocently. "Nothing at all."

Darkness had settled by the time we began our journey to Kinloch.

The luxurious carriage was fitted with clever seats that reclined to form beds. Velvet curtains had been drawn to create partitions between the beds. And the bedding itself was as soft and plush as any I had ever seen.

I lay for a time before I slept, considering this unusual turn of events and all that had happened in the short space of several weeks. Here we were, ensconced in deluxe accommodation, making our way with a group of warriors and noblewomen to a mythical Highlands keep where we would be greeted by the laird of their clan. It was so far removed from the backstreets of Edinburgh I almost wondered if I was in fact dreaming, if the harrowing events of recent weeks hadn't got the better of me. I blinked and took in my surroundings, fingering the fine thickness of the soft fabrics.

Hamish was curled up, already asleep, along the edge of my haven. I tucked the fur blanket more tightly around him.

I removed my dress to sleep in my shift, folding it carefully, knowing this was the only suitable gown I had at my disposal. But then I remembered that I wouldn't be expected to have a change of clothes—all my belongings had been stolen by a band of murderous thugs. I couldn't precisely tell whether our story had been convincing—or whether we had merely piqued their suspicious curiosity. Either way, Lachlan had not balked in the slightest at the thought of continuing through the night. He either knew our tale was fictitious or had such confidence in his own skills and those of his men that he was completely unperturbed by the possibility of conflict.

Time would tell whether our lie would catch up with us. I wondered if the esteemed Laird Knox Mackenzie was a clever and intuitive man. Would he be easy to deceive? Or would he see right through me and order me gone at his first opportunity? I would find out soon enough. For now, despite—or maybe because of—the gentle lull of the moving carriage as it pulled us through the night, safe and warm, I fell asleep more easily than I had in many months. But then the memories began to haunt my dreams, creeping up and closing in.

He was there, behind me. I could feel his presence like a tightening grip around my neck. I turned to him, all black eyes and evil intention. He was not an especially handsome man but it was true he had an air of importance, with his well-fed, well-dressed appearance and his smoothed dark blond hair. Beneath the glossy, urbane exterior lurked a vile soul. I was aghast but not surprised when he made a gloating announcement.

"I've taken a financial interest in your family's establishment, Amelia." The sound of my name, spoken in that dark, ominous voice, caused the tiny hairs on the back of my neck to rise. "In fact, I have just purchased a very decisive controlling share. Which means that you are now my employee. It is therefore my responsibility to ensure that you are suitably engaged, and as useful as you might possibly be." I

flinched back from the coldness he seemed to emit, but his hand stole to a loose curl of my hair, with which he played with two fingers. "I gave you several opportunities to act in your family's best interest."

I glared at him, and it was this defiance that challenged him. He was accustomed to fear, and obedience. That he could detect neither in me, I knew, provoked him. And fascinated him. I could see it there in his pitiless eyes: he wanted to break me. Each time I refused him, he upped his game. My determination to avoid him was having the opposite effect, miring me deeper into the control he was determined to gain.

"In other words, my dear Amelia, I now own the majority of this club." And you along with it, *was his unspoken implication.*

"Congratulations," I said. This was the worst news he could have delivered, but I'd be damned to the fiery depths of hell before I let him see any hint of weakness in me. That would be his victory.

"You could easily have relieved your family of their debts without forcing me to play this particular hand. I'm surprised you continue to refuse me. I've had to take somewhat excessive measures just to get your...undivided attention." His gaze was chilling, but his tone was deceptively light. *"And you look lovelier tonight than ever. Like a nymph with a siren's tendencies. Worth the price, I daresay."*

I glared at him, taken aback by his inappropriate flattery. Whatever I looked like, I was entirely inno-

*cent. I—and my sister, it had to be said—intended to
keep it that way for some time to come. My mother's
sense of propriety, for better or worse, had manifested itself tenfold in my sister; she watched me like
a hawk and refused to allow any man to court me,
perhaps because the selection of suitors we were
exposed to were, more often than not, married and
cheating, destitute, drunk or wanted by the law.
"There are more important things than money," I
said. "I would rather starve than give myself unwill-
ingly to any man."* Especially you.

*This made him smile, and it was a smile that sick-
ened me with fear. "Is that so?" he purred. His eyes
were uncannily emotionless.*

*I willed myself to hold my ground. Fear was
not something that troubled me often, but Sebastian Fawkes seemed to bathe me in it. His presence
clouded my confidence. Whenever he darkened our
doorstep, it was as though doom lurked around every
corner, waiting to ooze in and take hold.*

*"You know how wealthy and powerful I am. You
know how much of Edinburgh I own. Yet you refuse
to grant me one simple request. My patience has
grown thin. I have more important things to do than
chase after a stubborn, down-on-her-luck virgin. Yet
regrettably, my desire for you consumes me. And so
I have taken matters into my own hands. You will
be mine. Tonight."*

*God help me. Logic was telling me to submit to
his dark requests, but all I felt was fury at his insults.*

"I'm not down on my luck," I seethed, glancing at my surroundings, which suggested otherwise, a detail that only enraged me further. "And I have no interest or intention of submitting to you, Mr. Fawkes. I'm sure there are countless women who would jump at the chance to bed you. I'm simply not one of them."

His voice was low, laced with anger. Awful and severe. "I'm afraid I simply will not accept nay for an answer."

A wash of terror chased up my spine as he eyed his hulking, ever-present bodyguards, considering. My courage was false, but it was better than nothing; I forced a chuckle just to annoy him. "I'd rather bed the devil himself."

"Since he's not available tonight," he replied, his eyes simmering with frightening anticipation, "you'll have to make do with me."

"You're wasting your time, Mr. Fawkes. I'm neither interested nor available. I don't plan to be here this evening. Now, if you'll excuse me, I'm needed at the tables."

He laughed softly, the sound jarring for its lack of humor. His hand cuffed my wrist painfully, halting my retreat. "There you go again with your plucky refusals. I could take you now, if I felt inclined to force you," he informed me callously. "You know that."

I made a small sound before I could stop myself.

He leaned in close, whispering into my ear. "It would be so much more fun if you would beg for it,

Amelia. I could make you plead, you realize. For mercy."

I could hear the racing drumbeat of my heart. I leaned away from him, having difficulty breathing. "There is nothing you could do or say that would make me beg anything of you."

His eyes roved to the far corner of the room, where Hamish showed his newest card trick to the barmaid as Cecelia served a drink to a customer. Fawkes's smile was eerily devoid of emotion. "I believe there is one thing." The terror infused me, hot poison seeping into my heart. "'Tis foolish of you to put his life in danger, when you could so easily keep him safe."

Fawkes had been watching me, learning my motivations and the direction of my unwavering loyalties. It was the most effective threat he could make, we both knew this. I fought to keep my desperation at bay. I looked into his fathomless eyes. "Please. Please don't hurt him."

His eyes roved my body, painting me with fear and a horrid, overwhelming sense of dread. "I think we can come to an agreement that will ensure his safety. I have grown weary of this cat-and-mouse game you insist on playing. So I'm willing to issue you a very generous offer. Do as I say or I can no longer ensure the boy's safety. Now or at any point in the future."

Fawkes leaned closer, pausing before whispering in my ear.

"I will return after nightfall. I suggest you come to

*terms with the inevitable and be ready and willing in
whatever way I require." He brushed a stray strand
of hair from my cheek, causing my skin to erupt in
gooseflesh. "I always get what I want, Amelia. From
this day forward, you'd do well to remember that."*

I awoke with a start. My fists were clenched into
the soft furs, which I'd displaced in my restless nightmare. My skin was clammy with a light sweat.

My awareness returned to me as my eyes adjusted
to the darkness and my heartbeat began to slow. I
could see Hamish's sleeping form curled up alongside me. And I remembered: we'd escaped. We were
being transported by the kind-eyed, well-dressed
Highlands women and their trusty guards.

I forced my fists to unclench, and I gently touched
Hamish's soft hair to reassure myself, taking care
not to wake him.

Listening to the crunch of the wooden wheels on
the graveled road underneath me, I closed my eyes
and pictured starry skies and green hills and wid-
ening distances.

It was some time before I could sleep again.

At dawn, I was shaken gently awake by Christie, who
told me to dress and to wake Hamish. We would arrive at Kinloch within the hour. By the time we had
folded away the bedding and adjusted the seats, the
carriage was passing through the guarded gates of
the keep.

I felt sluggish and sullen from my broken sleep

and disturbing dreams. And weary from the continued separation from my sister. If only she'd come
with us. If only I'd been able to convince her of her
own vulnerability.

When I looked out the window of the carriage,
my resolve returned to me and my fatigue faded. My
purpose was clear. I knew exactly what I had to do,
and this place and these people were as fortunate a
discovery as I could possibly have hoped for. We
were approaching the most magnificent stone manor
I had ever seen. A shining loch curled around the
back of it, extending far into the distance, smooth as
a mirror, reflecting the cloudless purple sky. Quaint
orchards dotted the landscape with small trees so
lovingly tended they might have been topiary sculp-
tures. And beyond them, as far as the eye could see,
farmed hills rolled gracefully, striped with rows of
crops. Layered shades of earthy browns and greens
were so rich in promise and hue they looked as if
they'd been painted with an artist's brush. Sheep
and cattle grazed the farthest foothills, tiny dots of
red, black and woolly white. If I'd been asked to
dream up the most bucolic, heavenly setting I could
fathom, even my most grandiose fantasies would
not have captured the charm of the scene I looked
upon now. Kinloch offered the ideal blend of careful
cultivation and rambling nature, as though the combined vigor of the fertile earth and the breezy air had
found some sort of perfect alignment here under the
skilled hands of the Mackenzie clan. The tall stone

wall that circled the keep reached all the way to the far horizon, containing and showcasing the beauty and plenty of the landscape within it.

The manor itself rose impressively from the surrounding splendor. From its highest turrets, flags flapped in the wind. The flag of Scotland. And just below it, one that was unfamiliar to me, emblazoned with a stag's head. The Mackenzie crest, I guessed.

"I have never, ever seen anything so grand in all my life," I murmured, aghast. Hamish's head rested against my shoulder as he dozed.

It was Katriona who responded. "You're the daughter of a doctor from a prosperous family of Edinburgh. You must have seen grand buildings before."

My eyes disengaged from the scenery to rest upon Katriona's face. Her pithy comment stole a degree of beauty from the day, as though a cloud had just passed over the sun. Her impeccable grooming had suffered only minimally from the travel, her dark hair still neatly bound. Light shadows touched the hollows below her eyes, but her complexion was creamy and becoming in the pink light. Her slim, almost willowy figure was wrapped in a tartan shawl. She was not unattractive and if she had possessed even a shred of tenderness she might have been quite lovely. As it was, I couldn't help feeling slightly amused by her light but undisguised derision. It wouldn't do to return her rudeness. I was far too experienced with manipulative belittlement to rise to her bait. And despite the hours of sleep, I felt almost more tired than I had along the rougher days of our journey. I already knew Katriona disagreed with her companions about my invitation. She had agreed to it only because Ailie and Christie were kindhearted, a trait she might have admired and aspired to. I smiled politely, remembering my role and my story. I kept my tone mild and pleasant, which was much easier to do if I made a point of speaking to Ailie and Christie as well.

"I've seen many grand buildings," I said. "Castles and cathedrals. Modern hospitals and stately courthouses. Elite schools and domed, acoustically attuned music halls." *Rarely,* I didn't need to add. *More often, I've deliberated upon the interior décor of a decadent gaming hall, listening to the scuttling roll of a dice across a felt-lined table, feeling the supple glide of the deck of cards I hold in my hands as I shuffle the cards and deal them to unscrupulous men. In my quieter moments, I retreat to an unused private library where I find sanctuary in the pages of old, dusty books as I pursue my treasured ambition of learning, and of teaching: a dream that is as passionate as it is pointless.* "Many of them are architecturally designed masterpieces, of course. But they're all city buildings. I've never been out of Edinburgh before now, and I can only marvel at the beauty of the countryside. And *this* countryside is far more beautiful than I might ever have imagined. It somehow lends a completely different magnificence to a manor than rows of other grand buildings do."

Christie and Ailie seemed pleased by the observation; they appeared to take my comment about the glory of their home as a compliment, as it was intended.

"You've never been out of Edinburgh?" Katriona asked. To her, the information was clearly another strike against me. "What a pity."

I wasn't sure of her meaning. And I wasn't overly compelled to find out exactly what her meaning might be. I was too distracted by the commanding view of the fields and the mountains beyond.

The carriage was slowing, coming to a stop at the front entrance of the manor. Footmen opened the doors and helped us disembark. To Hamish's dismay, the guards had ridden off once we were inside the walls of the keep and were nowhere to be seen.

"Amelia," Ailie said. "Christie will show you and Hamish to your guest chambers. You'll be quite comfortable there for now." I remembered: I was to undergo an extensive interrogation by the almighty laird himself, and at his very first opportunity. I honestly didn't feel up to such an encounter at this present moment. My usually staunch self-preservation-at-all-costs outlook felt as if it had been somehow undermined, just slightly, by this vast, resplendent place. I wanted to be left alone, to drink it all in and appreciate it for a time.

Christie seemed to sense this. "After I show you

to your chambers, you can take a stroll through the gardens if you'd like. After all the traveling you've done, you might like to take some time, to settle in and clear your head before the noon meal is served in the hall."

I was very touched by her kindness. I smiled at her. "Thank you, Christie."

She returned the smile. She reached to finger a long ringlet of my hair that had come loose. "Your hair is the most outstanding color. Not blond, not red. Something in between. With a myriad of shades from rose gold to copper."

"Strawberry blond," clarified Hamish. It was what my sister called it. We had read the term in a book somewhere and we had mused at the fanciful-sounding word. In fact, we had no idea what a straw-berry was, or what color such a thing might be.

My nephew was in somewhat of a mood, since he'd discovered the soldiers had taken their leave of him. Christie had noticed his immediate attach-ment to the burly guards—and their weapons. "No doubt you'll have an opportunity later, Hamish, to visit the soldiers' barracks, and to meet with Lach-lan, and perhaps even Laird Mackenzie himself. He has the biggest sword of them all."

Hamish was placated enough by her comment, but it left me with a singular flush of unease. Knowing I would have to face this Laird Mackenzie—and his big sword—and spin my elaborate lie seemed less larkish than it had from afar, now that we were here within the walls of Kinloch.

Christie led us into the manor, through a grand hall that was being cleaned by a number of efficient workers and up a stone staircase. Every detail of this place shone with gleaming attention. Large candles sat in grooves carved into the outer edge of every second step, illuminating our path with a modernistic glow. Deer antlers had been weaved to make a rustic chandelier overhead. Tapestries depicting hunting scenes, the scenic loch I already recognized, a wedding and other stunningly crafted portraits of Mackenzie history decorated the stone walls. We were led to our private chambers, which was small but charming, and very clean. It was a narrow room with a large window at one end. There were two single beds laid with thick furs, a dresser between with a porcelain pitcher and bowl on top and a small table with two chairs placed by the window, which overlooked the orchards.

"'Tis very simple, but I hope you'll find it suitable enough during your stay," Christie said.

"It couldn't be more perfect," I assured her. "Much better than a hay wagon."

Christie smiled again, her white teeth small and neat. She was so pretty and petite. I was several inches taller than she was and much more voluptuous. I knew I had the kind of figure that won the attention of men—I'd had more than enough experience with their admiring glances and lascivious comments to understand that much. But now standing here next to Christie made me feel less like a womanly treasure and more like a prize-winning heifer. "Once you're settled, feel free to stroll the gardens as you like," she said. "A meal will be served at midday, in the hall. You'll hear the bell. When Knox is ready to see you, he'll send someone."

With that, she left us to it. I washed my face with some cool water and brushed my hair, tying it in a loose coil, but Hamish was too energized to stay cooped up in our room.

"Let's go, Ami. I want to explore the orchards and see if any of the fruit is ripe enough to pick."

"I would think it's still too early for the fruit."

But I was soon pulled at his insistence out the door and down the stairs. The workers took no notice of us. They were likely accustomed to guests and visitors. We found our way out-of-doors and into the day. The light was clear and golden, slightly hazed with the climbing heat of summer. The orchards themselves were something akin to a wonderland of lush green. Soft, waving grass carpeted the expanse. Compact, leafy trees created inviting little curling paths so exquisite that if someone had told me faeries were hiding among their branches, waving magical wands and leaving gold-dust trails, I would have believed him. Hamish ran ahead. I called to him, but he had disappeared. He wouldn't have gone far, I knew. *Let him be,* I thought. He needed to play, to run. To be a child for an hour or two.

I strolled along, thoroughly enjoying myself, taking a deep breath and feeling the air in my lungs and the sun on my face for the first time in…perhaps ever. This was a different sun from the muted light of the city. This sun felt healthy and restorative. I unpinned the clasp of my shawl to feel the warmth on my skin.

I heard laughter. From somewhere up above me.

"Come down from there," I told him. "You'll fall."

"I won't fall. You should come up here, Ami. I can see over the orchards. And at the very top of the tree, the apples are turning red."

"Pick one for me."

"There's one right above you," Hamish exclaimed. "On that branch there. You could reach it if you climbed across."

I looked to see where he was pointing. A thick, low branch was within my reach where it met the trunk of the tree, rising at an inclined angle as it grew outward. At the end of it was a very big, very red apple. It nearly glowed with its luscious rosy ripeness in the dappled sunlight. "You get it," I said.

"I'm all the way up here. You'll have to."

I'd never picked an apple straight off a tree before and eaten it when it was still warm from the sun. It simply looked too good to resist. This truly was Eden, I couldn't help musing, and I was Eve, overcome by temptation. Laying my shawl on the grass, I reached up and slid my palms over the comfortingly rough bark of the tree branch. Placing one hand farther, then the other, I inched my way along it until I was hanging several feet off the ground. My arms were already getting sore from the effort, but I was now determined to reach my apple. And I was almost there.

I was close enough to reach out, through the leaves...I almost had it. My fingertips brushed against its smooth, perfect surface. But then I heard a sound. Someone was clearing his throat. The deep rumble was so close behind me it startled me and I lost my grip, tumbling to the ground in an unruly heap.

Slightly dazed from my fall, I looked up to see the most striking vision I had ever laid eyes on.

A man.

He was very tall and backlit by the sun so that his lit silhouette was framed by a wash of bright, molten gold. The shape of him was somehow superb, as though he'd been carved by a master. I could see the colors of him and the details of his white shirt, loose and open at the neck to reveal the tanned skin of his throat. His shirt was exceptionally well made and of high-quality cotton but worn to the point of visible softness. Strapped around his waist was a thick leather belt that holstered two weapons: a gold-handled hunting knife and an exceedingly large sword that was not sheathed in a scabbard but slung bare and shiny into its looped harness. That exposed blade seemed to signify something, purposefully advertising not only its gargantuan size but its artful craftsmanship. *He has the biggest sword of them all.* His leather trews were tucked into tall boots. On his wrist was a wide leather band adorned with gold ornamentation and he wore a gold chain around his neck that was mostly hidden from view inside his shirt. His hair was a deep midnight-black and hung past the collar of his shirt in thick, sun-glinted skeins, curling slightly at the ends. He wore a small braid at either temple, as his traveling guards had also done: a Highlands warrior custom. I noticed all these details abstractly; it was his face and his demeanor that riveted me most of all. His posture was upright but relaxed, utterly confident. Power seemed to radiate from the wide set of his shoulders in heatlike, shimmery waves. The features of his face were bold but aristocratic, from the wide, straight nose to the carved, masculine jaw roughened by the light shadow of stubble. Strong, black, expressive eyebrows arched slightly with a note of absorbed assessment. And his irises, arresting in their charcoal-rimmed pale gray glow, as though alight from within. Long, thick black lashes brushed almost elegantly against his cheeks as he closed his eyes briefly. When he opened them again, there was a flash of bemused satisfaction. His full lips curved in an arrogant pout that wasn't a smile.

"And who," he said, his deep voice curling into me with unusual effect, "might you be?"

CHAPTER THREE

I REALIZED THEN what I must have looked like. My
gown was not only exceptionally low-cut, a detail
that had only become emphasized by the effects of
my ridiculous tree-climbing expedition, but also
bunched up around my knees. I had left my shawl
near the tree's trunk and fleetingly thought of scrambling over to retrieve it but didn't want to make even
more of a spectacle of myself than I already had
done. My hair had come loose and hung down, almost to my waist, in untamed coil-tipped curls that
did little to hide my abundant breasts, which were
practically spilling out of the tight bind of my gown. I
knew my face was likely flushed from my exertions.
And worst of all, I was still agog at the spectacle of
this…this *person* who stood over me with all the ad-
vantaged superiority of the lord that he was. I recognized instantly that *this* was the venerable Laird
Knox Mackenzie, not only from his vague resemblance to his sisters but also from the aura of authority that clung to him along with the fine, well-worn
clothing, the gold adornments and the immense, exposed steel sword. Power was written all over him.

He remained motionless for several seconds,

seemingly stunned. Or miffed, perhaps, by my brazen intrusion into his ordered world.

Then, after a brief bout of what appeared to be indecision, he held his hand out to me.

The gesture—and I noticed that his hand was large and strong-looking and he wore a gold ring on his right pinky, which struck me as incongruent to this overall impression of excellence: edgy somehow, as though he had a hint of pirate in him, or a little devil that lurked in the deeper recesses of his character—was enough to stun me out of my stupor. But I hesitated. I was almost afraid to touch him. I suspected—and it was confirmed as soon as I placed my hand in his—that his effect would be absolute. A flourish of warmth leached into me from the point of contact. The enveloping clasp of his hand pulled me to my feet with ease. Despite the fact that I was tall for a woman and was often able to look men in the eye, he outsized me considerably. I felt subtly dominated by him and, for the first time in my life, that feeling was not entirely unpleasant. But my initial stunned reaction was fading, and my usual resilience was returning to me. I had never been one to cower under the weight of authority and I met his unwavering gaze with my own.

He did not immediately release his hold on me. His gray eyes, from this closer angle, were startlingly vivid, the darkness of his thick lashes and the charcoal rim of his irises contrasting with the light, charged brightness of his keen attention. He did not smile, yet there were sparks of measured raptness in him, as though I had somehow caught him by surprise but he was too controlled to be visibly caught off guard. His gaze wandered then, lower, and I pulled my hand away, making an unsuccessful attempt to stretch the cloth of my gown up a fraction to cover myself. I ran my hands down the bodice of my dress, to smooth it, and my fingers found the length of a curl, which I played with idly, knowing there was nothing to be done about the state of my hair. The blasted blond-red curls were untamable.

Appearing to be mired in some sort of trance of his own, Knox Mackenzie licked his lips then. The way his did this was so unconsciously yet wickedly sultry, I was utterly hypnotized. His bottom lip was plump and wet. The sight of his mouth was unbearably...*inviting*. I felt an outrageous urge to *taste* those lips. Shocked by the turn of my own thoughts, I looked away, letting my eyes rest instead on the long length of his sword.

"I'm still waiting," he said softly. My gaze returned to his face. His manner was stern and solemn.

Waiting?

"What is your name," he repeated, "and how do you find yourself here at Kinloch, climbing apple trees?" It struck me that Laird Mackenzie would already have known my name and all the details about which he had just asked me. His sisters and his guards would have fully and immediately informed him of our story and the nature of our impromptu visit. Yet he wanted to hear the details as I offered them. This intrigued me, and seemed to hint at hidden facets of his very guarded disposition: he was wary and meticulous and practiced.

With that, he looked up at the apple I had been attempting to pick. In a move that seemed slightly incongruous to the inherent sternness in him, he reached for it with one hand, straining so that the edge of his shirt came untucked, exposing a glimpse of his torso, which was lightly tanned and muscled. The masculine *hardness* of his body made me feel inexplicably giddy. I laughed lightly at the state he had found me in, and at the image of my wanton dishevelment.

"Falling *out of* apple trees, you mean?" I said, my laughter lingering.

Laird Mackenzie did not return my smile but instead contemplated me with narrowed eyes. He held the apple out to me, but not close enough for me to easily reach it. I would need to take a step forward to do that. He was challenging me.

As imposing a figure as he was, I didn't feel intimidated by him. Quite the opposite. His expression, despite its commanding scrutiny, was not unkind. He was intrigued by me, this was clear enough, possibly enough to grant me leniency for whatever rules of decorum I might have broken, or maybe because of them. I did take a step forward, and as I bridged that narrowing divide, a tiny ripple of warmth darted through the low pit of my stomach. That peculiar

urge to taste his full lips returned to me as a most unfamiliar, compelling, barely there ache that seemed
to start in my mouth and infuse my body with a
lightly feral flush.

I took the apple, and the brush of his fingers
against mine caused the flush to flare. I'll admit I
was mildly disconcerted by this newfound sensation, but it wasn't unpleasant. Not at all. In fact, I felt
surprisingly spirited, in a soft, subdued way. I was
suddenly glad my shawl wasn't wrapped around me,
concealing me. My breasts felt rounded and plush.
Since I wouldn't have dreamed of acting on my urges
but was indeed feeling quite overwhelmed to taste
something, I took a bite of the ripe red fruit, which
was, as I had guessed, warm from the sun and the
heat of Knox Mackenzie's hand. And juicy. So very
delicious. I took another bite and the juice wet my
lips and dripped down my chin.

Knox Mackenzie was watching my mouth with
a glazed, spellbound expression that looked very
similar to how I *felt.* I didn't dare to presume he
was thinking the same thing I was, that his urges
might be mirroring my own. Maybe he was hungry.
"Would you like a bite?" I asked him, sucking some
juice from the apple.

I was somewhat surprised when he said, "Aye. I
would like a bite."

There was something increasingly sensual about
this exchange. He took the apple from my grasp,
watching my eyes as he bit into it with decadent rel-

ish. *God,* that greedy *mouth.* I had never found such a thing—or such a person—so fascinating.

"My name is Amelia," I said, almost breathlessly. "Amelia Taylor. I'm—"

"Who are you talking to, Ami?" Hamish's voice came from far above. I'd practically forgotten he was perched up there. Knox Mackenzie looked up.

"I believe I've just met Laird Mackenzie," I called up to my nephew.

"How do you know who I am?" Knox asked. Actually, it was more like a demand than a polite question.

"Everyone knows *Laird* Knox Mackenzie," I said, remembering Katriona's annoyance at my complete ignorance when his name had first been spoken of, and my thoughts at the time. "From the tribesmen of deepest Africa to the nomadic plainsmen of the Americas."

His dark eyebrows knitted together as he attempted to gauge whether I was mocking him, or something else. I wasn't sure either way if I was—I hadn't meant to—but I smiled at his expression. This man was not at all accustomed to impertinence of any kind whatsoever. *Tease him,* my little devil was whispering. *He doesn't know what to make of you.*

I wondered what he looked like when he smiled, and what his laughter might sound like. I suspected he did not smile often, and I wanted to try to inspire one. But I had no idea how to do such a thing.

Hamish had climbed down and jumped out of the

branch above my head to land lightly beside me. He appraised Knox Mackenzie with a critical eye, deciding for himself whether *this* was the genuine article, the laird with the mightiest weapon. When Hamish's eyes landed on Knox's sword, they widened. It was proof enough. "*You're* Laird Mackenzie?" he said.

"I am. And *you* are…?"

"Hamish—" with barely a pause "—Taylor."

"I've heard about you," Laird Mackenzie said. Hamish appeared stunned by this information, and the laird continued when Hamish didn't respond. "One of my most trusted officers told me of your nerve and your…creativity. He thinks you've the makings of a soldier."

I thought Hamish might burst with the praise. I smiled, but the laird's light note of sarcasm did not escape me. *Creativity.* Hamish's—*our*—tall tale might have been discussed between Lachlan and Knox Mackenzie. Knox's trusted officer had shared his suspicions with his commander, who was also, quite possibly, his friend. Of course he would have. It was wise to voice suspicions, to be alert and aware of newcomers who were residing within the walls of your own keep. This sort of practice, I suspected, was typical.

And Knox Mackenzie was a clever man. "Hamish, I need a message sent to my officer Lachlan, who is over at the barracks. Would you be able to deliver this message for me, lad?" Noticing Hamish's small wooden sword that hung from his belt, Knox added,

"In return for the favor, I'll see if any of the men have a smaller steel sword that they no longer have use of. You look man enough to handle an upgrade."

Hamish's jaw dropped open at the thought: that he might get a steel sword of his very own. It took him several seconds to respond. "Aye, Laird Mackenzie. *Aye*. What's your message?"

"Tell him I have a few things to discuss with my new guest. And after we've finished speaking, I will be having a similar conversation with her young brother. I'd like Lachlan to give you a tour of the barracks while you're waiting for Amelia, and see if any small swords are about. The barracks are that way," he said, pointing. "On the other side of the apple orchard. I will meet you in the grand hall after the midday meal has been cleared away. Have you got all that?"

"Aye," Hamish said, and he took off in a full run, disappearing from sight.

Knox Mackenzie was going to question Hamish and me *separately,* to see if our stories matched. A faint flutter of panic squirmed in my stomach, but I forced myself to remain calm. We'd already established the details of our tale, and we were both gifted and practiced with spinning lies, for better or worse. There was no reason we couldn't sail through our individual interrogations with ease.

But I felt far from easy.

"Would you join me for a chat?" Laird Mackenzie said, without waiting for an answer. The question was clearly not a request but understood in advance to be an order that would be readily obeyed. I almost felt a perverse inclination to refuse, but then he added, "I can offer you food and drink. You must be hungry after your travels."

Knox Mackenzie had a way about him that intrigued me. He was a blend of contradictions that somehow harmonized perfectly. His face was both rugged and refined, his tall form both relaxed and on guard. His expression showed no trace of humor. Yet there was a glint in his eyes that might have been described as charisma. He was comfortable with the upper hand that he undoubtedly always had, with whomever it was he happened to be with. He was laird of his clan, leader of his army, wealthy beyond belief, blue-blooded to the extreme and, as if that wasn't enough, he was also endowed not only with a wide-shouldered, perfectly proportioned physique that would intimidate even seasoned warriors, but also a masculine beauty that no doubt caused many women to swoon.

Luckily for me, I wasn't one of them. I could acknowledge that there was a definite allure to the supreme Laird Knox Mackenzie. If I'd been a hapless debutante with good breeding and a cultured sense of gentility, I might have described him as utterly dazzling. But I was not a hapless debutante. I was in fact a skilled and underhanded cardshark with few prospects beside the strength of my own wit and, perhaps, the occasional use of my own physical attributes. Attributes that had so far brought me more trouble than advantage. I could see the way his gaze lingered on the lavish curves of my body, gliding over my full lips, touching the long, feminine coils of my softly fiery hair and caressing the plush bounty of my half-exposed breasts. It was a look I was accustomed to, for better or worse.

It was glaringly clear to us both that I was at a distinct disadvantage in the universal scheme of things. Despite this, there was some indescribable thread of imbalance, in the opposite direction, as though he was deferring to me on a base level and in a way that flustered some inner sanctum deep within his psyche that had not been flustered for some time. I saw the light touch of craving in his eyes, and it was laced, oddly, with a profound flicker of sadness. Again, a subtle contradiction. He was an enigma and one that, against my better judgment, I couldn't help being drawn to. Knox Mackenzie was privileged but he was not at all unscathed: this was a pronounced feature of his mien.

So, he was clever. And so was I. I planned to explore these small intuitions, to use them to my best advantage. After all, they were the only advantages I had and were tenuous at best.

"Thank you, Laird Mackenzie. Aye, I am hungry. And thirsty. It has been a long trip."

He walked over to where my shawl lay on the ground and picked it up. He didn't just hand it to me but draped it carefully around my shoulders. A gentlemanly gesture—not something I was particularly accustomed to. I left the shawl where he had placed it, not bothering to fasten it yet with the pin. His eyes were on me and, as never before, with a sense of almost bashful amusement, I found I *liked* that he was watching me, feasting somehow on the look of me. It made me want to grant him whatever pleasure he might have been deriving from my femininity. After years of discouraging or altogether ignoring the forthright attention of men, this was an entirely new response.

He led me through the orchard to one of the side doors of the manor. There were servants and other clanspeople about, all of whom bowed to Laird Mackenzie as he walked by. They took little notice of me, beyond a light glance. In some circumstances, it might have been inappropriate for a young woman to be alone with a man. But lairds, I suspected, were above scandal. Either they were too highly respected to be accused of making untoward advances, or they were allowed whatever untoward advances they chose to make. I hardly cared. It wasn't as though my reputation was as pure as the driven snow. That I had managed to traverse the path of my young adulthood without experiencing even so much as a first kiss was all but a miracle. I wasn't afraid of being alone with Knox Mackenzie. And, in fact, I *was* hungry.

Our path was interrupted by the sudden approach of a young soldier, who was well armed and also bloodied and dirty as though from a fight. "Laird Mackenzie," he said, with clear urgency in his voice. "A dispute between Eamon and Fraser is in full force in the sparring ring. I fear one of them might take the other's life if they aren't persuaded otherwise. I've attempted to intervene, but they're in a blind, provoked rage. They've already injured themselves quite severely." Then, as though noticing me despite the circumstances, he took a quick bow. "If you'll forgive the intrusion, milady."

I was unaccustomed to being addressed in such a way, and I fumbled with my answer before I could give a reply that might have sounded appropriate. "I, uh, not...not at all."

Knox Mackenzie was too preoccupied—and annoyed, if I was reading him correctly—with the matter at hand to take notice of my response either way. "Isn't there anyone else who can break up two hotheaded recruits? Where's Lachlan?"

"I couldn't find him," the young soldier said.

Laird Mackenzie's manner had changed markedly, his resolute seriousness shielding any fleeting, momentary connection we might have skirted around. "If you would be so kind, Miss Taylor," he gruffed, "to wait for me in the hall, I will be with you shortly. This will not take long."

"Of course, Laird Mackenzie," I replied, and I was pleased with the gentility of my response; I sounded wholly proper, and suitably respectful. As I very nearly was.

As Laird Mackenzie retreated into the unsee-able distance with his soldier, I made my way to the manor, entering through the side door and finding my way to the grand hall, where the tables had been set with cheese, fruit and bread.

There was no one about. The servers must have been preparing the remainder of the meal in the kitchens.

My stomach rumbled at the sight of the abundant food. Tiny tufts of steam still rose from the fresh-baked bread rolls, and the heavenly scent was enough to break down my barriers of etiquette. Surely they wouldn't mind if I took something to eat before the others arrived. I *had* been offered food by the laird himself, after all, and also invited by Christie. My last meal had been a hearty one—more than twelve hours ago. And the apple…well, Knox Mackenzie had eaten most of it in the end. I'd always had a healthy appetite, yet more often than not I was left unsatisfied. And the bounty before me was simply more than my limited powers of resistance could handle. I picked up a small, rounded loaf of bread, breaking it open. I placed a hunk of the ripe cheese between the still-warm halves, watching it melt. Then I took a blissful bite. Unthinkingly, I reached for more bread, for Hamish, stuffing it in the pocket of my gown. And another. He'd be hungry after his morning in the barracks.

At that moment, Laird Mackenzie walked into

the hall, accompanied by not only Christie but also Katriona.

Oh, damnation.

How uncouth I must have appeared. It occurred to me that I could have been just a wee bit less eager about helping myself to this food on offer. I didn't believe they would *mind* that I'd taken a small bite of bread before the dinner bell was rung, but the way I was stuffing not only my mouth but also my pockets might have looked less than genteel.

Ah, well. My intentions were as true as they'd ever been: to look after my nephew as best I could, by finding food for him along my travels. Partaking in sustenance for myself was hardly a crime worth punishing, I reasoned.

I swallowed, brushing the crumbs from my chin with my hand, for lack of anything more suitable. All three of them were staring at me, of course. As I might have expected, this transgression would only fuel Katriona's scorn; she looked almost amused by my total lack of decorum, as though I had proven a point she'd been trying unsuccessfully to make all along. I thought of stuttering out some excuses, but that might make matters worse. Instead, I squared my shoulders and smiled gracefully.

Knox Mackenzie's face was virtually unreadable. This irked me. If it was pity he felt for me, or disdain, I wanted to be able to tell, I realized. But he wouldn't even give me that. He just leaned his shoulder against a wooden pillar to watch me, his thumb casually laced beneath the belt at his hips, as though to take his time and carefully assess whether I should be regarded as a thief, a beggar, a nuisance or something else altogether.

Christie stepped forward and laced her arm through mine. "I'm famished, too," she said conspiratorially, and I was grateful. Her benevolence was the most pronounced aspect of her character. I wished I might someday have a chance to reciprocate her kindness. "We didn't even break our fast this morning, did we, Amelia? You and your brother must be half-starved by now, after the journey you've had."

Before I could respond to her, to thank her for tactfully smoothing the awkwardness caused by my misdemeanor, Knox Mackenzie said brusquely, "Shall we conduct our meeting now, Amelia? I can offer you more food in my den…if you're still hungry." As if to imply that I might have already eaten my fill.

I thought of telling him that I could have eaten all the food in the room if he'd just leave me to it. Instead, I smiled and said, "As you wish, Laird Mackenzie."

Katriona's flicker of amusement faded. In a complete reversal, her face took on a note of mild anxiety and she offered, "I could bring the food to your den if you'd like."

Offhandedly, without giving her so much as a glance, Knox Mackenzie replied, "Call for one of the servants to bring it. Amelia, this way, if you will."

Christie patted my arm and turned her attention to Katriona, placating an apparent uprising of distress in her that I appeared to have a knack for inspiring.

I followed Laird Mackenzie through a door and down a candlelit corridor.

We entered a large, low-ceilinged chamber that was opulently decorated with well-crafted yet comfortable-looking furniture, woven rugs and a large circular table. Several shuttered windows were open and looked out upon the orchards. A servant came immediately to the door, and Laird Mackenzie asked her to bring us some food and ale.

I stood by the window, feeling increasingly on edge about the inquiry that was about to begin. Perhaps sensing my unease, the laird invited me to sit in one of two stuffed leather chairs that had been situated to enjoy the view. I was glad he hadn't asked me to take a seat at the meeting table. This cozy corner seemed more conducive to a casual, informal chat than a full-blown interrogation. The servant returned, placing a large plate of assorted meats, cheeses and breads and a pitcher of ale on a small table between us. Then she took her leave, closing the door with a heavy thud.

Laird Mackenzie poured ale into two goblets and handed one to me. I accepted the drink, even though I knew he was likely just trying to loosen my tongue, hoping to get me tipsy so I'd spill all my secrets. Wise to his ploys, I would humor him but I would not fall into his traps. I would drink. Very, very slowly.

But when I tasted the ale, it was so delicious, lightly bubbling with a hint of malty sweetness, and I was so thirsty that I ended up drinking half the goblet in one go. Even as I silently cursed myself for what would certainly be unwise, I couldn't resist just one more sip. A large one. I had never tasted anything so refreshing in all my life.

Knox Mackenzie watched me and it was the very first time I saw a hint of humor in him; his mouth skewed just slightly to the side. Not a smile, as such. But a sign that he was at least human. "You *were* thirsty," he commented.

I took one more sip, nodding.

He handed me a plate with some bread and slices of meat and cheese. "In case you didn't get enough in the hall." His gaze dropped to the rounded pockets of my dress, where I'd stashed the food for Hamish, then rose slowly upward until he was once again contemplating my face and my hair with lingering interest, a pastime that appeared to be one of his new favorites.

My stomach, in my mild anxiousness, suddenly didn't feel particularly hungry, but when I took a small bite of the offering, the flavors of it were so tasty that I decided I was in fact still quite famished.

The laird allowed me to eat for several minutes. But he had questions on his mind that he was clearly eager to ask. "Amelia," he began. Then he paused, looking measuredly into my eyes. "That *is* your real name, is it not?"

Already he was accusing me of lying and we hadn't even begun. This riled me. He hadn't even *heard* my story yet and already he was distrusting it. It occurred to me, aye, that my indignance was maybe, just barely, the tiniest bit absurd. After all, I *was* about to spin a partly fictional tale. But still.

"I heard your brother call you something else," he said. This eased my irritation by a degree. So he hadn't distrusted me—yet. He'd only heard Hamish's nickname for me.

"He calls me Ami. It means—"

"Friend," he finished for me. Something about the tone of his voice, so deep and impressive, touched me in a very strange place. A glowing burn settled below my rib cage, extending in seeping, brazen directions; this burn felt remarkably, and intensely, like *longing*. His eyes were fixed on mine, only compounding the effect. I was glad I was sitting down, and I took another cool sip of the ale.

"Aye," I replied softly. "Friend." Of course he spoke French, and probably twelve other languages besides. No doubt he'd traveled the world and read every book, too.

"You've come from Edinburgh. 'Tis a long journey."

"Aye," I agreed. "We traveled for six days."

"Tell me about it."

His soft command was patient and, even worse, *kind*. As though he was reading the difficulties of our journey and all that had come before it in the expression on my face. It was this note of compassion that found me uncharacteristically remorseful that I had need to lie to him. I knew with certainty that if he discovered the truth he would likely banish me from the grounds of his keep before I could even finish my drink. In a daft act of defiance, I took another sip of my ale, finishing it. And now I had two things to feel remorseful about. He'd tricked me! By serving me a drink so delicious there was no way I could resist it.

All right, so he'd won that hand. But I had no intention of giving away any secrets, ale or no ale. I knew I could handle my drink better than most. Ale and whiskey were plentiful at my family's gaming club, and although I rarely imbibed, I had once taken a game, and lost, against a regular client named Burns, a devilish brute who seduced rich women for a living and would frequent our club when he was between heiresses. He'd placed a handful of shillings on my table for a single roll of the dice, mine against his. It was enough money to keep our creditors at bay for at least a week, so I'd taken him on. He'd bet me I couldn't match him drink for drink and continue to resist his charms. I wasn't an heiress, I'd argued. For me, he'd said, he would let that small detail slide, just this once. His roll—two sixes—had been unbeatable. I'd taken the drinks, poured by Nora, one of the club's hostesses. It had helped that Burns had already been well into his cups when the challenge began. I'd taken four shots of whiskey before he'd passed out cold. *Well played, lassie,* Nora had laughed. *You've a hollow leg.* At the time I'd taken the praise to heart: it took a lot to impress Nora.

To my dismay, I realized that while Burns had merely become blurrier, Knox Mackenzie now had only become more...*beautiful* with the light effects of the ale. He was too masculine to be called beautiful, but it was a word that came to mind. His black hair framed his face, all thick and glinting. I'd never seen hair that richly black. The gold of the chain at his neck and the thick cuff bracelet he wore only added to his aura of nobility and sovereignty. *Damn him. Now he's trying to undermine my control with his regal allure.*

"Why are you traveling north and where were you headed when you were intercepted by my sisters?" he asked.

And so I began, offering as little information as possible, resolved to embellish and rearrange when the story required. I kept Hamish in mind, too, making sure to keep true to our plan as we'd made it, in the woods behind the tavern. "Our parents have passed," I said, with genuine feeling. This was, after all, true; at least in my case, it was a certainty. I didn't allow myself, in that moment, to even think about Hamish's parents. I tried to keep my voice steady as I continued. It was all becoming a bit more difficult than I'd imagined, this ruse, but I had no choice now but to follow through with it. "We were told by our father, in his final hour, that we have relatives in the Highlands, but we know none of the details of their identity or their whereabouts. So we set out to search for them."

"Until you were attacked," he continued, not sounding as concerned by the detail as he perhaps should have, "by masked bandits dressed in black and wielding silver-hilted swords."

I felt my eyes narrow just slightly. "It sounds like you already know all the finer details of the story, Laird Mackenzie," I said, vexed not only by the light dismissal in his tone but also by this ridiculous situation I'd landed myself in. How on earth had I managed to find myself on the run and at the mercy of this admittedly dashing laird in his admittedly idyllic empire, attempting to convince him that I'd been robbed by a gang of fictional thieves? "There's not much point in me repeating it to you if you've already been told, in intricate, itemized flourish, of our plight."

He ignored this completely. "Tell me more about these bandits. From which direction did they ride? Describe to me their features, their clothing, their weapons, their horses. All of it. What exactly did they say to you?"

Smug brute. He was domineering to a fault, I thought. The little devil in me wanted to somehow challenge his blatant attempt to intimidate me, and practically bully me into telling him what he wanted to know.

This was where he would discover the extent of

our deceit: it was all in the details. And I had a feeling Hamish would be explicitly imaginative when it came to the embellishments. So I kept it simple. The ale was, if anything, encouraging my dramatic flair. I willed myself to channel the fear I'd felt, when we'd fled Edinburgh, when I'd—only just—managed to slip through the hands of the man who hunted me. I believe I might have been somewhat convincing; the memory, to be sure, was still fresh and the terror was easy enough to summon. "I was so overcome that I can't remember all of it. I feared for our lives. I thought they would kill us, and—" *I thought they might hurt me. Violate me and break me in the most profound manner imaginable. And when I struggled and attempted to refuse, I thought they might kill Hamish.* I faltered, falling silent as I remembered.

He was coming for me. For us.

"You must take my son, and yourself, away from here." My sister grabbed my arm, pushing me away even as she pulled me closer. Her dark eyes shone bright with fear. *"Take Hamish, Amelia. You must get him out of Edinburgh. Take him far away from here, where they won't find him. And don't come back."*

"Cecelia, I'm not leaving without you."

"You must! For Hamish. He's not safe here, and neither are you."

"Nor you, sister. Fawkes will take out my desertion on you if I leave. Either I give him what he wants or we flee together."

My sister was as horrified as I was by the thought

of Fawkes possessing me merely to exercise his power over our family. Perhaps even more so. She remembered more vividly the lifestyle we had once led, of dignity and civility; she valued and coveted this ideal more than any other, as our mother once had. "You are not for sale, Amelia. 'Tis not an option."

"Neither is leaving you behind! You must come with us." Sebastian Fawkes was one of the most powerful ganglords in Edinburgh. A man who hungered for power and would go to any lengths to gain it. A man who enjoyed the chase, the game, the fear in the eyes of those he sought to better. Myself included. I had intrigued him from the start. My looks and my insolence had fueled his conquest. My family's predicament had given him the perfect avenue to gain the upper hand when I'd refused to engage him. He could have forced me, but it wasn't enough. He wanted to own me in every possible way. By whatever means necessary. "I'll not leave you here alone to fend for yourself."

"I'm not alone, Amelia. James has taken a shipment south, but he will return for me. If I leave, we'll lose what little we have left. My place is here. I have to see this through."

"Your place is with us!" I insisted. Not as bait, to lure me back. None of this mattered: this club, the shreds of our livelihood, this city, with its confining, unending hardships. My sister was much more involved in the underworld, mostly by default, than

I was. Her husband, James, over time, had fallen further and further into the abyss of debt. He had become a pawn and a runner in a dangerous game. Despite it all, Cecelia was loyal to him, for all that he had tried to do. My mother's ingrained sense of duty to home and husband, to keeping up appearances at all costs and to stubborn perseverance had manifested themselves strongly in her eldest daughter. Cecelia held doggedly on to some tattered hope that all was not lost.

And she would not listen.

"Please, Cecelia," I begged her. "Please come with us. I'll not go without you."

The banging at the door down below was growing louder, the commotion gaining momentum.

"You can, and you will," she insisted. "You are the strongest person I know, Amelia. You'll rise to the top no matter what you do, or where you go. Take Hamish, I beg you, and don't look back. They're coming. Hurry!"

The pounding at the door gave way to a smash and a flurry of voices. Fawkes was earlier than his promises had indicated. Much earlier.

The noise was getting louder. And closer.

"Take him!" she cried, urgent. "I know what Fawkes threatened you with, and what he's capable of. He's taken my husband to keep me here, to keep me quiet. I have to wait for James. You must go. Go and don't look back. Keep him safe, Amelia. Please. I beg you. Do whatever it takes to keep him safe."

Cecelia gave me a brief hug. And then she ran in the opposite direction.

There was no more time to argue with her. If I waited any longer, my opportunity for escape would be lost. It might already be lost.

I woke Hamish. Quickly and quietly, I led him to the library down the hall. Closing and locking the door, I pulled him toward the bookcase. I knew where the latch was. Behind a black leather-bound book about, of all things, the deciduous trees of the British Isles. I'd read it only once, in my quest to learn every shred of knowledge I could get my hands on. But it was hardly riveting material. Which was precisely why I had put it in this space, hiding the latch that would release the bookcase from its frame. I had discovered the secret portal many years ago, when I'd been searching for something to read. At that time, a small red book had sat there, almost conspicuously, bringing attention to itself. Its pages were blank except for these words: Be free. *The small red book became one of my most treasured possessions. I used it as a journal, to record my innermost thoughts and restless dreams, of a life far from Edinburgh's backstreets, away from the lowlife and the immorality, to a place more serene and forgiving. This small library had set me free many times over in my imagination, through books, fantasies and aspirations. Now it would, I could only hope, deliver a more literal sense of the word. I pulled the bulky shelf forward, exposing a hidden passageway.*

Loud banging on the door nearly undid me. I could hear Fawkes's voice. Calling for me. Threatening me with his vengeance and his obsession. My heart was in my throat. The lock was rusted with age; it wouldn't hold for long.

"Why are we running, Ami?" Hamish had whispered. "Where is my mother?" I pushed Hamish into the narrow passageway, barely fitting through it myself, pulling it closed behind us until I heard the click of the lock. We were in the dark staircase now. "These men have less than honorable intentions," I had replied to him, once I was sure we were well out of range of being heard. "For me. Your father is exporting a shipment to England and your mother waits for him. We will meet up with them again when it is safe to do so. Until then, we must find a safe place, far from here."

Feeling our way down, drawing our fingers against the rough-hewn wooden walls, we reached the bottom of the staircase. Cautiously, I turned the key, opening the door to a dark underground tunnel, which led us to a hidden doorway, far down the back alley and away from the building itself. There were shouts from around corners. Unseen commotion called for us, seeking us out. We ran through the backstreets, toward the northern edge of town, putting as much distance between us and them as we could. After a time, we'd stopped for a moment, out of breath. It was then that we saw a farmer's wagon, pulling away from a small stables, half filled with

*hay. We climbed on as it began to roll. And we had
done it. I had escaped him. For now.*

"I was so afraid," I whispered. And I was no longer lying. I *had* been afraid. More afraid than I'd
ever been in my life. The tears in my eyes were not
an act and they pooled before I even realized what
was happening. I had not cried since we'd fled, not a
single tear for the displaced disaster my life had become, or for my sister, whose fate I could not know.

I didn't know why I was crying now. I *did* feel
overcome with emotion, aye, but I also wondered
if I was reacting to Knox Mackenzie's authority by
playing on his manly concern. This was the sort of
reaction I might have staged in the past, although
this time my feelings felt unnervingly authentic. Annoyed with myself for showing such overt vulnerability, I wiped the tears away, wanting to temper my
weakness with a show of resilience. I had a job to
do, I remembered: deception in the name of survival.
I imagined telling him the truth, and his reaction.

*I'm a card dealer, Laird Mackenzie, and a gifted
one at that. I've resided in one of the less prosperous gaming clubs in old Edinburgh for the past ten
years, using my blossoming feminine wiles to deceive
the less-skilled, downtrodden gamblers, conning
them out of money to keep my family off the streets.
I can count cards, curse in French and drink a half-
inebriated man under the table. Are you charmed
yet? Offer me a job, Laird, and look after my nephew
for me while I travel unchaperoned back to Edin-*

burgh to see if my sister is being held against her will by an evil ganglord.

Nay, the truth would be best kept quiet. "We hid, and we escaped," was all I said on that topic.

Knox Mackenzie was watching me intently. Little rays of kindness seemed to be shining through the veneer of his staunch authority, as though he wanted to contain them but couldn't. "You're safe now," he said. "There's nothing to be afraid of here inside the walls of Kinloch."

Here he was, this prodigious, controlling laird and warrior, offering not only protection, but solace. Safety. It was such an unfamiliar mood for me: that of feeling buffered from all danger and difficulty. There was no way Sebastian Fawkes could gain entry to this place, not with an entire army protecting its walls and its citizens. I had food on my plate and, aye, stuffed into my pockets. I was warm and sheltered and my nephew was more well cared for and happily engaged at this moment than he might ever have been in his life.

It might have been the ale. In an unintentional gesture of gratitude, I placed my hand on Knox Mackenzie's.

The touch of that warm, comforting, calloused hand was unexpected and fed a fiery warmth into my body as though he was ablaze with currents of energy. The rush of my response was unnerving, and he, too, seemed struck. He exhaled lightly. And as he slid his hand from mine, I found myself simultaneously pulling back from his touch. I was afraid of my response to him: afraid of what I might *do*. I was wary of the volatility of my body's urges. Bizarrely, I felt the effects of Knox Mackenzie's touch as a squirmy, primal quiver in a most secret, womanly place. That lightly pulsing ache was wildly distracting.

Shockingly, what I wanted to do was to pull his hands closer, to feel the strength of them. Gripping me, overpowering me, holding me down as he lavished his magnificence all over me, in whatever way he chose to do.

Instead, I folded my hands demurely in my lap. I really might have been suffering some unexpected side effects to the stress of recent days that I made a point to discourage. I took a moment to focus on the light wring of my own fists as I squirmed lightly in my seat. I waited for the sweet, swelling anticipation to fade away. But the urges were so unexpected and so strong that I had to force myself to remain still. I was not well practiced in the art of restraint. I took a deep breath, summoning all my powers of control, composing myself as best I could.

After a minute or more, I looked up at him. The thick strands of his black-on-black hair framed his face in artful disarray, contrasting somehow with the unyielding seriousness of his expression.

He was waiting for me to continue, I realized.

"I'm sorry," I said. "'Tis difficult to speak of. All of it. We've had a number of trials to test our courage of late, and it all occasionally gets the better of me. I do want to give you the information you seek." It felt strange to apologize—something I rarely had need to do.

He might have been grateful for my apparent compliance. My tears, it seemed, had tempered the totality of his bravado and the forcefulness of his approach. I couldn't help noticing that the sudden gentleness in his manner, shining out from beneath his staunch exterior, only succeeded in magnifying his beauty tenfold, if such a thing were possible. He literally took my breath away with his stately radiance.

"'Tis I who should be apologizing," he said. "You've not yet recovered from an unspeakable ordeal and already I'm forcing you to relive it. I'm sure you understand that my motives are purely in the interest of the safety of my clan and all those who reside within the walls of Kinloch, you and your brother included. If there are threats to our peace, I need to know about them."

"Aye," I said, fairly overcome with the magnitude not only of all he had to offer but of all he was. Pure, somehow. Surly, aye, and stern, yet beautifully devoid of malice and spite.

Could it be true that he *believed me?* The possibility unfurled something in me. I *wanted* him to believe me, I found. Desperately. I wanted to give him the truth and only the truth. I wanted to forge a bond and earn his trust.

But I could not.

My secrets were too deep. My truth was too sordid. I twirled a long coil of my hair around a finger.

"I'm going to ask you one question," he said, "and I want an honest answer. I won't prod you further on this one point, nor will I ask you for any further explanation. But I ask for your honesty to spare my men unnecessary danger and my clan unnecessary work and worry." He paused. His silver eyes speared me with sincerity and also challenge. Causing unnecessary danger to his men and frivolous, possibly harmful distractions to his clan would not be taken at all lightly; this was clearly written across his swarthy nobleman's face. "I understand there are layers to your situation that may extend in directions you are not, as yet, ready to share. We all have details of our stories that are less desirable—or less *easy,* many of which are entirely beyond our control—than others."

Again he paused and I found myself disconcertingly drawn to him, for his patient diplomacy, his princely beauty, his sharp perceptiveness. If I hadn't had cause to reasonably avoid all involvement with him for both our sakes, I might have described this surge of emotion in stronger terms. I might have admitted that I was in fact *besotted* with Knox Mackenzie already. Or at least the *idea* of him. Of this heady combination of his glaring beauty, his righteous protection and the true north of his moral compass.

"One honest word is all I ask," he continued. "Can you give me that much?" His voice was ridiculously soothing, penetrative somehow, as though he had the power to peel back my defenses with just the velvety tones of a well-placed request.

"Aye," I said. I could give him that much. I could at least *try* to give him that much.

His steely voice matched his eyes. "Do these bandits truly exist? Were you truthfully attacked by masked murderers less than a day's ride from my clan and family's keep?"

I was watching Knox Mackenzie's mouth as he spoke, mesmerized by the perfection of it. And I had never wanted anything so much as I wanted to touch those lips at that moment. To taste him. To somehow connect with him in not only a physical way but a meaningful one.

"Nay," I whispered, transfixed.

And there it was. To my surprise, the contemplative pout of his lips curled into the very beginnings of a subdued smile. It faded almost instantly into a look of chiding approval. "See?" he said. "That wasn't so very difficult, now, was it?"

I didn't respond, looking down once again at my clenched hands. If I was glad I had, as he'd so eloquently pointed out, spared his men and his clan some undue danger and worry, the feeling quickly faded as the realization of my failure shone through. He'd tricked me *again!* With his beguiling, captivating charm, I was like putty in his hands! This simply wouldn't do. I needed to focus on my task, and *not* turn feeble and love struck at the first blink of his ridiculously long, dark lashes or the expression of fascination on his exalted face. Or the way his teeth bit gently into his sensual bottom lip as he waited for my answer. He'd combined these lures with a generous dose of well-timed and stealthily administered ale. And his tricks had worked!

Now I'd ruined our carefully constructed story. I'd doomed us even further. Hamish would be summoned before I could speak to him alone. Our stories wouldn't match. We'd be thrown out, to make our way on foot to the next tavern or the next town to find work, if we could, or to steal or gamble or starve. Once again we'd be on the run and unprotected from the wily and deadly men who were at this very moment—I had no doubt—scouring every inch of Edinburgh for our trail.

Damn this *Laird* Knox Mackenzie. He was clever indeed. He'd outwitted me with his crafty sincerity, finding my weaknesses with barely any effort at all. I would need to be smarter than this if I was going to keep my nephew out of harm's way. It was true that I didn't want to lie to Knox Mackenzie. But I remembered why I *must* lie to him.

And so I backtracked. I sat up straight and looked him in the eye defiantly. "What I *meant* to say, Laird Mackenzie, is that I don't know. I couldn't see clearly. It was Hamish who saw them enough to describe them. I was overcome, you see, and I wouldn't want to retell the events unless I was absolutely certain of all the finer details."

"My guard informed me that you were somewhat

elaborate in your description about your ordeal to him. In a tavern not far from here."

Damn that Lachlan! He'd recounted every minuscule crumb of our encounter with the Mackenzies in that blasted tavern.

I was flustered. I wanted to stand up, to gain distance from Knox Mackenzie. His closeness softened something in me. I wanted to go to the open window, to get some fresh air and to clear my head. As I stood, my shawl, which I had not fastened, slipped off my shoulders and onto the floor.

I leaned down to retrieve it, but he was quicker. He reached to pick it up with his hand. Then he rose toward me. We were both half-crouched, our faces close. Leaning forward as I was, without any covering but my low-cut dress, my breasts were very nearly escaping the confines of my too-tight bodice. My lush, creamy curves were in fact quite close to… his mouth. His sinfully beautiful, scornful mouth. His full lips were parted and he was so close I could feel the warm puffs of his breath on my skin. These light, sultry gusts were hypnotizingly rife with influence. His exhaling impressions seemed to seep into me like small, liquid darts of sensation. Where his air touched me, I became warm and somehow assuaged. My breasts became heavy and tender, their tips tightening into taut, wishful buds. *He could so easily release me, touch me, take my nipples into that surly, decadent mouth.* The thought only inflamed me more. Crouched as I was, with my knees slightly apart, the place between my legs became alarmingly responsive. I had never, ever felt anything like this. Some hidden craving within me was waking up: that's how it felt. An untamed, fledgling sprout of my womanliness had just taken root. *Right there.* We were frozen in place and his eyes were sparked with…something. Some simmering emotion I could not name. Something volatile and outrageously alluring.

What was happening to me?

I felt my pulse in that hidden place, and a quickening, damp heat that ruffled my composure enough to break the trance he held me in. Grasping for the tiniest thread of sanity, I rose in one quick movement and turned away from him. I faced the window and took a deep intake of the fresh breeze, and felt the tiniest bit better for it.

He was behind me. He draped the shawl around my shoulders. I clutched it together in the front in a vain attempt to shield and contain my blossoming desire. I needed to rein myself in, to nip this covetous yearning for Knox Mackenzie in the bud. He was not only a laird, noble to his bones and powerful beyond belief, but possibly at least ten years older than me. Maybe more.

I was a poor, indebted troublemaker who was more at home on the seedy city backstreets than in these fine, rich environs of the privileged. I assured myself that *that* was the reason I was having lustful thoughts of Laird Mackenzie: his wealth and the security he offered. It was impulsive, this desire, not rational. I was responding to his position and his lifestyle.

And his total, upright, virile glory. Damn him!

I couldn't even turn to him. I didn't want to see his face or the solid, sculpted outline of his shoulders. If I did, I feared I would do something wildly inappropriate. Like reach for those strong warrior's hands. Or beg him to put that pouting mouth on my… *on me. On that secret, flowering place.*

Oh, God.

I thought he might be angry, for my unhelpful reply and my muddled vagueness. But his reply was not angry. It was lenient and textured, as though he was reading my barely concealed turbulent response and attempting to calm it. "I can help you," he said.

I let that lofty, useless offer have its way with me. For a moment, I pretended it was true. I imagined him storming into Edinburgh with his army of honorable muscle-bound heroes, rescuing my sister, spearing Fawkes and his thugs and riding off into the sunset, but not before he swooped me into his arms, snuck me into a quiet stable and kissed me everywhere.

Nay. Do not think it. Do not act on it. Be calm and quiet and proper.

Neither of us spoke for a time.

I was glad of this, veering my concentration to the sweet song of a bird and the rosy glow of a distant apple. Then, to my intense surprise, Knox Mackenzie remarked softly, "Your hair is very…unusual. Colorful and wild. It suits you."

This did nothing to help me in my attempts to remain guarded and serene.

He might have been insulting me in a roundabout way. My hair was unruly, it was true. The golden-red curls could never quite be coerced into any real semblance of order. But his comment didn't sound like an insult. It sounded like…something else.

I turned to him. Rapt, even though I made an effort not to be, I looked up at his face.

Oh, bloody hell. He was staggering me again with that manly spark and that proud, brooding pout.

"And yours suits you," I found myself whispering. "I—I like it." It was an inane reply, possibly. But it was, at least, the truth. I did like his hair. I liked the way it fell in different lengths to frame his face in a wholly masculine mane. I liked the slight curl to it and the deepest, darkest blackness of it. I liked how he wore it somewhat shorter than the other warriors I'd met, still longer than the men's styles I was used to. I liked the small braid that was somehow exotic, fastened as it was with a small golden band. I liked how his hair was shiny and caught the sunlight in tints of blue. There was much *too* much to like, in fact, about Knox Mackenzie's hair. And everything else about him.

I noticed then that his gold chain hung partially outside his shirt, displaced when he'd leaned to pick up my shawl. I could see that a gold ring hung from it. In an unthinking, curious move, I touched the ring, gently pulling the chain out so it was fully revealed. He made no move to stop me, but he went very still.

"What's this ring?" I asked.

It was a moment before he spoke and there was a raw, rough edge to his voice when he said, "It was my wife's ring."

His wife. The words were heavy, as though edged in sadness. The steeped, somber tone of this single sentence left no doubt as to what had happened to her. She had somehow been taken from him, wrenchingly, leaving a black hole in her wake.

I held the ring between two fingers. It was a beautiful ring, solid and thick, artfully rounded. It felt warm. Knox's eyes were cast down, not focused on anything, clouded by memories and regret.

"This is her wedding ring," I said softly.

"Aye." I was taken aback by the edge of anger, not directed at me but at some unknowable force that had stolen her. "She died in childbirth with our son. I lost them both."

Such a simple explanation, yet one that echoed with profound, devastating loss. And there was that pronounced thread of vulnerability in him. *This* was the pain that cut him deep and shone through even the hard shell of his war-fired demeanor.

"I'm sorry," I whispered.

"It was several years ago. More than two years ago," he said, and I was struck by his quiet openness.

"I can't bring them back, so I must move forward, according to my brothers. 'Tis time to move on."

"Nay," I responded gently. "You won't ever truly move on. We can't move on from losing the people we love. They stay with us forevermore. They become a part of who we are."

He watched my face. He might have thought I was speaking of my parents and I was. But I was also thinking of my sister, whose fate I did not know. I prayed for her safety and I felt a burrowing connection with Knox Mackenzie. "Aye," was all he said.

"Your brothers," I said. "They are here at Kinloch? In your army?"

"Nay, no longer. They have both married and taken up lairdships of their own. Just recently, in fact."

Here was another stratum of sadness in him: he missed them.

It was a lot to carry around, I thought. Heartbreak, loss, separate and deep layers of loneliness. He was a formidable laird and nobleman. He was king of his kingdom, and what a kingdom it was. But there were large holes in the happiness such a position might have provided.

The urge was remarkably strong: I wanted to comfort him. I wanted to ease those aches and, oddly, I had the distinct feeling that I could.

It might have been the ale that obliterated my good sense and my propriety—neither of which, it had to be said, were overly developed in my character. Or it might have been his influence in all its complex subtleties: the outlandish draw, the vulnerable edges. I was still grasping his chain in my hand. I curled my fingers around it and pulled very, very lightly, drawing him closer to me. He followed my lead, his eyes a striking contrast of light and darkness, until his face was close to mine. His close presence trickled into my body from where his breath touched my face, leaching through me in a red-hot stain of fervor.

In a daring move that I could not have held back even if I'd wanted to, I reached up to finger a longer strand of his black hair. It felt thick and satiny to the touch, like coarse silk. This was a man who had been blessed in all manner of physical flawlessness, aye, and not only that. He was privileged, rich beyond belief, well bred and practically glowing with power. But he was scarred. And it was that fissure of vulnerability in him that drew me to him more than anything else. *That* was the part of him I could relate to.

It was the part of him I could touch.

In every other regard, he was so loftily endowed I'll admit it was somewhat intimidating—and I wasn't a person easily intimidated. But this secret sensitivity in him seemed to put us on suddenly level ground.

He was watching my face—my mouth—with a look of complete absorption. My closeness had somehow peeled away the layers of his utter authority to reveal a demeanor that was no less beautiful and no less dominating, but vastly more *approachable*.

I wanted to do much more than approach Knox Mackenzie. I wanted to immerse myself in him. To drink him in. I loved this *choice* I was being given, the freedom of it. There was no force involved, nor imbalance. The equality of our unexpected, tumultuous attraction was irresistibly empowering.

And he was getting closer. It wasn't just the light pulling pressure of my grip on his chain that drew him to me. He was leaning in. His lips were close to mine. And he was waiting for me. I could see the light challenge in his eyes. The beguiled, confrontational glimmer. He was daring me to kiss him. Daring me to make this outlandish move that we both knew was miles out of my depths, and possibly his. I returned the challenge, daring *him*. Let *him* be the one to fall, to succumb.

I held back from him, but our breath mingled in an erotic tease. Neither of us would either relent or surrender. This mutual fascination was going to be a test of wills, so it seemed. Knox Mackenzie was used to getting his way, in whatever it was he happened to pursue. I had no doubt that any woman he conquested would be instantly and willingly subservient to whatever request was made of her. He was mourning the death of his wife but it seemed to me that he was taking his brothers' advice to heart: *'tis time to move on*. He seemed charged with some sparked emotion that shone out of his eyes.

The moment was deliciously laden with possibility, yet neither of us moved. We were entranced yet stubborn. Conflicting urges warred in me feverishly. I desperately wanted to bridge the divide, to ease closer and touch my lips to his. I was imagining the softness of them, the taste. I knew if I surrendered myself to his touch I would be overcome with raging, riveting responses that I badly wanted to experience. I was on the edge of a thrilling precipice. Just one more step…

But then he would win yet again.

"Give me what I want," he whispered.

I felt my breath quicken. What was his meaning? What *did* he want? A kiss? Something more? Or something else entirely? And his quiet command provided exactly the impetus I needed to resist him. That frank, arrogant authority. My assumed obedience.

I always get what I want.

The implications of his certainty—that I *would* give him what he wanted—incited me to do the exact opposite. I stepped back, breaking the spell he held me in. I could see that this small, new distance displeased him. His brimming satisfaction in the face of my enthrallment turned and his mouth curled in a light scowl.

"This interrogation isn't proving quite as informative as I had hoped," he said.

The comment bothered me. Was *that* all he'd wanted of me? Had he staged the attraction between us as a ruse to lure me and tease me into giving him the information he was after? Very likely, I realized. A man like him wouldn't truly be interested in a woman like me. Look at the state of me, I thought. My hair was a wild mane, my dress barely covered me. I was curvy and windblown and unrestrained. I was a wanton mess compared to the slender, elegant refinement he was used to.

You bastard, I thought. *You scoundrel.* I was cornered, bracketed by his muscular thighs and the big bulk of his body. My inner angel and devil were distracting me with irritating banter, mostly because I was having trouble deciphering which was which. In fact, I knew Knox Mackenzie was neither a bastard nor a scoundrel. Far from it. He was questioning me in the interest of his clan and his family. *He's playing with me, deceiving me by pretending to want me.* Perhaps not. Perhaps his urges were as genuine as they seemed, as genuine as my own. *There's one sure way to find out. Kiss him. Kiss his surly mouth.*

The combined forces of his allure and his cunning felt downright dangerous. There was no telling what I could be talked into under this kind of influence. I could feel my heart racing in a staccato thrum, not with fear but with lingering sympathy and, most of all, with flooding desire. I wanted to cry for him and his losses, and for my own. I wanted to be suitable for him, knowing only too well that I most likely never would be. It wasn't something to pine over. It simply was. I knew only too well the uselessness of futile wishes.

"I want the truth from you," he said. As though I owed him something. His low, sincere tone was quietly commanding, as always. But my unruliness and my caution had been provoked. I wanted to rebel against this total control he couldn't help but issue.

First false desire and now subtle intimidation.

"Go to hell," I heard myself whisper.

He didn't even flinch. But his eyes flashed. "I'm already in hell," he replied darkly.

My lips curled in a cynical smirk that was more about self-preservation than anything to do with actual cynicism. I guessed he was talking about his losses and his loneliness, but even with those crosses to bear, his lot was still one of the most fortunate I had ever encountered. I glanced over his shoulder, out the window to the picturesque orchards beyond. "Well, I suppose hell is relative, in that case. All *I* can see is paradise."

His transfixed gaze was on my parted lips, roving lower, to the swell of my full, rounded breasts. I realized my shawl had come loose again in my distraction. The absurdly low cut of my gown was emphasized by my unsettled, breathy stance as I leaned back from him, my back arched. I almost felt a small triumph at the entranced look on his face. He looked deep into my wide eyes as he repeated softly, "All *I* can see is paradise."

It was then that Knox Mackenzie leaned closer.

I prepared myself for the most intense sensations of my life even as I thought smugly: *I won. He can't resist. He relented first.* I felt giddy and triumphant before he even touched me, with superfluous glee and intemperate anticipation.

A sharp knock rapped on the door, spearing the moment.

He stepped back abruptly at the sudden interruption.

Knox composed himself, but I could detect an irate incredulity in him. Something about his reaction was almost comical; it was just so different from anything I was used to. I imagined the translation of his expression along these lines: *my loyal subjects know better than to trouble me in this way.* I couldn't hold back a smile at the thought, which did not escape his notice. He stared at me and, with intense effort, I smoothed my face into an expression of innocence. Something about his incense was crazily endearing, and mixed as it was with my heady reaction to him, the effect entertained my little devil to no end. I tried to restrain myself, but a small bubble of laughter escaped me.

He contemplated me coolly, clearly annoyed and baffled by my small outburst. "I can't imagine why you would find humor in any of this," he seethed, to which I giggled again, lightly clapping a hand over my mouth.

Knox strode toward the door and I pitied whoever it was that had interrupted him—*us*—in the throes of…whatever it was we'd been in the throes of. One of his underlings would surely be subjected to some unwarranted wrath. But it wasn't one of his officers or servants at the door. My small nephew darted under Knox Mackenzie's arm, which was still outstretched and holding the door open, and ran toward me.

"Ami!" Hamish said, reaching me and holding up a small yet very shiny metal sword. My nephew was out of breath but triumphant with his prize. The weapon was well crafted, I noticed, even though I had no experience in the craftsmanship of swords. It looked solid and attractive, as these things go, and was the perfect size for Hamish. A new belt hung around his waist with a leather scabbard attached. This, too, was artfully designed and inlaid with threaded etchings in swirled flame-shaped patterns.

Hamish displayed the sword, held up with both hands for my appreciation. Pride and undiluted excitement were written all over his face and I felt indebted to Knox Mackenzie. For providing such an easy fix. Hamish had not had an easy life, especially recently.

Hamish's father's financial struggles were such a constant that they seemed more a part of James's character than a result of external forces. Unbeknownst to us, his crippling debts had plagued him since well before my sister had married him. Cecelia had married James, who was ten years her senior, because he had offered a refuge for us at a time when we had been utterly desperate. Our parents had died, only a month apart, and left us a surprisingly meager inheritance that had mostly been eaten up by various creditors. My father, despite his respected status as a gifted doctor, was a kind and softhearted man, a truly compassionate practitioner who treated the infirmed whether they could pay him or not. He never turned a patient away. People would knock on our doors in the dark of night. We could hear their pleas from our beds, high above the street. *Please, Dr. Taylor. I beg you. Please take pity on my child. Please take pity on my wife, my cousin, my mother.* My father might have been a saint, but he died a poor man. In the days before our stately home—almost entirely owned by the bank—had been sold, Cecelia and I huddled together in the candlelight, shivering against the wind at the windows. I remembered it vividly, the sudden emptiness of our lives, and the terrified uncertainty. *What will become of us?* I remembered asking my sister at the time. *Where will we go?* James Scott was known to my sister. For a time, he had pursued her. At first she'd brushed off his advances, claiming he was shady. After the death of our parents, however, when the winter grew colder and the money ran out, she gave in to his proposals. And so Cecelia had taken her vows, believing him to be a successful businessman whose assets would shield us from poverty. I don't know if he lied to her at the time, or embellished the extent of his endowments to lure her. Whatever had taken place, James

Scott's financial situation was far less attractive than it might have first appeared, and only continued to deteriorate. I could no longer go to school to pursue my dream of becoming a teacher. We were forced to live in the gaming club, rather than at a separate, more acceptable residence. And James was forced to turn to the darker side of business, resorting not only to gambling, but to smuggling, illegal trading and worse.

Hamish, who knew nothing of the more refined side of life, except through the books I read to him, had never felt an affinity for his father. Even as a very small child, he seemed to understand that his father was lacking in traits that he valued. My nephew learned the tricks of the trade, as we were forced to do to survive, but his interests were in the pages of the adventure stories we read together. Honor, bravery, loyalty: these were the ideas that captivated him. And now, with his angelic face lit with delight, I could detect that he had found aspects of that fantasy here, in this unexpected reality. His wooden sword had served him like a talisman, a link to a world far from the backstreets of Edinburgh, where men aspired to greatness, where heroism was the goal, not deceit. And this new shiny metal treasure seemed to embody something that had been missing from his life. Not hope. Hope tended to be disappointing, for the most part. This sword glimmered with something more concrete. Escape. And attainment. With *this* sword in his hand, Hamish could truly aspire to the ideas of valor that had so captured his imagination.

That symbolic weapon, clutched as it was in Hamish's grip, seemed to signal a change. For him, and for us. Hamish could begin to protect himself, as he would have need to do, against the evildoers that sought him out, if they were ever to find him. That small sword felt wildly auspicious, and I was grateful to Knox Mackenzie for providing it. For somehow introducing a real glimmer of fortunateness into our lives. In that moment, I resolved to leave Hamish here, at Kinloch. My journey was not yet over—I had yet to find out what had happened to my sister. But Hamish would be safe here, I felt certain. Knox Mackenzie might be arrogant and self-important, but he was also honorable. And, surprisingly, *caring*. He had read the simple desire of a nine-year-old boy and had gone out of his way to grant it. Without any obligation to do so, at all.

I felt like throwing my arms around Knox Mackenzie and giving him a very appreciative kiss.

But, of course, I did not.

"You're early," Knox commented, to Hamish.

My mind was whirling, hatching a plan. Now that I had found a place to leave Hamish, where I knew he would at least be fed and protected behind guarded clan walls, I could begin to plan my return to Edinburgh. I would need money to pay for food and possibly transport. I remembered Knox's sisters' offers to help me find work, and I thought I might go to them, to ask them if there were tasks I could perform for them here at Kinloch in exchange for some coinage.

"Amelia." Knox's voice trod through my thoughts, scattering them. "I might ask if you'd enjoy a stroll through the flower gardens, just to the west of the orchards. Or you might prefer to return to your guest chambers for a rest after the trials of your long journey. I will speak to your brother for a time, and then he can join you."

Part two of the dreaded double-pronged inquisition. The one in which our lies could very well be revealed.

Now that I knew the extent of Knox Mackenzie's keen intelligence, I felt a jab of panic in my heart. Best if I waited until the verdict was reached as far as our fate at Kinloch was concerned. It was likely that Laird Mackenzie would uncover all our dark secrets within the hour, and immediately banish us from the sanctuary of his clan's keep. The thought distressed me for a number of reasons. First, it would delay my trip back to Edinburgh, since I would need to start from scratch in my search to find a safe haven for Hamish. Second, I found the thought of leaving this idyllic, magical place unsettling. We'd only just arrived, yet I was already becoming addicted to the pleasure this place delivered to my senses. The *beauty* of it was supreme. The calm, peaceful safety of it was nothing less than sublime. Third, well, I didn't bother dwelling on my fascination with the aloof and dazzling overseer of this veritable utopia.

That was a fixation I needed to decisively rid myself of before it could firmly take hold.

And it *hadn't* yet taken hold, I assured myself.

I thought of Cecelia, alone and unprotected. James's assignments had become increasingly dangerous, I knew. He was now involved in the smuggling of weapons, whiskey and opium. These were excursions that could—and did—prove lethal to some. My sister was resolute in her decision to wait for her husband, stubborn as she was, but how long would she have to wait, alone and unprotected? And at what cost? Would James even return at all? Had Fawkes taken out his anger on Cecelia when he'd discovered my desertion? These were questions I was determined to return to Edinburgh to find out the answers to. A part of me was troubled at every glimpse of beauty in our new surroundings, every round apple and singing bird and warm bun, knowing that my sister might be suffering. Aye, she'd insisted that I flee, and for good reason. But any pleasure I might have derived from the idyll that was Kinloch was always going to be undermined by my worry.

I was glad to see that Hamish, with his newfound fortification, seemed wholly in control of himself. As though the small yet undeniably lethal weapon he clutched in his fists had given him a reinforced confidence. He seemed to have grown a little, and in that moment I could see glimpses of the man he would one day become. I wondered if I would live long enough or live free enough to see him grow into that man.

"Would you prefer an escort?" Knox said with forced patience. I had momentarily forgotten: he was waiting for me to leave so he could question Hamish. "I could call for one of my sisters." From his tone, it was clear that he wanted to get on with this inquisition so he could return to all the importantly, lairdly tasks that were awaiting him.

"Are you sure you wouldn't like me to stay?" I asked him, knowing full well what his answer would be. "I haven't been very helpful. I could try to elaborate more on what I remember."

"Nay," he said brusquely.

It was that note of abruptness that saw me, mostly unintentionally, inviting a challenge. I wanted to exasperate Laird Mackenzie, oddly, and I also wanted to hear Hamish's version of the story. I needed him to get it right. I needed *us* to get it right so I could return to Edinburgh as soon as possible. Thoughts of my sister made me feel restless and disobedient. "Because now that I think of it, I actually do remember a few more details of—"

"Thank you," Knox interrupted. "I will summon you at a later time if I feel the need for more information."

And he was holding the door open for me, even taking it so far as to gesture with a little sideways movement of his head toward the exterior corridor as though encouraging me to exit posthaste.

Slightly incensed by the curt dismissal, I fastened my pin to hold my shawl more modestly in place and I brushed my fingertips against Hamish's shoulder in a passing gesture of encouragement. *Stick to the story. Our lives—and hers—could very well depend on your persuasiveness. I love you. I'm sorry.*

I wasn't sure if the graze of my fingertips conveyed any or all of the sentiments I'd hoped, but I knew he understood.

And I made my leave. A very solid thud of the door closing behind me echoed through the stone hallway as I retreated to the out-of-doors.

CHAPTER FOUR

I HAD AN IDEA. Curiosity had overcome me.

I couldn't stop the conversation that was taking place behind the closed doors of Knox Mackenzie's private den. But I might be able to *hear* it. The windows were open, after all, and I now knew which ones they were. They were at ground level, horizontally placed rectangles that looked out to the orchard, which I just so happened to now be walking through.

I experienced a moment of conflicting urges. I didn't want to eavesdrop: it wasn't really in my nature to spy. Only under extreme circumstances. And I knew what was at stake here. I crept closer to the window, approaching it from the side so I wouldn't be seen.

Through the window, the deep tones of Laird Mackenzie's voice drifted, and Hamish's chipper reply. But I couldn't quite make out what they were saying. With my back against the stone wall of the manor, I slid closer.

It was then I happened to notice a large man approaching. None other than the guard Lachlan. He was carrying a small child. A dark-haired girl, who was holding a red apple in her hands.

As soon as I saw him, I stepped away from the manor wall, strolling casually out into the orchard as though to pick a piece of fruit.

"Amelia," he said, bowing his head slightly in a gentlemanly greeting. "What a surprise to find you here." I couldn't be sure of it, but I detected a hint of sardonic reproach in him. Had Knox Mackenzie suspected I might attempt to eavesdrop and specifically assigned his guard to watch me? Surely not. Was I such a spectacle of distrust? I found the thought didn't vex me as much as maybe it should have. I was a complete stranger, after all. And the thought seeped through my mind, even though it was probably completely off the mark: I might have been being guarded for an altogether different reason. It wasn't entirely out of the realm of possibility that Knox wanted to ensure that I was kept safe. I knew it unlikely, but still, I allowed myself a very brief respite from doubt and skepticism.

I liked Lachlan's company. And the small girl he held in his arms was one of the most beautiful children I had ever seen.

"This is my wee Clara," Lachlan said. "My wife is a weaver with a project to finish. So Clara and I are taking a stroll through the gardens to keep the little lass occupied while her mother finishes her work. Since there are no wars to wage this afternoon."

I smiled at Clara, quite taken with her wide brown eyes, her tiny bow-shaped lips and petite, perfect features. "I'm glad to hear it."

It caught me off guard somehow, this big, strapping warrior, armed with a holstered knife and sword, all fierce and manly in appearance yet holding this exquisite child with absolute gentleness. I might have expected these Highlands soldiers to be gruff and rough, barbaric and brutish. But the few that I'd so far met had been anything but barbaric. They'd been all about their beguiling contradictions and unexpected lightness. Instead of warriors obsessed with war or wrath, what I found was men who were not only intensely loyal to one another, but also radiated a distinct sense of harmony. As though the heat of battle, or the threat of it, had tempered their awareness, concentrating their perception to that which truly mattered: the peace, the beauty and the beloved.

It was such a refreshing outlook, compared to what I was used to.

This scene, with Lachlan and his young daughter, was unexpected to me and utterly enchanting. I knew it was a moment I would recall, when I needed to take refuge in memories, in frozen moments in time that had touched me in some way, and comforted me.

"Stroll with us," Lachlan said, putting Clara down, holding her small hand in his large one. Not an order, as such. A request.

"I'd love to," I said, watching as Clara reached up to touch a long strand of my hair that hung to my waist. She was a beautiful little creature, tiny, with lightly curled dark locks and the pink flush of health on her skin. Her clothes had been carefully hand-made and were woven from fine wool.

She twirled her finger through the coiled curl and said softly, "You're the prettiest lady I've ever seen."

My heart melted. "And you," I said, "are the prettiest lady *I've* ever seen."

Clara's wide eyes grew even wider. She looked up at her father. "Can we take her home, Da?"

Lachlan chuckled, picking her up once again, as though he couldn't resist her. "Aye. If that's what you want. We'll take her to meet your mother."

I was very pleased at the thought and I felt touched that they would invite me in this way. I knew Lachlan suspected that the story Hamish and I had told him was not entirely truthful. I could detect, though, that he also suspected we had good reasons for fabricating our lies and was giving us the benefit of any doubts. He held the proof of his understanding in his arms. If he was suspicious about me, he at least did not consider me a threat. I sensed that he viewed my possible discretions not as devious but as protective; just as he would go to any length to protect Clara, so would I to protect Hamish. The reasons behind my white lies were not devious, nor frivolous, and I could sense that Lachlan had understood this from our very first encounter.

We walked through the orchards, past the barracks, where soldiers milled about, sharpening weapons or sparring in a large, dusty ring. Several of them eyed me curiously as we passed. We walked farther, down a lane flanked on either side by dotted stone dwellings. These, it seemed, were the homes of the soldiers with families. Feminine touches were noticeable, from the neat, flowering gardens to the patterned drapes lining the interiors of the windows.

Lachlan led us into one of the nearer houses. As soon as we entered the gate, Lachlan put Clara down. She grasped my hand and skipped alongside me. "This is where we live," she said, smiling up at me. Her voice had the bell-toned clarity of a morning bird. She reached to pick a purple flower and held it up to me. Lachlan opened the door of the house and we followed him inside.

The house was larger than it looked from the outside, quaint, homely, lovingly decorated—and full of activity. Five women were seated around a loom that took up a large square side enclave of the house. A sixth woman was stirring in a pot on the hearth. A seventh elderly woman sat in a rocking chair in one corner, holding a sleeping baby. They all looked up as we entered and Clara ran to the woman seated at the far end of the loom, the one that was holding the wool-wrapped skittle: clearly Clara's mother. Clara climbed onto her mother's lap and the young woman kissed her and settled her into position so Clara could help send the skittle through the stretched wool strands that had been wound through the loom.

Clara's mother was a gorgeous woman, with long dark hair and wide brown eyes like those of her daughter. She looked up at Lachlan as he nodded a brief greeting to her, conscious of the careful attention everyone paid to their connection. Lachlan did not approach his wife, since he would have had to displace several of the weavers to do so, but his eyes and his smile conveyed a smoldering pleasure at the sight of her. His wife. And it was clear he was most satisfied by that fact. It seemed an entire conversation passed between them without a word spoken, and I was fascinated by their silent bond.

What would such a thing feel like? Not only to be connected by marriage, to share a house and raise children together, but to also *revel* in that closeness. To count the minutes until you could drink in the sight of your loved one, to be alone together, face-to-face, skin-to-skin, heart-to-heart.

Because it was fairly obvious to all that *that* was on Lachlan's mind, in the way he was riveted by her, momentarily lost in the sight of her, as though no one else was present.

This was such a different dynamic to the marriages I had witnessed. My sister's marriage, to be sure, offered her little joy. Cecelia rarely sought James out other than to relay messages from creditors, or to alert him to the arrival of a ganglord's demand, or a drunken brawl, or a cheating patron. I'd rarely seen anything resembling love pass between them; her loyalty to him was an instilled remnant of her upbringing, but her affection was reserved for her son, and for me. My parents had married for love, in part, although the considerations of class and occupation had surely been the more pressing considerations. They had run their marriage with rigid, proper civility and with a mutual respect that dwindled over time as the money began to run out.

This was something different. The emotion that passed between Lachlan and his wife like a sultry, fervent channel was complex. Understanding. Concern. Devotion. Attraction. These were the sentiments that seemed to pass between them as their eyes met and held.

It wasn't surprising that everyone else in the room was watching the exchange, as I was.

Several of the women sniggered at Lachlan's reaction to his wife. "Lord above, he's at it again," one of them said.

"You've been married for five years, Lachlan," another chimed in. "Aren't you ever going to grow weary of the sight of our lovely Marin?"

A third continued. "We're just finishing up, so you'll have her all to yourself soon enough."

Lachlan smiled at their gentle teasing, which seemed to break his trance. "Marin, ladies, let me introduce Miss Amelia Taylor. She's a guest to Kinloch for the time being. Amelia, my wife, Marin. And this is—"

"Good Lord, don't hold the lass to remembering all our names," one of the women seated at the loom interrupted. "She's barely just arrived."

"Look at that hair, would you?" the one at the stove said, walking over to me, circling me and taking a coil of my hair between two fingers. Her interest set off an enthusiastic exposition on the topic of my appearance.

"The color is outstanding," said another of the ladies. "Like gold mixed with a light, burnished copper."

"Aye, and touched by the sun," added the old woman.

"So wavy, too. Look how it curls into ringlets at the ends, hanging just past her waist."

"I'd wear it long, too, if I had hair like that."

"And look at her *figure,*" one of the ladies exclaimed. "God's teeth, woman, your dress is barely holding up."

"Yet she looks to be very young," commented another. "She has a fresh face. How old are ye, lassie?"

"Twenty-one," I said, feeling unusually shy under all the outspoken scrutiny.

"'Tis a good thing your husband is so smitten, Marin," the woman who still held a lock of my hair teased, "or you might have a bit o' competition on yer hands."

To this, Lachlan replied good-naturedly, "If my wife had anything to worry about in that regard, Fionne, you know it would be *you* I'd be running after."

The woman named Fionne cackled, thoroughly delighted by his flattery. "Oh, he's a charmer, Marin. God smiled down on you the day this man strutted into your life and swept you off your nimble feet."

The baby being held by the older woman began to fuss, and Fionne went to her, gathering the infant and taking it to Marin. Clara was transferred to another's weaver's lap.

Marin had not yet spoken, but she appeared amused by the banter. Her smile at Fionne's comment suggested that she agreed wholeheartedly. "Aye, He surely did. Welcome to our keep and our house, Amelia."

"Thank you," I said. "Yours is a beautiful home."

She murmured a gentle thanks, somewhat distracted by the assistance of several of the women who were helping her attach the baby to her now-exposed breast. With some adjustments, the baby mewed and settled, latching on.

"Will you be having some stew, then?" asked Fionne, turning her attention to us now that the baby was content.

Lachlan, who appeared somewhat dazed at the sight of his wife's abundant, creamy breast, focused—at Fionne's insistence. "Lachlan?"

"Oh," he replied. "Nay. Clara and I were entertaining Amelia before the noon meal is served in the hall, as Laird Mackenzie had other business to attend to. He has asked that I escort her and return her to his care." So Knox Mackenzie *had* asked that I be 'entertained,' as he suspected that I might…well, do exactly as I had done.

This inspired another raft of lively discussion. "Oh, he *did,* did he?" Fionne smiled knowingly.

"So it's the laird himself who's taken an interest in the lovely Amelia, is it?" said the woman holding Clara.

"Not surprising, I suppose," added another. "Given her generous…endowments."

"Aye, perhaps you're just what he needs to pull him out of his ongoing melancholy," continued Fionne. "God knows that bony Katriona could hardly offer much comfort to a man like Laird Mackenzie."

"Fionne," chided Marin quietly. "You shouldn't disparage her. She, too, is grieving."

"Oh, I don't blame her for trying," Fionne countered. "I just don't think it's a good match. He needs a woman who can pull him out of his mood, not mire him deeper into it."

"Aye," agreed the old woman. "And he'd have acted on his urges by now if he was interested in Katriona, to be sure."

"Well, maybe Amelia can bring him up to scratch," another of the women said.

I was following their conversation but not entirely understanding the depths of their meaning, and I wanted to assure them that the situation was not at all as they speculated. "I'm not… I don't—"

But they were neither easily deterred nor willing to give me time to sputter out my futile protests. "Anyway," Fionne said, with authority, "Laird Mackenzie will decide who, when, where and all the rest of it. He is, after all, the *laird*. And if he's asking for your company, lass, you'd be a fool not to partake, maiden or not."

The mention of my maidenhood and the way the topic was being bandied around was enough to shake me out of my inarticulate muddle.

Several details of this exchange were beginning to rile me. First, the mention of Katriona and Laird Mackenzie. That Katriona had intentions for him did not surprise me; it explained her apparent animosity toward me, as an intruder who might vie for his attentions. But I didn't give their connection or lack thereof excessive consideration now. I was even more irked by Fionne's suggestion that I should willingly jump into Knox Mackenzie's arms, and bed, just because—and *only* because—he was the all-powerful laird of Kinloch. Perhaps it was true. Maybe I should be grateful for any attention I could get from a man like that. I could admit that I'd been attracted to the almighty Knox Mackenzie. But I had bigger concerns than my own misguided urges. I had to think of Hamish, and Cecelia, and the task at hand: to house Hamish here behind Kinloch's walls, secure some funds for my return to Edinburgh and take my leave. And Fionne's comment only served to rouse my ever-present defiance in the face of authority. If Laird Mackenzie *was* asking for my company, and for *that* reason, the last thing I wanted to do was make it as easy for him. "I'm sure Laird Mackenzie has no designs on me," I said evenly. "He's merely interested in my history as it relates to the safety of Kinloch. Lachlan will no doubt agree."

"Aye," he said distractedly.

"There's the call now," said Marin.

Everyone went momentarily silent. In the distance, the sound of a horn could be heard. Once. Twice. A third time. "That's the signal that the noon meal has been served," explained Fionne.

Lachlan blew his wife a kiss, a subtle gesture that was meant only for her but that was nevertheless savored by all. Several of the women sighed.

"Let's go," Lachlan said to me, somewhat gruffly.

I bid the ladies farewell and followed him.

"You have a beautiful family," I said to him as we walked back past the barracks.

"Aye," he muttered, still mired in sweet memories, already pining perhaps for the company of his wife. But then, he turned his head to look at me and said, "Thank you. I am fortunate."

"And deserving, I'm sure. You've been very kind to me and I appreciate it," I told him. It was true and I wanted him to know that.

He didn't reply, but as we continued on our way through the idyllic rambling pathways of the orchard toward the manor, there was a lightness to our companionship that felt richer than it had even moments ago. There was something meaningful about recognizing and acknowledging that a person was trustworthy, and decent, and that an inkling of that trust might be returned.

We approached the Mackenzie manor. The double doors of the grand hall were opened to the warm breeze and I could see and hear that the hall was crowded, already filled with people enjoying a good meal and the camaraderie of their clan. The sounds of laughter and conversation filled the sunlit air.

It took my eyes a few moments to adjust to the relative dimness of the interior space after the brightness of the day. Lachlan led us to a table where Christie, Ailie and Katriona were seated, near the end of a long table, among others. I noticed then that there was a tall chair at the head, empty.

At that very moment, Laird Mackenzie entered the hall through the door at the far end, followed closely by Hamish. Laird Mackenzie's eyes scanned the room, searching. As soon as his eyes found me, his gaze bore into me, unrelenting. I was struck once again not only by the size of him but by his shape. His shoulders were broad and he held himself as though he were the king of the world but that the weight of his responsibilities required strength he had to summon from the deepest corners of his soul. His face, as he watched me, was not friendly but stern, serious, uncompromising, assessing.

I walked toward him, remembering what Lachlan had said: that I should be returned to Laird Mackenzie's care. When Lachlan had mentioned it in his cottage, I had not been particularly pleased by this pronouncement, but now, under the watchful heat of Knox's gaze, I found I was breathless and quietly excited. I couldn't be sure about this, but something about his expression suggested he'd been thinking about me, and seeking me out. If the superiority of him goaded me, the superior*ness* of him enthralled me. He stood there like a masterpiece. He was easily ten times more radiant than anyone else in the room. And all this with a scowl on his tanned, distinguished face.

As I drew closer to him, our eyes remained locked. It was an intense, charged response. I remembered the connection between Lachlan and his wife I'd just witnessed. Whereas that glance had been one of affection and love, *this* was alight with challenge—defiance in the face of heavy authority—and mutual curiosity. Not only curiosity, but a strange, unexpected *relief.* I could read it in his expression as I could feel it in the layered tumult of my own emotions: I was glad to see him. My eyes and psyche were thrilled somehow by the vision of his arresting arrival.

I stood close to the fireplace, which was unlit owing to the mildness of the day, unsure of where I was supposed to sit. He had not moved and was now several feet away from where I stood. His eyes did not leave me. And his scowl did not soften. This hardness in him, studded with arrogance and advantage, ruffled me. I felt out of place in this grand, polished setting, with its servants and banquets and picturesque views. But I was good at pretending.

Or at least I had been until recently. Irritatingly,

something about the presence of Knox Mackenzie seemed to undermine my controlled, dramatic prowess. I did not look away from him, but I took an unsteady breath.

"Laird Mackenzie," I said in greeting. My polite respect, even to my own ears, sounded somewhat overdone. "I trust your meeting with my brother went well, and offered you more information than your rather disappointing conversation with me."

His eyes narrowed, but I thought I detected a glimmer in their light gray depths. "Let's just say he offered the information much more freely than you did."

"I'm glad to hear it."

"He's a bright spark," he said. "I believe he'll make an eager student in the barracks."

The comment reassured me to such an extent I smiled in spite of myself, breaking our aloof little standoff, or whatever this was. Not only would Hamish be protected and entertained, but he would be learning a valuable skill, and one that would challenge him, make him happy and most important, equip him. He might even forgive me, eventually, for leaving him. "I thank you for that. I know he would be very willing."

"I am always in need of young recruits that might strengthen my future army," he said. His remark struck me with its arrogance. I almost laughed at the innate loftiness of him. I held back my laughter, but I believe my smile might have curled into the mildest of smirks. He noticed, of course, as eagle-eyed as his attention was. And he reacted with a retort that found my smirk fading almost instantly.

"At least, that is, until we locate your long-lost relatives. The cousin of one Michael Taylor, a surgeon from east Edinburgh who died only a month ago. I will send out messengers on the morrow, to see what information we might be able to gather."

Hamish had done well, if our interests were still to fabricate as many details of our history as possible. My father's name had not been Michael, but Robert. He had not been a surgeon, except in extreme, dire situations, but a general practitioner. Our home had not been located in east Edinburgh, but in the northern quarter. And he had not died last month, but ten years past. I remained silent, both in an attempt to keep my expression smooth and also because I was experiencing an unfamiliar pang of guilt. *I will send out messengers on the morrow.* Lachlan or someone like him. A posse of men with wives and children who would rather be spending their days with their loved ones than prowling the hills in search of information that would—unbeknownst to them—never surface.

I found myself saying, "Laird Mackenzie, please. *I* will search for my father's cousin. Please don't trouble yourself—"

"You?" he interrupted sharply. "Alone? What do you intend to do, lass? Take a stroll across the Highlands knocking on doors?" His mouth twitched in

admonishing amusement. But he didn't smile. His voice grew quiet, so low it was almost a murmur. "In *that* dress?"

I looked down at my dress. I hadn't realized it but my shawl had shifted and was not covering me as adequately as it possibly should have been in such noble company. I adjusted it somewhat indignantly. His constant mockery was nothing short of infuriating. "If that's what I must do, then so be it. I had hoped to find some gainful employment to pay my way, *Laird* Mackenzie. That is my intention."

He scowled at my barely disguised insolence.

"What about the *bandits?*" he said softly, and his eyebrows rose briefly at the word as he uttered it, as though emphasizing his suspicion on the subject. A subject, to be sure, I now wished we had never, ever dreamed up.

I lifted my chin in a small movement of dissent, but I did not reply.

Knox Mackenzie seemed to read my silence as another win. He studied my face with sanctimonious satisfaction. Then, as his eyes remained locked on mine, he said, "Come. Sit. Have some food." Overly commanding, once again, but this time I was glad for the change of subject. I was also interested to see that he was placing a chair next to his own. Not only that, but he had repositioned his own large chair at the head of the table to the side, just slightly, to fit me next to him and also to make a space for the stool he put next to my chair, for Hamish.

This act seemed significant: that he would displace his own kinglike position at the table to make way for *me,* for us. A few other people seated at our table also noticed. This caused several in the group to study me, and the laird, more closely. Katriona was among them, and I wondered at the comments I'd overheard at Lachlan's house. *I don't blame her for trying. I just don't think it's a good match.* This suggested she had designs on Knox Mackenzie but that the relationship had not gone according to her plans. I had no thoughts on this. I, certainly, was no competition for a cultured woman of her standing, nor did I particularly want to be. *You're lying to yourself,* my own internal contrariness said. *You want him. You want to kiss him and touch his hair. You want to feel his mouth and his hands on your body—*

Nay. It wouldn't do. I would remain aloof. I would focus on the task at hand, that of securing a small amount of money that would pay for my way back to Edinburgh or at least some food along my journey.

Laird Mackenzie gestured for me to sit.

"To what do we owe the honor of Laird Mackenzie's esteemed presence today, brother?" said Christie, who had been one of our keenest observers throughout the shuffle of chairs. "You usually only join us for the evening meal."

He appeared mildly provoked by the question. "I can enjoy the company of my clan and the offerings of our cooks during the day occasionally, can I not, Christie?"

Christie and Ailie both looked at me, and at the placement of my chair, which Laird Mackenzie was holding out, waiting for me to sit, in a gentlemanly courtesy. They exchanged a loaded glance, both smiling, and Christie replied, "Of course you can. Whenever you like, Knox." Whereas everyone else in the Mackenzie clan clearly deferred to their venerable laird, Christie's role was one of playful instigator. She was not intimidated by him in the least and the dynamic between them was one of good-humored mischief, on her part at least, and mutual affection.

Katriona was also watching Laird Mackenzie, but her expression was far less amused.

Hamish ran inside, joining us, absentmindedly grazing my shoulder with the light touch of his fingers as he sat. I could see that Laird Mackenzie was interested in both of us, in the way we interacted: anything that might give him more clues as to our characters and our mysteries.

Christie, however, was not yet finished goading her older brother. To me, she said, "Knox is not always so attentive to guests, Amelia. I daresay my brother is intrigued by your city origins, is that not so, Knox? We don't get all that many visitors from Edinburgh—"

"Speaking of Edinburgh," Knox said, decisively cutting her off, speaking to the group in general. "I didn't hear how your trip went. Did you accomplish everything you set out to do?" He sounded bored by his own question, as though he couldn't care less about the trip or the tasks, nor could he recall what the tasks might have been.

"Actually, nay," Christie offered without hesitation. "I mean, we were able to find the fabrics we needed for Ailie's designs, and in more variety than we expected. But Katriona was not so lucky in her pursuits."

"'Tis true, unfortunately," Katriona agreed. She was lovely, I thought, if somewhat severe. Her dark hair was almost black, and shiny. Her skin was flawless. If she had allowed an inkling of humor or liveliness to permeate her manner, she would have been all the more appealing. As it was, she seemed relentlessly dour. I remembered another comment made by the women in Lachlan's cabin. *She, too, is grieving.* If she had designs on Laird Mackenzie, I reasoned that she must have lost her husband, as he had lost his wife. She had reason, therefore, to be saddened by this. I made a point of trying my best to like her, and to sympathize with whatever her hardships might have been.

Knox glanced at her blankly, distracted. His distraction seemed to displease her. "I had hoped to secure a teacher for my children," she said to him. Her tone suggested she had told him this before, and that she was miffed that he had forgotten.

"And you weren't able to?" he replied vaguely.

"Nay, alas. 'Tis surprisingly difficult to find someone who has the required qualifications," Katriona commented. "And etiquette."

"Several of the young women you interviewed seemed very good, to me," Ailie said. "But we know you're exceptionally particular when it comes to your children, of course. As you have good reason to be."

Katriona's eyebrows knitted together at the memory. "Aye, well, I was hoping to get someone just a bit more experienced than some of those—"

"Amelia's a qualified teacher," Hamish offered, through a mouthful of food.

Everyone at the table quieted for a moment, glancing at me. Despite my early elite education, I was qualified to do nothing more than deal cards at a crooked gaming club, and even that had been disputed by some (those who lost), since it wasn't a role usually fulfilled by a woman. These, however, were details I would refrain from elaborating upon to Katriona. I had been crushed, at first, when I had learned that I would no longer be able to attend school, to train and to one day get qualified as a teacher. The dream had never faded, and over time, I had read every book I could find, on instruction, on method, on every subject from arithmetic to aviation to apothecary. And I had used Hamish as my student. As I had always allowed him his dream of someday becoming a soldier, reading him stories, feeding his fancy, he had likewise encouraged me. He'd willingly let me use him as a test case, obediently completing grammar exercises, taking the little examinations I drafted and then improved.

He knew all my stories. Including my shameful

attempts to create a false paper qualification, which had, in fact, fooled several upper-class women into letting me tutor their children. For a few short weeks, I had been able to escape the confines of the gaming scene and work at a real and wonderful profession. But the ruse had ended abruptly when one of the children's fathers happened to frequent our club. At first the man couldn't place where he knew me from. He'd offhandedly mistaken me for an extramarital conquest he'd bedded. But then it had dawned on him. I had, needless to say, been fired on the spot. Hamish had been the one to comfort me and encourage me to try again. But secretly, I'd almost given up a little. No one would ever want me teaching their children. I hailed from the backstreets, not the esteemed halls of learning. I could play the part convincingly enough, but it was disheartening at times to lie so constantly, especially to children. Lying could be exhausting. The convolution had the power to test one's wits.

I was beginning to feel weary of all these lies, then, and now. My nephew, however, was only getting warmed up.

Hamish swallowed and took a drink, sitting up straight and blotting his mouth with a cloth with suddenly perfect manners. "She attended one of the most exclusive schools in Edinburgh," he continued. "She's read more books than anyone I've ever met. And she has taught me everything I know. *Je parle français, bien sur.* And I know Latin, too. *Actus non facit reum nisi mens sit rea.* I—"

"An interesting choice of phrase," Laird Mackenzie's smooth, deep voice interrupted. He understood it, as I did.

An act does not make a person guilty unless his mind should be guilty.

Perhaps, in hindsight, it wasn't the best phrase he could have chosen to recite. The laird was watching us both.

Hamish recovered admirably. "Thank you, Laird Mackenzie," Hamish said. "If you prefer, *aut viam inveniam aut faciam.*" Better perhaps.

I will either find a way or make one.

Laird Mackenzie was eyeing Hamish with something close to bemusement. I got the impression that the laird was mildly impressed by my nephew, that there was a tenuous fellowship taking hold between the two of them. I was glad of it. Given that I was planning to leave my nephew in the laird's care, this was a fortunate development.

"Da mihi factum, dabo tibi ius," Laird Mackenzie said to Hamish, testing him, perhaps.

Give me the facts and I will give you the law.

"In somnis veritas," came Hamish's quick response.

In dreams there is truth.

Hamish might have passed the test. Either way, the laird took a sip of his ale, his eyebrows almost imperceptibly raised. And his steady gaze watched us with unwavering, calculated curiosity.

Hamish continued his pitch on my behalf. "I can

read and write as well as most fully grown men and my skills with mathematics are legendary. Ask me a sum," he said to the women. When they hesitated, he encouraged them with a beatific grin. "Go on, ask me."

Christie humored him. "Eight hundred and sixty-two plus four hundred and twelve."

"One thousand, two hundred and seventy-four," Hamish said without hesitation.

Christie thought about it for a moment, then smiled at Katriona. "He's right."

Katriona appeared stunned. Her mouth opened and closed like that of a fish out of water. The thought that her own children might be in any way at all associated with this little heathen seemed to render her temporarily speechless. "I couldn't possibly…sums aside, the boy is a—"

"He's a darling," interrupted Christie.

Ailie sensed Katriona's reservations. "He's just been through a string of trials that would bring out the rougher edges of any child, or any adult for that matter. But he's clearly well educated. Edward would love a playmate, and Greer might like a child her own age to speak French with. Have they been taught Latin?"

Katriona stuttered. "Nay."

I almost began to protest. I would be leaving soon, to return to Edinburgh. But the truth of the matter was, I needed money. And this would be gainful employment. Not only that, but teaching was something

I did know how to do, even if I didn't have a piece of paper to prove it. It was a calling of mine. A passion I'd never had the fortune to officially pursue.

All eyes were on me. "Would you be willing, Amelia?" asked Christie. "You did say you were looking for a job."

"The boy certainly appears to be well taught," said Ailie, in a further bid to convince Katriona.

"Aye," agreed Laird Mackenzie. "He does. But of course, Amelia won't be staying at Kinloch. She has kin who will no doubt be overjoyed to hear of her fortuitous arrival in the Highlands." His sarcasm did not escape me, nor did the slightest hint of roguishness. If I didn't know better—and I *didn't* know better: the scalding memory of our near kiss still touched me in secret, pulsing places that I preferred at this moment not to acknowledge—I might have thought that Knox Mackenzie was flirting with me, in a deeply buried, against-his-better-judgment kind of way.

"At least she could keep herself busy until they are located," urged Christie. She seemed genuinely concerned about my plight, and I decided she was one of the kindest persons, if not *the* kindest, I had ever met. "What say you, Katriona?" she asked. "Amelia could meet the children tomorrow morning. If they find the arrangement agreeable, she could teach them until you find someone permanent."

Katriona fell silent for a moment, appraising me with cold condescension, which I found somewhat annoying. She didn't, in fact, *know* that I was worthy of her condescension, even if I was. "I suppose we could try her," she said.

"Fine," declared Laird Mackenzie. "Then it's settled. Amelia will be kept busy during her brief stay here at Kinloch with her new appointment as Katriona's children's teacher, assisted, as it were, by Hamish, who will spend his afternoons learning swordsmanship in the training grounds. I will send a message to Magnus Munro on the morrow, to begin the search for the elusive relative. And—"

"I told you I would prefer—" I began my protest, but Christie interrupted Laird Mackenzie at the same time.

"Oh, that's wonderful news! Isn't it, Ailie? Invite them here for the meeting. A visit from the Munros is always welcome. Perhaps we should make an event of it. We could request some parties from some other clans, too. The Macintoshes, maybe. We haven't seen much of them lately."

Ailie's eyes were bright with an emotion I could not identify. Katriona's expression was easier to read: an embroiled attempt at diplomacy. Christie continued to chatter happily. And I felt a small glimmer of accomplishment. I would earn some money, and Hamish would be safe and well occupied.

My plan was falling into place.

"COME WITH ME," Hamish said after the midday meal had been cleared away and the Mackenzie clan had returned to their afternoon activities. I would meet

Katriona's children tomorrow morning, and this afternoon, Hamish and I were free to wander the manor and grounds as we pleased. We were back in the orchards, this time among a quaint cluster of pear trees. "I want to show you the barracks," he added.

"The barracks? I'm not going to the barracks."

"But, Ami, the armory is the most outstanding place I've ever seen. I want to show it to you. A whole building dedicated to designing, making and storing all kinds of weapons. Shields, pistols, knives of every description and more swords than you've ever imagined. Long ones, short ones, scabbards, belts. Scythes and blades and these round, sharp throwing devices, and—"

"Hamish," I interrupted. "First, I'm not a weapons enthusiast like yourself, and second, I'm not sure I'd be welcome in the—"

"All the soldiers are either hunting or sparring this afternoon," Hamish told me. "No one will take any notice of us. They're busy." My nephew was pulling me by the hand, past a row of trained bean vines, a walled garden adjacent to the manor, and out into a cleared glade. I could see a number of buildings in the distance and a fenced ring where several well-occupied soldiers were circling each other, swords raised. They wore masks and held shields and were being encouraged by a small assembly of young men. "I just want to show you this sword I saw. If I ever get to be a trained soldier, it's exactly the sort I hope to have. I saw one in a book once that was similar, but this one is even bigger, and sharp enough to slice—"

"What if I'm seen? I'm sure women don't frequent the barracks." But I was walking along with him, around the side of one of the buildings. We were now hidden from view of the distant soldiers. It would be handy, I supposed, to have a weapon in my possession, once I began my journey. Who knew what kind of trouble I might run into along the way? And once I reached the city, well, it didn't bear contemplating. I preferred not even to think that far ahead, but it did occur to me to ask Laird Mackenzie if I might borrow a knife, perhaps. I would need to come up with a suitable excuse. For sharpening the children's broken quills, perhaps. Or cutting the parchment into small, useful squares. I could at least have a *look* at the sorts of things that were on offer.

Hamish led me into one of the buildings, closing the door behind us. He was right: there was no one else inside. The interior was dim, save for the afternoon light through one small low-slung window and the eerie gleam of hundreds of blades. The air smelled of steel and leather and sweat but was not unpleasant.

"Have you ever seen any place so miraculous in all your life, Ami?" Hamish whispered, running his fingers along one, then another, of the swords. The weapons were stacked and hung from rows of cleverly constructed storage racks. There were shelves and sharpening stones. A large firing pit and elevated chimney loomed sooty and black in the center of the room. And the walls were pinned with hundreds of drawings and writings, advertising the thoughtful innovation that had gone into the plentiful arsenal.

"Be careful," I scolded Hamish, but he took no notice.

"Look at this one," he said, circling his small fist around the hilt of a gargantuan silver beast of a sword that had been not only etched with intricate designs but studded with a single glass jewel. The grandeur of the object made me wonder then: was it glass? Or a genuine ruby? "Lachlan said this one has killed a hundred men. The laird himself has used it, and his father, as well. Laird Mackenzie's father was killed in battle only a few years ago. By a man named Campbell."

How sad, I couldn't help considering. *Another loss. Another tragedy to bear for Knox Mackenzie. He must get so lonely.*

"This is the one," Hamish continued, sliding a middle-sized, gold-handled sword from its rack, not without effort. I watched him, fascinated. It was an impressive-looking weapon, to be sure. Beautifully crafted. Simple in design but elegant, too. And by all appearances, very, very sharp. Its metal length glinted as Hamish lifted it. "I could take it back to Edinburgh," he said. "And kill them all."

The comment horrified me. I watched him swing the heavy blade carefully in the dim light and imagined the repercussions of his boyish intent. Fawkes's thugs would overpower him easily, small as he was. They would hurt him. Or they would kill him.

And I would never, ever let that happen.

Shouts from the soldiers reached us through the small window. "They sound like they're getting closer, Hamish. Put it back. Let's take our leave before we get caught."

He swung the sword a few more times and I helped him lift it back into place in its rack. I went to the door and attempted to lift the latch.

But the door would not open.

"Hamish. The lock is stuck."

"Let me try."

Hamish was equally unsuccessful in his attempts to open the door.

"It might be one of those automatic devices," he commented, "that locks from the inside. To thwart thieves. The Mackenzies are skilled at making those sorts of inventions. This morning I saw—"

"But how will we get out? They'll find us in here."

"We were only looking," he said.

"I know, but it…it doesn't make a good impression." I was starting to think I was incapable of making any sort of impression that wasn't windblown, wanton or wayward.

"We'll go out the window," Hamish suggested.

I looked at the small rectangular window. A nine-year-old boy might fit splendidly through it. I, however, would clearly have some difficulty. The wooden frame was dirty and dusty, as well. "Even if I do manage to squeeze myself through, my dress would be ruined."

"Take it off," Hamish said cheerfully. "I won't look. And you'll fit more easily."

My nephew was already shimmying his way through the tiny portal, until he dropped from view. Then his dirt-smeared face appeared. "It's easy," he announced. "Take your dress off, fold it and hand it to me carefully. Then come through."

Damnation! Why did I possess such a knack for miring myself in ridiculous situations?

I had no choice but to follow Hamish's instructions. I unbuttoned my dress and stepped out of it. I wore only a thin shift beneath it, worn to the point of sheerness. The garment was positively indecent, but at least it hardly mattered if it was dirtied by my escape. I folded the dress and carefully handed it through to Hamish's waiting hands. "Don't look."

"I'm not. My eyes are closed."

"Step away. Give me some room."

Placing my hands on the dusty wood, I poked my head through the small window, eased my shoulders—and the rest of me—through the narrow gap, maneuvering my way out, falling into a heap on the hard leaf-strewn ground. It wasn't a far distance to fall, but I felt mildly winded from the entire experience. I rose, regaining my equilibrium, and began to brush myself off. Before I could remove all the dirt and leaves from my shift, I heard the unmistakable sound of footsteps. I looked up to see two men standing not three paces from where I stood.

None other than Knox Mackenzie and one of his officers.

I WAS SO shocked I couldn't move for several seconds.

Knox's fair-haired guard had no such compunction. He was tall and well built, as all the Mackenzie warriors seemed to be, thoroughly kitted with hunting garb and enough weapons and other contraptions strung to his belt to arm a small community. He had a friendly face and green, smiling eyes. His brow registered suspicion, but he was clearly entertained at their discovery: me, and my unusual predicament. Bright curiosity softened his fierce appearance. Knox Mackenzie himself, however, let out a low, strangled-sounding sigh, which caused the guard to glance at him, as though it was a sound that was out of the ordinary.

I was only too aware that my outfit left little to the imagination. Knox Mackenzie's imagination, and every other facet of his self-important personality, appeared utterly stunned. His jaw had dropped and his widened, silver eyes appraised me with all the delicacy of a starving hound who'd been denied its meat for weeks on end. A detail that was clearly highly comical to the accompanying soldier.

"Knox?" the soldier goaded lightly, elbowing him.

Still Laird Mackenzie did not respond. His gaze remained riveted on…well, on the thin film of a garment I happened to be wearing and all that it failed to conceal. "What…" he stuttered.

It was all frightfully rude, I thought. "If you don't *mind*," I began, then looked around for Hamish. "Hamish?"

My nephew appeared from around the side of the building, clutching my dress, which he handed to me as he walked over, his eyes remaining locked on the men. He addressed them sunnily, seeing nothing out of the ordinary here at all. "Laird Mackenzie," he greeted. "I was showing Amelia your swords. I simply *cannot* believe how many there are. 'Tis an outstanding collection indeed. If you're in need, I just know I'd make an excellent apprentice. I could help sharpen the weapons until they're the most lethal in all of Scotland." To me, he said, "I was right, Ami. The door opens from the outside. I checked. I could have let you out that way."

I could have saved myself this irritation and embarrassment? Why hadn't that occurred to me before? I cursed myself for being not only dim and overly curious but also half naked. *Damn it all to the fiery pits of hell!*

I didn't realize I'd spoken my oath aloud until the smirking guard said, "What was that, uh…milady?" As though he thought the address somewhat misplaced. Never mind that it was; this only fueled my indignation.

My tone was, regrettably, somewhat stirred. "What I *meant* to say is that if you wouldn't mind at least turning your back while I dress, I would live out my days in state of eternal gratitude for your *abounding gentlemanliness*. Sir."

By this time, I had managed to hold the dress up against myself as a shield of sorts. The barrier did little to unstun the eternally composed Laird Mackenzie, whose flummoxed shock was quickly turning into a grand source of amusement for his officer. Through a smile, the officer nonetheless gave Hamish a clear command, "Lad, that arsenal's off-limits unless you're accompanied by a soldier." To his laird, he said, "Knox, I realize your self-imposed sentence has taken its toll—a less scrupulous man would have crumbled many times over by this point—but let's give the lass a moment to make herself presentable, shall we? Then you can intimidate her into all manner of confession and otherwise," he said, winking at me amiably.

Laird Mackenzie snapped out of whatever variety of bewilderment he'd been mired in. He glared at me. "That won't be necessary," he grumbled, and without so much as a backward glance, he turned and walked off.

"Stormed away" would have been a more accurate description, in fact.

The jovial officer gave me one last grin before following his laird. "I don't know who you are or what in God's name you're doing, but you've well and truly ruffled Laird Mackenzie's unruffleable feathers. Well done, lass. 'Tis about time."

With that, he took his leave.

CHAPTER FIVE

KATRIONA'S CHILDREN WERE surprisingly delightful. Edward was a boy of ten years of age, bright-eyed and dark-haired, and eager to learn. He was quieter than Hamish, and more serious in demeanor, but they struck up immediate conversation. If Edward had ever entertained an interest in the military, he was thoroughly discouraged in this pursuit by Katriona—which she pointed out to me before I was to begin. "The children's father was killed in battle," Katriona said. "I will not allow my son to follow his footsteps into the bloody ravages of war and an early grave," was what she had to say on that topic. Edward seemed content to follow this particular guideline and had expressed an interest in farming. "He is being trained to be an overseeing farmer," Katriona explained to me. "A landowner who will experiment with new technologies and agricultural practices. He needs good counting skills and the ability to speak well, to the groups of people he will lead and instruct when his education is complete."

Katriona had very definite plans for her children, which I was to do my small part to help them achieve during my short stay and my very temporary assignment.

Greer was a girl of eight years of age, with fair hair and dark eyes. She did not smile upon our first meeting and, apparently, was somewhat headstrong. "She'll marry well, of course," commented Katriona. "She must learn etiquette, French, calligraphy, as well as discipline and reserve. These are skills she has not yet mastered."

"I have," was Greer's somewhat surly reply. I could see Katriona's disdain in her, but above all, I could see a contrariness that I could relate to. I had learned this long ago: to find common ground with my students. It was the first step toward building a successful relationship. Learning their interests would help me inspire them, by offering them information they could use to build upon those interests.

"You look very disciplined to me," I said. "Sit with me under this apple tree, and tell me what you'd like to learn first."

I had requested to spend the first lesson out-of-doors, in the orchard, where I could get to know the children in a more relaxed setting. I would teach them in the mornings, and they would be otherwise occupied, with apprenticeships and play, in the afternoons. "We will meet you at the midday meal," I told Katriona.

She looked a little taken aback by my undisguised dismissal. But she obeyed my roundabout request and took her leave.

The morning passed quickly. I learned that Greer's passion was drawing, she enjoyed French and one day wanted to be an artist. She didn't care about marrying well, or etiquette, and she had an active dislike of discipline. "We'll avoid it at all costs," I told her. "And we can decorate your calligraphy work with your drawings."

By the end of the morning, Greer's hand was latched in mine, Hamish had taught Edward seven Latin verbs and we'd recited the multiplication tables four times.

I, I could admit, was in my element. The day was bright, Hamish was safe and happy and he would spend his days of the foreseeable future learning and playing and training at the one thing he was passionate about. I was earning money and pursuing a life-long goal, and I was doing it honestly, without need to cheat or to steal. There was real satisfaction in gainful employment, I already knew, and was glad I could be useful in this way while getting one step closer to rescuing my sister.

This was the one looming dark cloud on my horizon: my return to Edinburgh, where I would have to seek out the only person in the world who truly terrified me in order to ensure that my sister was not being held against her will, or worse. At this moment, she would be afraid. Afraid of the wrath my escape had brought upon her. Afraid for the life of her husband, her sister and her son.

As I had been afraid. To the very depths of my soul. *I could make you plead, you realize. For mercy.*

Something about the fresh, misted air of Kinloch eased the restlessness that had always been a part of my character. When I found her, I could convince my very urban sister, with her visions of civility and sophisticated comfort, that we didn't need to cling to the tatters of a life that had died a long time ago. That there were new frontiers to explore that were luxurious but at the same time wild and free: no better combination existed, as far as I knew.

Of course, the undertaking was daunting. I would be alone. I knew I could steal rides from hay wagons as we had done on our northbound expedition, but I was not looking forward to the bumpy rides or the sleepless nights. Or the hunger.

Edinburgh itself would be another story completely. I would need to hide, to seek information, and if I was unable to find any, my last resort would be to confront Sebastian Fawkes himself. This was a scenario that haunted my dreams. He would be waiting for me. He knew that my sister and I shared a close bond and that at some point, I would attempt to find her.

He also knew I was wily. Wilier than he had first given me credit for.

And I doubted he would make the same mistake twice.

I knew his plans for me, and I knew what lengths he would go to in order to prove his upper hand.

Power fueled him like a drug and had gained him the fear and respect of much of Edinburgh's underworld. I understood that, unless I used every weapon of intelligence, stealth and craftiness in my limited arsenal, he would have me.

I always get what I want.

A light chill crept up my spine at the thought of him. The icy touch of his fingers as he trailed them up my arm before I could flinch back from him. The heat of his appraisal that had then, and even now, repulsed me to my bones. I would give in to him if it was the only option. I had already resolved to sacrifice myself in this way. If such a sacrifice would save Cecelia's life, then so be it. My sister's life was worth more than my happiness.

I was glad Hamish would be well protected and far away from whatever confrontation took place. My trip would be lonelier, but that hardly mattered. His safety was paramount.

And so my thoughts trod as a little girl held my hand while she drew pictures in the summery air with the daisy she held in the other. The boys climbed trees and sparred with long sticks. In the muddle of dread over my own uncertain future, I took strength from my nephew's laughter and the pollen-speckled rays of the warm sun.

We returned to the manor and took our midday meal with Katriona, Christie and Ailie. Laird Mackenzie was nowhere to be found. I was glad of this. My humiliation over being gawked at as though he were a starving man and I the banquet had faded, but I wanted to keep my distance from him nonetheless. He was a distraction I could neither afford nor endure. Our meetings had so far been fraught with all manner of the absurd. Just the thought of running into him again had me on edge. I made a point of keeping my clothes thoroughly buttoned and my pockets appropriately empty, just in case. He was as stealthy as those jungle cats I'd read about; you never knew when he might suddenly appear out of thin air.

"Since your possessions were stolen, Amelia," Ailie said, "I wondered if we could gift you with some new gowns. Since you have only the one you're wearing."

"There's no need—"

"Please, you must let us," interrupted Christie. "We have so many. Ailie's a seamstress, and she's not satisfied unless each and every man, woman and child in the entire keep is immaculately dressed. I'm afraid you really have no choice in the matter. She'd love to fit some of the gowns for you, and you won't hear the end of it if you refuse her. She's obsessed and very bossy. Please oblige her, for all our sakes."

"I have several I think would be perfect," Ailie continued, as though the matter had already been agreed to and ignoring her sister's comments altogether. "Blue to match your eyes, and a green one, too."

"She's very talented," added Katriona, whose manner seemed to have softened toward me somewhat. Maybe she had found my way with her children more satisfactory than she'd hoped. There was an unevenness to her warmth, though, that I couldn't quite put my finger on. "Even the Edinburgh designers were asking her for advice."

"I didn't realize it was you who made these gowns," I said. "I admired your designs the very first time I saw the three of you. In the tavern."

"Then you simply must agree to a fitting," said Ailie, eager. "Please," she added. "Are you finished with your meal?"

And so it was, I was whisked to the sisters' large private chambers, which had an adjoining workroom, where there were dozens of garments in various stages of completion. Katriona had taken her leave to attend to the activities of her children.

"I was thinking this one," said Ailie, holding one of the gowns up to me.

"Try it on, Amelia," urged Christie.

I did, and Ailie busied herself making adjustments, pinning and sewing with the talkative assistance of Christie. "You've such a lovely figure, Amelia. So feminine. I'd wager the men of Edinburgh chase you."

Aye, they do, I thought but did not say. *I'm often propositioned at the gaming tables with suggestive offers. And at least one murderous ganglord has placed a handsome price on my capture and ownership.* "Not particularly."

"Well," she said, "I can assure you the Highlands men will."

"Christie, hold this," said Ailie, perhaps so used to Christie's chatter than she barely noticed it.

"One Highlands man in particular seems to have noticed you quite a lot," Christie said, a comment I could not respond to as I was currently being cinched into my gown with some insistence. Had Knox Mackenzie noticed me? I remembered our first meeting, under the apple tree. I was inexperienced in every way except one. I could read the look in a man's eyes as easily as words in a book. He'd more than noticed me. His guarded fascination was encrypted into his every glance. And in his den, the charged connection as I'd pulled on his golden chain, drawing his princely face close to mine. The challenge and emotion. As for the incident in the barracks; aye, he'd noticed me. There was little doubt about that. I almost smiled as I remembered his stunned, speechless stupor. The almighty laird lost for words. A first, perhaps. I couldn't help feeling a tiny flicker of accomplishment.

"I…I'm sure I don't know what you mean," I protested inarticulately. Even now, as I recalled our shared enthrallment in his private quarters, I felt the lingering effects of Knox Mackenzie's masculine charisma in a most secret, fluttering place. Even so, as much as I might have liked to let my urges lead me where they may, I was resolved to ignore whatever whimsical allure the laird might have held for me. It was entirely possible that my journey southward would not allow me to return this way again. I hoped that it would, of course, but the dangers of my mission could not be understated.

"I'm referring to Laird Mackenzie, of course," continued Christie. "Wasn't it obvious at the midday meal, Ailie? He couldn't tear his eyes away."

Ailie smiled calmly as she worked, reading my unease. "He might have just been taking a professional interest in our new and very interesting guests."

"Nay," insisted Christie. "There was much more to it than that." She had reclined on one of the big fur-strewn beds, propping herself up on one elbow in a relaxed, girlish pose. She really was lovely, with her sparkling, youthful air and easy smile. Her hair fell around her shoulders in radiant waves. "He's very intrigued by you, Amelia. Even if he hasn't yet admitted it to himself. We all know how self-controlled our powerful brother is. And it's the first time I've seen cracks in his armor for…well, for some time."

"I was terribly saddened to hear of his loss," I said. "Of his wife and child. 'Tis an unimaginable tragedy."

"Aye," Christie replied. "That was a dark day indeed. One of the darkest this clan has ever known." After a pause, she asked gently, "Who told you of that?"

"Kn— Uh, Laird Mackenzie himself," I replied.

"He mentioned that he had lost them. Two years ago, he said."

The sisters exchanged a glance.

"He doesn't often speak of it," Ailie said quietly.

"He doesn't *ever* speak of it," Christie amended.

"I had asked about the ring he wears around his neck," I explained.

These details seemed highly intriguing to Ailie and Christie. There was a pronounced thread of concern to Ailie's interest, although Christie's manner was lighter, almost gleeful with the information I had offered. "Knox keeps that ring well hidden," Christie said. "However did you get him to even reveal it to you?"

"I… He had leaned down to pick something up that had dropped," I said. "It fell free of his shirt. I saw it and I asked him about it." Nothing untoward in those events as I described them. Nor even as I recollected them. An innocent conversation, that was all it had been.

"What else did he say?" Christie asked, curiosity lighting up her face.

Before I could reply, Ailie began to speak. I thought she might reprimand her younger sister for being overly inquisitive, but instead she said, "Amelia, I hope you don't mind our questions. It's just that Knox has been acting…out of the ordinary since you arrived. We have his best interests at heart, of course. And yours."

"Aye," added Christie. "We suspect it might have something to do with his reaction to you."

Their kindness and their clear concern for their brother made me want to open up to them, to help them in any way I could. "I'm sure it's nothing to do with me," I said. "Except perhaps that I seem to annoy him beyond belief. He's probably just anxious to be rid of me. And he won't have long to wait, fortunately for him. I'll soon be on my way." It sounded abrupt, the way I'd worded it. "Once my relatives are located, that is," I added.

"It will be wonderful when they're found," Ailie said. "After all you've been through, it'll be nice for you to find your kin once again."

"I wonder who they'll be," Christie said. "Or if they might be neighbors of ours. Wouldn't it be grand if your relations turned out to be the Munros, perhaps, or the Macintoshes? Looking at you, you really could be a Munro, couldn't she, Ailie? Practically everyone in the entire clan has red hair of some description. The Buchanans, too, come to think of it."

"There's little point speculating on those grounds alone, Christie. Every clan has red-haired people in it. Even ours. I could list twenty easily."

"Whoever it is," continued Christie, "it won't be a hardship to any of us if it takes some time for you to find them. You are quite welcome to stay here as long as you like."

"I thank you for that. You are so very kind." Something occurred to me at their mention of the neighboring clans. "Your other brothers. They have taken up lairdships of their own clans recently. Are they nearby?"

"Kade leads the Morrison clan now, a day's ride from here. Wilkie is farther away. Ossian Lochs is nearly a three-day ride. We don't see him as often." Again, Christie paused before asking, "Knox told you of them?"

"Aye," I said. "He mentioned that they had married only recently. He was speaking of some advice they had given him."

"What advice?" Christie said.

"Oh. Just that it was time for him…to stop grieving. To move on."

The sisters were silent for a moment. Their eyes met and an unspoken thought passed between them.

"With that, I have to agree," said Ailie, making one final adjustment. Then she stepped back, surveying her work. "There," she said. "Perfect."

I had to admit: it *was* perfect, clinging to my every curve, accentuating and flattering my feminine shape. Low-cut but not indecently so, softly decadent, at the same time meticulous and winsome, it was truly a work of art, a dress that made me feel beautiful, comfortable and desirable all from the way the velvety, sky-blue fabric was fitted expertly to my body.

"And if he didn't take notice of you then," Christie continued, thoroughly immersed in her own lighthearted line of thought, "he certainly will now."

I allowed their fussing and their adjustments as they fitted my clothing and brushed my long hair, but, in fact, I was more mired in the thoughts of my imminent departure from Kinloch than I was enamored by their review of the attentions of their oldest brother.

A knock on the door quieted the discussion and a young woman who appeared to be a servant appeared. "The lass has been summoned by Laird Mackenzie. She is to meet with him in one hour, at his request."

"Already?" mused Christie. "He's not wasting any time at all."

My heart skipped a beat at the news of my summons. What did he want me for, again, and so soon? Had he unearthed our lies during Hamish's inquisition? Was he going to order us off the premises immediately? Or did he have some other complaint? Maybe he was angry at our break-in and subsequent break-out of the arsenal. Whatever the subject of his ire was this time, I needed some time to prepare myself.

I thanked the sisters once again and excused myself. "I think I'll take a rest in my guest chambers before I meet with your brother, if you don't mind. My long journey seems to have caught up with me."

"Of course, Amelia. Take your rest. We'll see you later."

After I took my leave of them, I walked through the stone passageways of the manor in the direction of my guest chambers. I passed a small arched window, which revealed a glorious afternoon. Surveying the magnificent view, I felt the call of the sunshine and the beauty of the landscape. Instead of returning to my room, I decided to go down to the orchard. I knew Hamish would be occupied in the barracks until the evening meal, and I felt drawn to the splendor of the gardens. The idyll of the place had touched something in me, and I knew my time here was limited. I wanted to savor the peacefulness, the dappled light through the leafy foliage, the plump fruit and the appealing juxtaposition of the cozy orchards and the vastness of the distant, neatly crop-lined hills. I wandered through the trees and farther. A lone gardener was tending several of the trees and I waved to him as I passed by.

There, a graceful slope led down to the loch, which was large and mirror-smooth, reflecting perfectly the image of the landscape. I couldn't resist a closer look. I walked down to it, along a raised stone shelf that overlooked the water. The level stone ledge was moss-covered and soft. I sat for a time, to revel in the quiet moment and appreciate the view. It might have been the most beautiful place I had ever seen.

At the far end of the loch, I could see a small boathouse. A number of men were milling about it, and appeared to be building or repairing a boat that had been propped upside down on a wooden stand.

Beyond the boathouse, there was a stone bridge that spanned a small south-flowing river.

A boathouse. A south-flowing river.

I felt simultaneous surges of both elation and distress. I could use one of those boats to make my escape. A boat would be faster than hitching or stealing rides on hay wagons. At least for part of the journey, my travel would be swift, and smooth. My plan was revealing itself piece by piece. Once I secured a small amount of money, I would sneak down to the boathouse, when no one was about. I would take my leave in the dark of night.

I wished I could stay here to hide away in this little utopic Highlands world for a long time to come. But it was not meant to be. My sister needed me.

It was so serene by the loch's edge, so soothing in the sunlight. I leaned back, delighting in the peacefulness of the moment, lulled by the calm rhythm of the water's lapping caress against the rocks. I hadn't slept well on a regular basis for weeks, if not more, and I lay down.

Within minutes, as I watched the birds glide in lazy circles overhead, I fell into an enchanted doze.

I AWOKE TO the sensation that someone was watching me. The warmth and light of the sun had been blocked by something large.

I opened my eyes.

Again, as the first time I'd seen him, his perfectly formed silhouette was illuminated by a low-hanging sun. The auburn light painted the tips of his black hair. *Holy Ghost, he's beautiful,* was the thought that didn't just come to mind but somehow infused my body from the inside out. I thought I might be dreaming him. Surely no earthly human could possess such overblown magnificence.

None other than Knox Mackenzie.

The light had changed. The sun was hovering over the horizon in a molten circle, leaching orange light into a purple-stained sky. The reflection of the water doubled the effect, reflecting an iridescent mirror image. A spectacular sunset over the water, just beginning.

"I've been looking for you," he said.

I took a moment to drink in the sight of his big, lean frame. His striking face, that rich, gold-tinted hair. Well dressed in his aristocratic yet rugged clothing. Refined but simmering with a masculine tempestuousness. His arms were folded in an assertive posture. Hardly necessary, really, since I was reclined and peaceful before him.

"And you've found me," I replied, sitting up, smoothing my hair and my dress into place. I'd slept, it appeared, for several hours and the deep, restorative slumber still clung to my outlook, mellowing it. I felt relaxed and supremely calm.

He stood rigid and expressionless, still blocking my sun.

"What is it you wanted to meet with me about, Laird Mackenzie?"

"I asked that you come to my meeting chambers. Several hours ago."

"Aye, I was on my way to you, but I was early, and I—"

"Let me guess. You got distracted, and wandered off."

If I hadn't been feeling so sanguine and replete from my recuperative sleep, I might have risen to his reply. Not quite an insult, as such, but not far off it. So I was easily distracted by the cornucopia of delights this new world had to offer, what of it? That he was assuming to understand me and my tendencies did not offend me. Inexplicably, I didn't mind this little familiarity between us.

I countered his rudeness with an invitation. "Sit here with me. Tell me of this urgent issue I must immediately be briefed with."

Knox didn't move, nor did his expression change. He appeared to be weighing up my motives for such a request.

After several moments of scrupulous decision-making, he sat next to me, but guardedly, as though wary I might do something unpredictable. And it was that spark of caution in him that made me want to do just that: catch him off guard.

Tease him. Ruffle those unruffleable feathers again.

In my mild, sleep-drowsed state of mind, I savored the closeness of his bulk and his beauty. I felt the subtle but unmistakable pull of him. At this point and against this backdrop, his arrogance was more amusing to me than offensive. The man was even more picturesque than the view. Now that I understood that his stubborn sternness was a mask that protected his deeper vulnerabilities and hidden desires, I imagined myself removing that mask, and comforting him. Breaking down the blockade of his severity.

"You must have been tired," he said. It was a more personal comment than I was expecting.

"Aye, I was. Did you try to wake me?"

"I've been standing here for several minutes. You were deeply asleep."

He'd been watching me. Quietly standing over me as I slept. Had he been thinking of the way I looked, disheveled and immodest by the weapons shed, with only the sheerest of coverings? I remembered the look in his eyes before he'd managed to rein in his self-control; the pure, undiluted lust.

Now he looked composed. Or close to it.

"I haven't been sleeping well of late," I confessed.

"'Tis hardly surprising." There it was again: near empathy from Laird Macstaunch. As reserved and vigilant as he was, he possessed that same innate kindness as his sisters; his was shielded behind the layers of his ingrained authority, but there nonetheless. And it was *this* that drew me to him more than his dazzling looks or his protective promise, that tenderness that he couldn't hide even though he clearly wanted to.

My reactions to Knox Mackenzie were very different from anything I'd ever experienced. Always before, I'd felt the need to hide myself, to discourage uninvited attention from the many men who gave it. Here and now, my responses to Knox's nearness were dynamic and disconcerting. That he was not immune, despite his stony facade, intrigued me and stirred my new, womanly inclinations. Mischievous urges were effervescing within me, filling my head with scandalous thoughts.

Never one to actively deny the direction of my compulsions, I secretly allowed these new cravings to take hold. I let them wash over me as I lay dreamy yet awakened in that inspiring sunlight. The pliant fabric of my dress molded to the shape of my full breasts and my beading nipples with candid honesty. Instead of hiding the shape of my body from Knox Mackenzie's gaze, I reclined in a languid, almost-arching movement. My fingers eased under the velvet of my neckline, unintentionally playing with it.

You want him. You want him as you've never wanted anything in your life. You want him *to be the memory you take within you into an unknowable future.*

Shocked by the boldness of my own thoughts, I concentrated instead on his mouth as he spoke.

"I have sent a messenger to Laird Magnus Munro," he said, his eyes watching the gentle glide of my fingers. "His clan is a wealth of information. His brothers and cousins travel widely and convene regularly with most clans of the Highlands. They pride themselves on their connections."

I returned his genteel conversation, even as my body continued to ignite. "You have made inquiries to him about my father's cousin."

"If anyone knows of Michael Taylor, it will be the Munros," he said. "I've issued an invitation to them, and others, for this weekend. They…" He paused as I rubbed my shoulder gently in a restless caress. His breathing became more rapid. "They might have gathered some information by then and you can speak to them directly."

The information he presented relieved me slightly, that his men would not be needlessly scouring the hills for my fictional relatives. There would be a gathering of clans, friends meeting with friends. A few questions asked of well-traveled acquaintances. No one would be unnecessarily dispatched for days on end on my behalf.

"I truly appreciate all the trouble you've gone to, for us," I said, and it was true. My gratitude, combined as it was with an unusually placated state of mind brought on by sleep and warmth and the dazzling presence of Laird Knox Mackenzie, was, if truths were being told, driving me a wee bit mad. I wondered if he could detect this. Could he know that I was suffering a most perfect, divine, swelling sensation in the most private place imaginable? A light throb condensed there, and I could feel its echo at the tips of my breasts. I felt as if I'd been dipped in warm honey. "'Tis especially thoughtful of you to come strolling out to the loch to speak with me. No doubt you have a thousand other priorities to contend with, as important as you are."

His eyebrows furrowed in that I-cannot-tell-if-this-thoroughly-outranked-lass-is-in-some-way-insolently-mocking-me-and-I-find-this-infuriating kind of way that I was now becoming accustomed to.

"That you would take the time to locate me personally is very thoughtful indeed," I continued, enjoying his mild confusion over my tactical female complexities. I wasn't sure exactly what my tactics were, but I was enjoying them nonetheless.

"I had asked that you come to see me, several hours ago," he said, his brusqueness again pronounced. Aye, we'd determined that: I'd missed his appointment. His curt, husky remark was doing nothing to tone down my desire. I *wanted* him to be gruff and rough and unyielding. In one forward direction.

What was happening to me? All I could think of was the shape of his long-fingered hands, brown and scarred and strong-looking. His grip would be punishing. The hardness of his straining, muscular arms would be stunning.

Oh, holy high heaven. Any residual traces of propriety or virtue instilled long ago by my once-cultured upbringing were crumbling. I was falling, but my soul was flying. *Touch me,* I wanted to say. *Hold me down. Put your mouth on me.*

"My apologies, Laird Mackenzie, for keeping you waiting," I said, my politeness tinted with soft provocation. "'Tis unforgivable on my part and I will make sure never to displease you again. Ever."

His tentative confusion lingered. "Good," he finally said.

That he would think that my assurances were sincere was enough to find my laughter bubbling up. I tried to stop myself. I covered my mouth with my hand, yet I couldn't prevent a small laugh from escaping.

He frowned, contemplating my face, but his expression was inflected with a new openness that encouraged me. His fascination was connective; it made me want to inspire more of it. I still had yet to see him smile. I wanted to change that and I wondered how I could. I had no idea, so I decided to just be myself. I had the distinct sense that my reaction to him was not only noticeable but pleasing him on a deep and wholly masculine level.

"I was teasing you," I said softly. "I'm not really going to try not to displease you. I can't."

His silence lingered, and his eyes were unwavering. "You can't," he finally repeated. After a moment, he said, "And why is that?"

I had a strange conflicting urge to both rile him and entice him. "What I mean is—" I almost called him "Your Majesty" or "Your Eminence" but held myself back. "I'm sorry I cannot offer you blind obedience, like all your loyal subjects. I will try to please you, but not because you order me to."

His gaze bored into me, but I refused to look

away. His eyes wandered to the creamy curve of my exposed shoulder, where the neckline had fallen as I'd played with it, to the cling of my new and very flattering dress. It was some time before he spoke. "How?" he said.

"How what?"

"How will you try to please me?"

"I—" I wasn't sure how to answer this. He was testing me, and quite possibly inviting me. I couldn't entirely tell. In my zealous state of heightened, heated sensibility, my response was breathy, almost coy. "How would you like me to try to please you, Laird Mackenzie?"

Our eyes were locked. Once again we were linked by this mutual challenge. "I can think of several ways to answer that question," he said. "All of which are best kept to myself, for now."

The shape of his mouth was having that same effect on me as it had once before. Twice, actually. That mesmerizing impact that funneled into my secret places, already moist, painting them now with a sweet, throbbing softness that caused me to squirm. "I think you should tell me all of them," I said. "Honestly and with all the solemnity and grandeur of your unequalled lairdly position."

And there it was. His mouth curled into a laconic half smile and he exhaled what might have been a light chuckle. And if I thought Knox Mackenzie was handsome in all his severe seriousness, it was nothing to this brief flash of heartbreaking radiance. He literally took my breath away.

I found myself leaning closer.

The sun was dipping below the horizon now and the light of day was beginning to fade.

The enveloping purple-tinged dusk was comforting to me and stoked a growing inner boldness. The combined effects of this new, heated ache in my deepest depths and the graceful curve of his eyelashes as he looked across the water were feeding an intrepid abandon. His profile might have been carved from marble by a genius. It was this unearthliness to him, this utter perfection that found me reaching to touch his hair to smooth a wayward strand back into place. The texture of it was rich and wildly appealing. So thick. Coarse yet soft. I fingered the small gold band that held his braid in place. He turned to look at my face and his light, dark-rimmed eyes speared a bolt of longing directly to that dewy, secret place that was brimming with fluttery intensity.

"Is that why you came to find me?" I said softly. "To tell me of the Munros?" I let my thumb rove to the ridge of his jawbone, feeling the prickled beginnings of his beard. *I was touching his face.* I had never touched a man this way before. I didn't know why I was touching him now. Actually, I *did* know. The craving to do so was severe, studded with anticipation and rife with a reckless need. Spurred by this unexpected, stunningly romantic setting. "Or for something else?"

His lips parted as he watched me. *That mouth.* "Something else," he whispered, almost too low to hear. He was leaning closer, accepting whatever invitation I was issuing. My fingers slid farther, touching his jaw and his cheek. His breath mingled with my own and I breathed him in, the scent of him unfurling something in me. Every unrestrained inclination I had ever had was concentrated here and now, gathering momentum.

"How can I please you, Knox Mackenzie?" I said, leaning closer still, so my mouth was only inches from his. My breasts strained at the soft fabric of my gown. His draw was too strong. I couldn't fight this, and I didn't want to. Very, very slowly, I touched my lips to his in a single, featherlight kiss. "Does this please you?" I whispered.

He remained utterly, perfectly still, but his breathing was heavier, his eyes lustrous with heat. I could sense that he was holding back, willing himself to resist.

I was not so disciplined.

I had never kissed a man before and I had no idea how to do such a thing properly. My instincts guided me. Touching my lips to his once more, I nipped gently. The feel of him was so decadent, so resplendent, I dared to touch my tongue to the velvety softness. *I am tasting him.* I gasped lightly at the revelation of him, the drugging flavor of his lips. He tasted too good. It wasn't enough. I licked the tip of my tongue into his mouth to get closer, to taste more of him.

He made a sound. A soft sigh. Of fathomless longing and of near surrender.

I could feel him relenting. I could *taste* his desire. His self-control was unraveling. He fought for command and I, in my abandon, wanted nothing more than to break through his authoritative barrier. I knew he was on the verge of succumbing to an insatiability that was so profound and so ravaging that it was equally daunting and necessary. I wanted him to react so feverishly I was surprising even myself with my vehemence. I curled my hands around his neck, into that thick, silken hair, holding him in place.

His fingers entwined in the long coils of my hair. "You can't be real," he whispered. "I'm dreaming."

"I'm real," I said, kissing his lips gently. "I'm real and I'm here. I can help you. I can please you." I remembered how he had spoken the same words to me, and it was true: I knew I *could* help him. I could temper his grief and help him heal.

It was entirely possible that my life would be forever changed by my impending journey back to Edinburgh. The removal over past days of the heavy, compounding threats of destitution and disgrace had changed me. I *loved* this place. I loved its peace and most of all, its peacemaker. I wanted *this* experience to hold on to, to remember when the darkness closed in. The beauty of this moment and this connection was one that I could take with me to my grave or my imprisonment.

Did I dare? Would he relent?

It was then that the night air rang with the curling note of a far-off horn.

Knox pulled back, albeit with some reluctance, glancing back toward the manor.

"What is it?" I said.

"A summons. For me. I'm needed."

Of course he was. He had an entire clan awaiting his directives. A fleet of underlings requiring his commands. In the distance, voices could be heard. They were looking for him.

I wanted to lead him away, beyond their call, to keep him all to myself. *Ignore them,* I wanted to say. *Make this—make me—your priority. Before it's too late.*

He disengaged, but not before smoothing a curl of my hair back from my face. The gesture was tender and dreamlike: a still, treasured moment in the fading daylight.

With that, silently, Knox rose to his full height, looming once again, the shield of his leadership already firmly reestablished. So much so that if my lips weren't tingling and sultry from the kisses I might have thought I'd imagined them. The little devil in me was irate not only at the interruption but at the abrupt reappearance of Knox's emotionless shield. My more logical side, however, was barely grateful. *You've only known the man for two days. What will he think of you? Already you're offering your-self to him like some desperate hussy from Madame Blondeau's brothel! You can thank your lucky stars that he's an important laird whose presence is sought out, or at this very moment you'd likely be either scorned and humiliated or, worse, naked and thoroughly, massively compromised!*

Oh, Jesus. I fought against the fierce longing to actually *be* naked and massively compromised. Right now. *Pinned down by his big, sculpted body. With his strong hands gripping and his hard—*

The horn sounded again. And again. The voices were getting closer and shadowy figures appeared in the distance. The subjects were impatient for the return of their king.

"Walk with me," Knox said. Then, as though realizing how terse he sounded: "If you would, milady."

I stood, and my mood was fiery and discontent. I'd been so very close to reaching him. I'd felt it, the first stones of his fortress walls beginning to crumble. All that was gone now, replaced by his full composure. He extended a hand in a gentlemanly offer, but I refused it, scrambling to my feet unassisted. I wanted nothing to do with his courtesies.

He regarded me as we walked, his eyes as churlish as I felt.

A messenger was quickly approaching as we made our way.

"Laird Mackenzie," the young man puffed, winded from his run. "We've been looking for you."

"For what, Sully?"

"A visitor has arrived, the letter carriers have returned from Edinburgh and there's a matter with one of the children. The lad."

"Which lad?" Knox said.

The young man looked at me. "The lady's brother."

"Is he all right?" I asked urgently, cold panic flooding me. *A visitor? Had they arrived? Had Fawkes found us? Had he taken Hamish?* I grabbed the young messenger's shirt at his throat with both my fists. "Where is he?"

Sully seemed taken aback by my overwrought reaction. "He's fine, milady. Unharmed. There's been an argument, that's all. He's being reprimanded by one of the women."

My panic had eased but now my hackles were raised. "Reprimanded?"

"Aye, milady," said Sully.

Damned if I didn't know *which* of the women had reprimanded my darling nephew. I glared at Sully, fuming.

Knox Mackenzie's smooth, deep voice was close behind me. "There's no need to manhandle my messenger, lass," he said. "I'm sure the matter can be resolved easily enough."

"Oh," I said, flustered by my inappropriate outburst. I released Sully, patting his shirt back into place, taking a step back from him. "I— Of course. I must go see him at once."

I turned and began walking toward the manor at a brisk pace. The messenger had given me a fright. The thought of something happening to Hamish, of the dark threats infiltrating this haven and drawing us back into the abyss of fear and adversity, was enough to put me on edge. I wanted to see Hamish, to reassure myself that he was safe and well.

Knox and Sully kept up with me easily, walking with me. Knox was looking at me sideways in a nonchalant yet curious manner, as though something I'd done had surprised him. I ignored him, now thoroughly frustrated and incensed. Which one of my misdemeanors had piqued his interest this time? The list would soon need its own scroll to fully catalogue it.

Knox's absence had drawn attention. People were gathered. A man opened the door for us as we neared it and I strode through without hesitation.

The hall was crowded, clustered with groups of clanspeople enjoying a drink, celebrating the end of the workday, preparing for the evening meal. Near the fire, I could see Hamish, seated in a chair. He never sat that still. Near him, Katriona stood with her hand on Greer's shoulder. Ailie and Christie had just arrived and were entering the room from the opposite door.

I walked over to Hamish, followed closely by Laird Mackenzie, who was being spoken to with questions and news as he made his way through the gathering; I took little notice. I was focused on the situation at hand and my nephew's face. He looked less than remorseful. He also looked healthy, I couldn't help noting. His cheeks were flushed with sun and activity. He did not leap up and run to me, but remained seated as though he'd been instructed to. I touched my finger under his chin, tipping his face up to mine. "Are you all right?"

"Aye, Ami. I didn't mean any harm."

I turned to Katriona. "What has happened?"

Katriona looked at Hamish pointedly. He frowned, and held out his hand, revealing two small objects cupped in his palm. Katriona didn't immediately speak, but her expression was indignant as she stared at the evidence, then at me, as though the two small, white cubes were explanation and incrimination enough.

"Dice," I stated.

"He was teaching Greer how to use them," Katriona accused dramatically. "To determine which of the two would get the last spoonful of honey. I will *not* have my children gambling and I will now have to seriously rethink your appointment as their temporary teacher."

God help me—I almost laughed. *That* was his crime? Hamish and I used the roll of the dice all the time, to decide any minor dispute we were confronted with. We had several pairs, one undoctored, one that was weighted from within to always roll double sixes and one that would roll double ones: snake eyes, we called them. The ones he held now were, I knew from sight, the double sixes. It bothered me, of course, that Hamish was using these die with the intention of cheating his way to his prize. But I could hardly fault him for that. We played such tricks on a daily basis against our patrons until they grew wise to us. This trick alone had been enough to keep us from going hungry many a winter's night.

Hamish had let his guard down and forgotten to act his part. Something I, too, was admittedly having some difficulty with.

"Give them to me," I told him.

"Why?" he protested. "I always carry dice. It's how I settle my disputes, Ami. As you showed me."

"Hamish," I said softly, smiling, shaking my head as though amused by the follies of a naive child. I could feel our audience jumping to conclusions, and I did my best to brush off their eagle-eyed judgment and play my role. *Think, think, think,* I willed myself. *Come up with a convincing cover.* I smiled at the assembly: Katriona, Christie and Ailie and Knox, among others. "'Tis a technique that was taught to me by one of my instructors at the teaching college," I explained. "For mathematics. The count of the dice is good practice for sums. As for the decision-making technique, that was in jest, Hamish. You know that. We make our decisions by considering the wisest option, the most altruistic option, the option that will better not our own situation but that of our fellow man. We consider our legacy and our reputation, always. Now give me the dice so I may put them with the rest of my teaching instruments. So the matter may be settled."

Hamish handed over the dice. I could see that he understood his mistake, and had, for now, learned from it. We were always going to have the odd glitch in spinning the perfect lie. He was only nine; he couldn't be expected to have the consistency of a saint. Nor could I, for that matter. I could only hope that I'd smoothed over the incident without any permanent damage to my plans.

And I was silently congratulating myself for the calmness of my response. I'd felt inclined to throttle Katriona, or at the very least warn her to leave my nephew alone. He was neither her charge nor her concern. But the fact of the matter was that I was leaving. I could not afford to create any animosity whatsoever. Hamish was an innocent child to be protected and nurtured, and I would soon no longer be on hand to do either.

"Please forgive me, Katriona," I said. "This misunderstanding is entirely my fault. 'Tis true I have used the dice regularly with Hamish, to work on sums. And I regret that I did once settle a small contest between us by employing them. But it was all done in the spirit of play and with the educational value of the game in mind. I'll make sure it never happens again. If you prefer, I will remove the dice altogether."

Katriona smiled, moderately appeased. "Aye," she

said. "I insist that they are removed from any and all lessons with my children."

"Of course," I conceded gracefully.

Before I was further tempted to strangulate either one Mackenzie or several of them, I took my nephew by the hand and ushered him out of the hall and up the stairs that led to our private guest chambers for a much-needed hour of peace. Most of all, I needed some time to quietly savor the consuming memory of my first kiss, the effects of which had changed and charged the very alchemy of my soul.

THE VISITOR WAS a man by the name of Thane Macintosh. He had a dark mane of wild, wavy hair and a handsome face. In his eyes lurked the possibility of danger, even malice, but he was civil enough. He had stopped in at Kinloch on his way south, to Edinburgh, where he was visiting an acquaintance he did not name.

We were seated at the evening meal, and I had made a point of sitting far from Laird Mackenzie, whose frequent, loaded glances I refused to acknowledge. I couldn't bring myself to feel humiliated by my own behavior by the loch. Shamelessly, my only regret was that we'd been interrupted before I'd been able to conquer his reserve.

"Is there any news you need delivered to Edinburgh, Knox?" asked Thane. "I should reach the city within a few days."

I was almost tempted to ask for a ride, but it was

too soon. I hadn't yet secured the money, and truth be told, I didn't like the idea of traveling alone with a man like Thane Macintosh. On my gauge of men's characters, I had one ideal and one nemesis. If I'd had to assess Thane's placement on the spectrum, my instincts suggested he skewed toward the latter, and I had no intention of putting myself at the mercy of any man. *Save one.*

"We have messengers that ride every few days, Thane," Knox told him. "For trade and communication."

The conversation faded out as I considered Knox's statement. It was unwelcome information for two reasons. First, it meant that questions about my identity, and Hamish's, could easily be researched. It also meant that traveling parties could be summoned to seek out a missing person, or one that happened to be on the run. I remember the boathouse I'd seen from the distance. If I could launch a boat when the builders left for the day, I'd have the whole night to sail, to hide the boat and to disappear altogether before the boat was discovered to be missing.

I thought I might have to act sooner than later. Maybe I could do without money. I decided that I'd sneak down to the boathouse this evening to see if there was a boat light enough to drag and launch on my own. Then I could solidify my plan one way or another.

"He's quite enigmatic, isn't he?" said Christie, after the meal had been eaten and cleared away.

"Who?"

"Thane Macintosh. Very mysterious. Inscrutable."

I wouldn't have picked Christie as one to find intrigue in the brooding type. It was true that Thane had watched her sporadically throughout the meal, although many people did: she was a bright spark, full of sunny, gentle laughter and kind praise. Thane Macintosh was a man whose dark side was a prominent feature of his countenance, and I was somewhat relieved, on Christie's behalf, when she said, "I'll be glad when he takes his leave of Kinloch."

Katriona had disappeared with Greer. And when Edward was summoned to bed in the boys' communal sleeping quarters, it was suggested that Hamish accompany him.

"'Tis typical for the noble boys aged ten to fifteen," explained Ailie.

"I'll be ten soon," piped in Hamish. "In only two months and four days."

Christie added, "Those are the lads Hamish will associate with as a fledgling apprentice soldier while he's here at Kinloch. It might be good for him to meet them, if you'll allow it, Amelia."

The sisters might have thought I was reluctant to be separated from Hamish, and I was, but I could see the value in his inclusion. Ailie continued. "The boys rise early to help with chores allocated to them by the men of the keep. Those who will become their teachers and their guides in whatever trade they're being trained to master. Their separation from their mothers is considered a rite of passage, so the boys can become well acquainted as workers and future leaders of the clan."

I knew it was an exceedingly fortunate position for Hamish to be in, and I encouraged him to go with the other boys. He would be well protected as one of the nobles, and he would finally, for the first time in his life, be able to enjoy the regular company of children his own age, and with similar interests. I was sad to be separated from him, but this would become his new lifestyle, fending for himself within the Mackenzie clan. Best to let him begin.

Knox, as always, was central to the activity. There was always someone waiting to speak to him, to ask his advice, or to serve him. Christie and Ailie, too, were popular members of the clan and were sought after for conversation, and gossip.

And so it was relatively easy, once Hamish had left with Edward and the other boys, to quietly excuse myself from the hall and make my way back to my chambers.

There, I waited for a time. When the activity of the clan had quieted somewhat, I wrapped my shawl around my shoulders and silently made my way down the corridor, belowstairs and out the back entrance of the manor. I was careful, and I went unnoticed. The night was balmy, but the breeze smelled like rain. How enchanting to detect such a thing. The breeze in the backstreets of Edinburgh smelled like coal, manure and whiskey.

The boathouse was, as I'd hoped, quiet. The boat I had spied from the elevated vantage point of the bluff was still perched on its stand. I could see now that it had a hole in it and was being repaired. There was a larger craft moored near the shore, but I dismissed it immediately. It was a fishing vessel and was too large for what I needed.

I went inside. The boathouse was large enough to hold upward of ten small wooden boats, which were stacked on specially designed racks. Each had been paired with several oars of different designs, smooth and beautifully made, as everything here at Kinloch seemed to be. People of this clan were especially talented at design, innovation and organization. They took every tool and detail of their environs to heart, and I admired this about them. I knew Hamish would, too. I knew if I left him here and wasn't able to return, he would learn to appreciate these values, as well. He would succeed and prosper without me, if need be. The thought vexed me, of course, but it could hardly be helped. I refused any wavering doubts or regrets.

And here was my escape. The boats were small enough for me to drag off the racks and down to the water myself. I could launch one of them and row down the small river, to make my way south, to find rides on hay wagons or to pay a passing carriage, if I had earned enough.

I could leave now.

But nay. I needed to say goodbye to Hamish, without actually revealing my intentions. I wanted to explain to him, in a letter, that I would come back to him as soon as I could. And I wanted to tell him not to look for me, or try to follow me.

Money, I knew, would be very useful. I wondered where the Mackenzies kept their bank. *It would make your journey easier, and quicker.* But nay. I wouldn't steal. I'd rather go hungry now than steal from Knox's clan. I would try to wait until my first payment from Katriona for the teaching, and then I would take my leave. I hoped I might receive my dues the next day, or the day after.

Outside, the rain began to fall. It was a heavy downpour and I could see the million droplets spiking the loch in a dancing, magical spectacle. *Damn.* I would get soaked walking back to the manor. At the edge of the horizon, above the jagged peaks of the Highlands, the sky was lighter. I thought the rain might ease shortly and decided to wait it out. One of the larger boats was supported by a swinging sling of sorts, strung low. It was lined, I could see, with blankets. I climbed into it, lying back for a moment, listening to the sound of the rain and hoping the storm would soon pass. The boat swung gently, lulling me.

My mind roved through a labyrinth of hopes and fears and aspirations, until I might have drifted into a brief, dozed revelry. But the dream was not a memory. From the shadowy depths of my hazy trance, it felt like a premonition.

The door was locked. The room was dark.

"Amelia."

I knew that voice. Its devil-tainted rasp reached into my throat and grabbed my heart. I couldn't breathe.

"I knew you'd agree to my demands eventually."

Nay! I wouldn't agree! Ever. I tried to scream and fight back, but I couldn't move. My limbs felt weighted and powerless.

"Take off your dress."

I would not allow this! "Please." *Hot tears wet my face.* "Please leave me."

"Ask me to take you," he commanded. "Beg me to be the first to possess you. Do it now. I own you and I intend to take what is mine."

I was swamped in terror. Black doom overcame my rage, engulfing me in its inky mire.

"Or I'll have the boy's throat cut," came the un-thinkable, horrific warning. "We found him."

Oh, God, nay. Please. *"All right," I sobbed. "I'll do anything. Anything. Please."*

He was there, leaning over me. His hand reached out—

A bloodcurling scream pierced the darkness.

Mine.

Strong hands grabbed me, shaking me awake. "Amelia!" came the familiarly gruff reply. *"'Tis me, Knox."*

"Knox?" I breathed, taking in heaving lungfuls of air. "Knox." My awareness gave way to rage. "What in God's name are you *doing* here?" I cried. "You nearly frightened me to death!"

He had climbed into the boat with me, and was clutching my shoulders with his hands. And he was equally furious. "The question is not about what *I* am doing here," he seethed. "I was told by one of my guards that you were seen—*yet again*—wandering off into the distance. Are you *mad?* What are you doing out here in the middle of a stormy night...in a *boat?*"

Damn it. I'd taken great care not to be seen. How had they noticed me? "I—I like boats. I was admiring the craftsmanship."

He stared at me as though I truly had gone mad. "You...*like boats?*"

Oh, hell. I couldn't have given a more idiotic answer if I'd tried. "I've never been in a boat," I added. "I'd fancy a sail out on the loch one day, if it's no trouble."

He blinked incredulously. Those long lashes really were a work of art, I couldn't help reflecting. "Oh, you would, would you?" he said.

"Aye."

He was not fooled, however. He used his most authoritative tone, carefully, as though to make sure I understood his dictate. "You're up to something and I want to know what it is. I *insist* you tell me exactly what you're doing here. What is it you're hiding from me, lass? Why is it that you seem incapable of being *honest* with me?"

Lord, how I wished I could. But my dream was still thrashing in my mind.

"Is Hamish all right?" I said, my heartbeat still thumping riotously in my chest.

My abrupt change of the subject clearly annoyed him. Hearing the genuine worry in my voice, perhaps, he allowed my question. "Hamish is fine," he said. "He's in the boys' quarters, fast asleep, I would assume, with all the other boys. Being looked after by the matrons and guarded by twenty-foot stone walls and a four-hundred-strong, enviably well-trained, astoundingly well-equipped army. Does that ease your mind?" he fumed with cutting vehemence.

Nay, I wanted to say. It does not ease my mind. Not in the slightest.

Knox was crouched over me in a somewhat aggressive position, almost pinning my shoulders to the floor of the boat, which was swinging slightly. And we were alone. In the dark of night, with the sound of rain patting rhythmically on the slate roof. In the aftermath of my nightmare, his giant presence might have been distressing.

In fact, it had quite the opposite effect.

What I felt under his riled glare was a profound, soul-drenching relief. *'Tis me, Knox.* I silently thanked God and the thousand choirs of angels for that. My traumatic hallucination only shed light on my impending trek into some very dangerous territory, which, once I faced it, might end badly.

But I was here now. And so was Knox Mackenzie.

CHAPTER SIX

NEITHER OF US MOVED. He was straddling me, holding me down, his rage and also his concern illuminating the pale inflections of his eyes. They were extraordinary eyes. Dark-rimmed and lightning-bright.

He might have been making a point, showing his dominance as he waited for me to answer the question he had every right to ask.

Despite his grip, or because of it, the tension eased from my body. I lay quietly, supine yet receptive. My restless sleep had displaced my shawl, and my gown, which was loosely tailored across the shoulders, draped in a revealing, delicately haphazard line.

I could feel the flaming heat of his body through the layers of our clothing.

A note of pleasant discomfort under his weight caused me to shift and I arched slightly. The movement accentuated the fullness of my breasts, encased as they were in the snug, flattering fit of my borrowed gown. I wanted to irritate him, or stir him, as he so easily did to me. Already, I was responding to him. The very core of my body throbbed lightly with a warm, sly pulse.

I placed my hand on his chest.

Something wild and restless was taking place between us that I could neither explain nor deny. Behind the sober civility, larger forces were at work between myself and Knox Mackenzie that were both thrilling and mesmerizing.

I want him. I want him to infuse me with his glory. Before I disappear to do my duty and risk my life, I want him.

My hands slid higher. Over the nape of his neck. Into that thick black hair. I pulled him down to me, until his face was over mine. Reaching up to him, I kissed his mouth in a seductive claim. I arched closer and our bodies met in tantalizing harmony. Rigid, uncompromising hardness over supple, inviting softness. I moved against him as my tongue touched his lips.

It was then that Knox Mackenzie submitted to my sultry demands with sudden, fierce surrender.

I had broken through the floodgates of his desire. He kissed me and the force of him was enough to overwhelm me completely. He took my mouth aggressively and his hands slid over my breasts. He was big and rough and hungry. His mouth fed on mine in long, erotic kisses, deep, ravenous and all-encompassing.

My hands had wreaked havoc in his hair and he was unfastening the top button of the bodice of my gown. We were both shaking, too absorbed to stop or to question. He made a savage sound, like a growl-edged purr. Leaning down, he kissed my breast, searching for the tip. Finding my nipple, he drew it into his mouth in firm, articulate tugs. Each pull sent a bolt of sweet, bountiful pleasure to the very center of my being that threatened to somehow spill, or overflow.

"Knox," I breathed. *"Oh, God, aye."* I couldn't hold back my impassioned pleas. I wanted to tell him how good he felt, how much I wanted him. *"You feel so good. I want to feel you everywhere. Everywhere. Aye, touch me. Put your hands and your mouth on me."*

He was pulling my dress lower, feasting on my body like a starving man.

And he, too, was gushing, equally overcome. "Amelia," he was murmuring against my skin. "God Almighty, lass. You're driving me to the brink of madness. I haven't slept since I saw you hanging from that tree, spilling to the ground and out of your gown, eating that juicy apple. I wanted to take you right then and there. You're so lovely. Too lovely. I want you more than I can bear."

It felt good to finally give him my complete honesty. "Laird Mackenzie," I whispered into his ear, nibbling and kissing him as he groaned. "You are, without a doubt, the most beautiful man I've ever seen. So brave and good. I wanted you then as I want you now. Take me. Take everything." My hands grabbed fistfuls of his shirt, pulling it loose from his leather trews. He removed the garment, sliding it over his head and tossing it away impatiently. In the humid air of a rain-soaked night, the dark skin of his torso gleamed. He looked bigger and more muscled without his shirt, capable of overpowering me and dominating me completely, and the realization only stoked my frenzy higher.

Knox's strong grip was on my bare leg, the fabric of my dress somehow bunched now around my upper thighs. My hand found the hard muscle of his upper arm, where the brutal power of him rippled and flexed. The sheer size and raw strength of him was stunningly arousing. Knowing I was wholly at his mercy, to do with as he pleased. I wanted him to do all of it. I wanted him to have his way with me, to take and to give. *Him, him, only him.* He was crouched above me. He pulled my legs open roughly, his hand gliding higher. The cool air on my hot skin made me gasp. And then he was there, searching into the slippery softness between my legs.

All my energies focused on this sinful, beautiful touch. I moaned at the invading glide of his fingers, the gentle skate of his thumb as he found and teased the hidden, honeyed nub of my sex. *"Knox,"* I cried out. *"Oh, Knox. Oh, God in heaven."*

"Aye, lass, moan for me. I'll give you everything you want."

He *was* giving me everything I wanted. The sensation was the most intense I had ever experienced. He was kissing my lips, still crouched over me. His fingers delved with expert intent, reading the pleasure points of my body as though he'd invented them.

One of his hands was on my breast and the other continued to explore tenderly between my legs. His mouth took mine with supple insistence. In a careful rhythm, he coaxed the rise. His tongue prodded silkily into my mouth as his fingers pulled and twirled my nipple, elongating the sensitive peak. With his other hand, he sustained the circular momentum, spurring a starry, feverish throb of pleasure that began to consume me in a tidal surge. His fingers pressed and slid, delivering a gush of ecstasy so severe I lost myself. My intimate flesh spasmed in delighted, furtive bursts around his invading fingers as though my body was trying to draw him deeper.

My entire being was focused on that fluttering place where his fingers played. It was some time before I could think, or speak. My arms were wrapped around him.

"Laird Mackenzie," I whispered.

"Aye, I'm here. I'm here with you." He removed his touch, laying himself over me as though to protect me.

My mind was muddled, still overwhelmed by the lingering, feverish sensations of my body. "That was…what *was* that?"

"Pleasure, lass. Relief."

"Oh." More than pleasure. Ecstasy as I had never known it. "Knox?"

"Aye." He was kissing the skin of my throat, licking and tasting.

"What of *your* relief? I want to give you pleasure."

"You are, lass. You are."

My hands slid to his strong neck. I was fascinated by the lines of him, the curved muscles that defined him so elegantly. He was regal and beautiful to such an extent that I felt awed by him.

And he had come to me. There was a tender tightness in my chest and my throat at the realization. This beautiful, important man had chosen to be with me in this moment. In all his considerable power, he was power*less* to resist me, here and now. I felt mightily encouraged by this, by his close, heavy presence. As though he had somehow transferred some of his power to me. I felt strangely *invested*. In us. I knew this feeling would likely pass, when the dictates of our lives and realities once again defined us.

But here, on the gilded shores of his moonlit loch, we were untouched by all that. We were alone. He was on top of me, shirtless. I lay naked but for a loosened, shredded gown that covered only the middle of me. I loved the feel of his hair against my skin and the big, masculine weight of his body bearing down on mine. The night air caressed my bare thighs, reminding me of the echo of a blissful, undulating pleasure. I wanted more of it. I wanted to please him, too, and feel *his* pleasure.

"Knox?"

"Hmm?"

I kissed him again, taking his delectable lower lip gently between my teeth. I wrapped my bare legs

around him. My hands wandered over the smooth,
quilted muscles of his back. Down to his thick leather
belt. I was curious. The way he felt, so big, so un-
yieldingly hard. I knew very little about the intricacies of male anatomy, but I wondered if he had
somehow…escaped the confines of his trews. What
if I was able to *feel* him and touch him so intimately,
so inspiringly, like he had touched me?

He lay more heavily onto me, effectively stopping
me. "Amelia," he warned.

"I want to… I want you to—"

"Nay, lass. Not like this."

Maybe he was having second thoughts.

He didn't *feel* as if he was having second thoughts,
however. With his body pressed against mine, I knew
that there was more to this story than playful banter or soothing caresses. He was stunningly hard.
Everywhere.

"Unleash your madness upon me," I said, burrowing my fingers farther, touching the hot skin of
his hip. "I want to feel you."

His hand clamped around my wrist in an unbreakable hold before I could reach far enough to answer
any of my questions. "Amelia," he said again. "It
would pay not to push me past the point of no return."

I looked up at him. I couldn't deny that my current outlook was tainted by a sense of impending
doom, held at bay by the calm, formidable beauty of
this man in this moment. It wasn't fair that he might
pull away, and revoke the pervading sense of safety

his presence provided. What I wanted him to do was infuse me with his effect, to fill me and imprint me with his influence so I could feel that colliding perfection, and remember it.

Knox Mackenzie's desperation was very different from mine. It was there; I could feel it. It lurked behind a carefully honed sense of discipline. In brief glimpses, that wild longing was detectable. I had tasted it when he kissed me, that exotic flavor of uncontrolled desire. But now his emotion was being corralled once again, restrained behind some judicious, lairdish, infuriating defense. The removal of this touchable, yielding connectivity was no less than infuriating to me.

Squirming underneath him, I tried to free my hands. But he held them tighter, his hold unbreakable.

I caught the soft flesh of his earlobe between my teeth, biting him. He exhaled a light growl and stilled for a moment, allowing us both a moment of reprieve. Into that stillness, my urgencies spilled, silent and abounding.

"Stop fighting me," he said, looking deep into my eyes.

"I don't want to *fight* with you, Laird Mackenzie."

"There's plenty of time. These things shouldn't be rushed into."

Such was my petulance, it took a few moments before I realized that Knox Mackenzie was smiling. In the rippling darkness, I could see the shine of his teeth, the dazzling amusement on his extraordinary face.

It was the sight of him, I think, that unraveled me. The gleam of his hair and the shape of his mouth. Or maybe it was the sanctuary of his embrace that did it. Either way, I felt the slide of a tear down my cheek.

His smile faded and he contemplated me with thoughtful concern.

I hadn't meant to weep. Not at all. It was something I very rarely did. I wasn't one to give in to my own vulnerabilities; my life didn't afford me with the opportunities or the inclinations to indulge myself in this way. This whim, now, felt not like a weakness but, oddly, as a strength. There was relief in it and also empowerment. As though I was capable of more emotion and more depth than ever before, like hidden cloisters of my soul had been discovered and they were enchanting places that housed love and laughter and seductive ecstasies the likes of which were yet unknown on this earth. I wished Knox Mackenzie would allow me to grant him one of these secrets. "We can never know what time has in store for us," I said. "This moment is our gift. A beautiful, magical gift. I don't want to waste it, or deny it."

His answering smile was kind, touched by that unruly desire that shone from his eyes with liquid, volatile fervor. The compassion in him was backlit by fever. He kissed me, touching his lips to mine. He might have known that giving himself in this way would calm me. I loved the feel of his mouth. The shape of it, the soft texture and the sensual intent. I responded to him, relaxing and submitting. Only then did he touch the tip of his tongue to mine. A hot current shot from the tip of my tongue to my silky core, renewing the sweet, eager pulse.

"I saw you from my window today," he said, pulling back to study me. "I saw you walking toward the bluff. When the time for our meeting had come and gone, I followed your trail. I saw you there, asleep, and I sat with you and watched you for some time."

Another sweet, slow, sensual kiss.

"And I was thinking to myself, as you lay so still and so peaceful, that there was something I wanted to do." A lengthy pause. "To you."

The curiosity was nearly unbearable, especially in the midst of his sly, prolonged pauses. "What did you want to do?"

He was tormenting me intentionally by stalling, playing with a curl of my hair. "Your hair, with all its winsome, vibrant curls. The inviting contrast of you, of innocence and supple, womanly beauty. The milky, flawless smoothness of your skin. Aye," he mused. "There were quite a few things, in fact, that I *fiercely* wanted to do."

He wanted me urgent and inquisitive, I knew. So I made a point of attempting patience and feigning disinterest.

And he continued, his voice condensed with feeling. "Your cobalt-blue eyes, so bright. Your delicate, rosy mouth. Your tempestuous, fiery spark."

He paused again.

I simply couldn't resist prodding for more. "What…what *kinds* of things?"

He smiled at my insistence, my insatiable curiosity. And he indulged me. "Lurid things," he whispered, as though we might be overheard. "Shocking. *Lewd,* even. All manner of debauchery, aye. Completely and utterly inappropriate, each one of them."

Shocking? Debauched? *Lewd?* I waited, even counting in my head in an attempt to stall my outburst, trying to think of anything but him and his lurid things. I tried to stop myself, I truly did. Despite it all, the soft bid came spilling out. "*Please.* Tell me."

His eyebrows furrowed in thought, as though he was uncertain whether or not he should share such clandestine information. He traced the wing of my eyebrow with his finger. "Perhaps, if you wouldn't mind…perhaps I could *show* you instead."

It went against his principles to debauch me here in this boathouse, yet here he went again with his promises. And I was on the verge of yet another ecstatic collapse, just from his gentle threats and the sublime rock-hard pressure of his damn manhood.

I could see that Knox Mackenzie was conflicted; this was easy enough to read from the juxtaposition of his furious desire and the entrenched discipline that he could intermittently control. I didn't want anything to do with his conflict. I wished he would rid himself of that infuriating control. All *I* wanted of him was a furious abandon. So I said, almost demurely—although that particular act was admittedly ridiculous considering my state of undress and the still-rippling effects of his weight and his touch—albeit breathlessly: "I might allow you to show me one."

"Only one?" he murmured, disarming me once again with a barely there half smile. Each time his mirth shone through, the sparkly night seemed to take on a new radiance. "All right, then. Just one."

He raised himself up, lifting with his arms. I felt both relief and lament at the removal of his closeness and his warmth. His muscles bunched and coiled with his movement as he prepared to do whatever it was he was going to do. *Damn him,* I thought as I regarded his face, the mane of his hair, the outline of his broad, muscled shoulders. The man was an absolute specimen of masculine magnificence. Sculpted and dominating and silver-eyed.

"Close your eyes," he said. "Lie still."

I was still somewhat incensed by this inequality. That he would pleasure me but that I would not be allowed to return the favor. But I was too curious— *and too aroused*—to refuse him. Knowing what I now knew about the extravagant pleasure he was able to give, my refusals were difficult to summon. My pulsing, secret place was brimming with honeyed anticipation. Would he touch me there again? *Oh, Holy Ghost,* I hoped he would. I was almost shaking with the crave and the covet of my anticipation.

"Relax," he murmured. "I promise you will enjoy this."

Obediently, I tried my best to do as he asked.

"Keep your eyes closed," he commanded, and this time, the forcefulness of his authority only fueled my excitement.

Still perched above me, he kissed my parted lips. I opened to his soft demand and he kissed me with long, lush, heated tenderness, taking his time, finding ever more intimate angles until I was beyond the threshold of rationality, existing in an altogether different realm of lust and beauty and serene, willing acceptance.

He kissed a trail to my jaw, then my neck, biting gently, licking and nipping a path to my breasts. He took one, then the other, wetting them, pulling them into the fiery deliverance of his mouth. I was moaning, but I took care not to plead, nor to beg. I didn't want to do anything that might give him pause.

His momentum had not slowed. His tongue dipped into my navel, making me squirm with the delicious torment of his ravishing. And he was moving again. Lower. He was pulling my gown higher, revealing all of me. He would see how wet and wanton I was. How ready. He would know that he had done this to me, and made me want him so very much. I didn't care. He could win every game and every challenge, *this* way.

It was then that Knox Mackenzie kissed me, *there,*

in that most intimate, aroused, delicate place imaginable.

"Holy God," I moaned.

He chuckled against my skin. "'Esteemed laird' will suffice."

I wound my fingers through his hair. He was gentle, at first, just kissing me. He was murmuring something. How good I tasted, how beautiful I was. But then his tongue began to lick, burrowing and exploring. And then his lips closed over the tiny, piqued nub of my sex, licking and sucking that acutely sensitive peak into his mouth. With careful, insistent deliberation, he sucked in furtive little pulls as his tongue flicked and delved. The pleasure began in my belly, rushing up in a building, excruciating surge that consumed me in dazzling bursts. My ecstatic core clenched around his invading tongue as he continued to tease every ounce of rapture from my body.

I couldn't move, or speak. I willed him, silently, to give me more, to release his manhood and possess me fully, aggressively, right now.

"*Now* I know how to quiet you," he said, a satisfied smile in his voice.

I realized he was covering me with my dress, pulling it back down to my knees. Then he began to button my bodice. "What are you doing?" I asked.

"We're going back to the manor. It's getting late."

"I don't want to go back to the manor yet. I'm not ready."

"You're ready," he said, and every ounce of superiority had returned to him.

To my intense dismay, it seemed that he had completed all the acts of lewd debauchery he was going to bestow. I began to protest. "I'm not going yet," I said, sitting up and smoothing my regrettably now-fastened dress into place.

"All right," he said, sitting next to me. He leaned forward to place his elbows on his knees to watch me, his head tilted and propped on his supporting fist. There was something so strikingly masculine about the stance that it inflamed all my feminine wiles. What would it *take* to undermine his mulish self-control?

I twirled a strand of my hair distractedly.

He looked out across the water and I followed his gaze to the smooth, twinkling surface of the loch, which shone brightly with the cast of lively moon-glow. The sight was festive, almost heartbreakingly beautiful.

"'Tis not at all gentlemanly of you," I commented.

"What isn't?"

"You know," I said.

He chuckled. At least, I reflected, I had succeeded in figuring out how to make him laugh. My own frustration was clearly highly amusing to him. "I believe I have been *quite* gentlemanly," he countered. "And restrained."

Aye, *too* restrained. Therein lay my problem. "A gentleman would return the favor."

"What favor?"

I hesitated, but *my* restraint was all but a distant memory. "A gentleman would allow me to indulge *my* lewd, debauched list, as I have allowed you."

His smile remained, but his expression was serious and tender. "I'm afraid allowing that would most definitely compromise your virtue, lass. And *that* would not be gentlemanly of me at all, now, would it?"

"I'm…" This was somewhat difficult to express but also, at this point, I thought rather obvious. "I wouldn't mind my virtue being compromised. By you."

"I gathered that." Lord, but he was a smug bastard! Unfortunately, his arrogance was no longer offputting to me. Not at all. In fact, the effects of his haughty self-importance were, conversely, having their way with me, again. One might have thought I would be satiated by now. But nay. In the presence of this glorious hunk of righteous masculinity, it seemed I had no limits where boundaries of desire were concerned. "Nonetheless," he continued. "*I* would very much mind your virtue being compromised. Not only that, but if *I were,* in fact, to compromise your virtue, that…well, it changes everything. For me." His gaze returned to my face. He repeated the word, for emphasis. "Everything. And I'm not sure you're ready for those consequences. Especially if you plan to be on your way in a matter of days. The Munros will visit this weekend and we'll likely

locate your cousin soon after. And if we were to…
compromise your virtue, then I couldn't…" The venerated and always eloquent Laird Knox Mackenzie
was having difficulty articulating whatever it was
he was trying to say.

"You couldn't what?"

"I couldn't allow you to leave."

Fascinated by this assertion, I contemplated him,
noticing once again that flicker of vulnerability beneath his staunchness. I was physically innocent, but
I had been raised in a red-light city district, after all.
I understood that acts of the night (and sometimes
the day) needn't be binding. Knox Mackenzie was a
glorious man, worthy of all varieties of female adoration, and his wife had passed more than two years
ago. I had a strange certainty that he was admitting
a preference, a lifestyle, a wholesomeness that was
certainly not something I had so far encountered in
a man of his status. Not that I'd met many men of
his status. Not that I'd met *any* men of his status.
For this reason, I doubted my own intuition, at first.
Was he suggesting that his wife, and *only* his wife,
had been the recipient of his sensual…gifts? Until
now? I, too, was stumbling over my words. "Surely
you've allowed *others*…to leave?"

"I have never had need to allow or disallow…
others."

Maybe he only convened with women of his
own clan.

"I'm afraid," he continued to explain, "I'm a hopeless romantic at heart."

"A romantic," I repeated, not fully understanding his meaning. "A very *lewd* romantic," I added.

His white teeth gleamed in the moon-bright night. "A very faithful, particular, singularly devoted and only occasionally lewd romantic," he corrected, looking into my eyes, communicating his point. "Who has recently encountered a reason to reconsider the direction of my...devotion."

And I understood what he was revealing to me: he was not promiscuous. He had honored the memory of his wife alone, and was choosing, only now, with *me,* to rediscover this type of sensual communion. This admission was somewhat of a revelation to me.

He had chosen me.

The realization was daunting, to be sure, and also vexing. If he had chosen me, to renew whatever activities he'd been missing out on of late, then why wasn't he following through on this choice now?

He's just explained to you why, I scolded myself. *He doesn't take this sort of thing lightly.*

And neither did I.

In any normal situation, I would have feigned my role as a proper lady and refused his progressive advances. It was true that it had been many years since I'd occupied a social standing or situation that called for propriety, but my early childhood had been confined by these rules and the vestiges of civility remained firmly placed like stern sentinels in the back alleys of my psyche. My mother's teachings and reprimands visited me often: whispers through time and from beyond the divide of this life and a shadowy past one.

This, however, was not a normal situation. First, I was soon—within days, if not hours—to face the most perilous journey of my life, to be greeted by a sinister foe whose demands might very well extend into issues of my propriety or lack thereof. Second, the vision before me was of no ordinary man. He was a pinnacle of beauty and position, loftily endowed in every way it was possible to be. I wanted *him* to be the one to compromise my virtue—as he insisted on putting it—before my virtue could be compromised by anyone else. Before I returned to the snake pit of my former life.

Of course, I could not explain to him why I wanted him so urgently. I imagined what the truth might sound like: *Knox, please take my innocence here and now by the shores of this enchanting loch. Please allow me to know what the ultimate pleasure feels like, with you and all your impressive magnificence, before I disappear and sacrifice myself to the untrustworthy mercies of a madman in order to save my doomed sister.*

I thought of falling to my knees, clutching at him and begging like some pathetic, lust-blinded wench.

I did not give in to this impulse.

Next, I thought of rising and returning to the manor as reservedly as was possible after such revelatory sensual enlightenment and amid this torrent of emotions.

I wished I could even the score. I wished I could make him so mindless with need that he had no choice.

At the present moment, however, he seemed fully possessed of his self-discipline. Annoyingly so.

"I would welcome any devotion of yours," I said. I turned to look at his face and he was watching me intently. I heard myself admit: "I would, in fact, *invite* your complete and uninhibited devotion right here and right now."

I was almost getting used to his smile and the accompanying dart of pleasure it pierced my gut with each time he granted me the privilege. "I have just explained to you why I cannot accept your invitation, milady, despite the fact that doing so would give me more joy than I have experienced in…well, I could even go so far as to say ever. There is something so intensely delightful about you that I can hardly draw even a shred of comparison to this night and any other night of my entire life."

I could see why he was king of his kingdom, throwing around phenomenally persuasive flattery like *that*.

"Which is why I would, respectfully," he continued, "request that you accompany me to the manor at once so I may deliver you to your private bedchambers, where I would recommend you securely lock the door before I lose my mind and my self-control completely and divest you of your virtue with such enthusiastic and thorough dedication that you might very well weep or faint or see God, or possibly all three."

I was mildly taken aback by his candor.

With that, he climbed from the boat. I climbed out after him, but I did not accept the touch of his hand. That could quite possibly be disastrous. Touching him now would likely lead to severe embarrassment involving begging of some description. I could and would accept his impassioned dictate. With as much grace as I could muster. Which, admittedly, wasn't all that much.

We walked in silence for a time.

"You'll thank me tomorrow," he said, grinning casually. In a distinct turnabout from my earlier intrigue, I now wished he would *stop* smiling. His infernal entertainment over the subject at hand was beginning to rile me.

"I'll thank you for nothing," I said, regretting the childishness of my surly reply.

"You can at least thank me for one thing," he teased.

I did not slow my pace, nor even look at him.

"Actually, *two* things."

Nay, I would not indulge him, nor respond to him at all. He was attempting to lighten my mood, to accept his infuriatingly sensible decree. So I would. I'd return to my chambers, where I would proceed to securely lock the door and forget about Knox Mackenzie. I would concentrate on my duty as a sister. My journey. The darkness, the hunger, the despair that would surely color the days and nights of my immediate future. I would forget all the twinkly beauty of the night and the loch and *especially* the man.

"Two very *lewd*—"

I stopped abruptly and turned to face him, my hands on my hips, a gesture my mother had often attempted to scold me out of, but never quite succeeded. Knox's expression was calm and faintly mischievous. He was no longer smiling, but he looked… happy. "Must you?" I seethed, turning from him to resume my bid to escape before I was reduced to tears or pleas or some humiliating combination thereof.

"My sincere apologies. I promise I will redeem myself."

"There is only one way you can redeem yourself, and since you have avowed that you are too 'romantic' to indulge me, then I believe this conversation is well and truly over." I continued to march up the hill.

He kept pace, watching me with that bemused fascination, as if I might have been a mermaid that had crawled up from the loch.

We were nearing the manor and there were people about. When we reached its grassy lawn, I turned to face him. I knew Knox would likely leave me here, to wander farther, around the corner to where the closest door of his den was located.

Our moment had come to an end. Our sweet,

sweet passion was dissipating in the populated shadows of the Mackenzie manor. Tomorrow we would pretend this had never happened. We would forget. We would act as we were supposed to act, feign graciousness and carry on with our lives as a laird and his barely welcome visitor.

"Good evening, Laird Mackenzie," I said graciously.

Slowly, he leaned closer, placing the lightest, most stealthily erotic kiss I had ever experienced—and I'd now experienced enough, damn him, to know erotic—right on my mouth. His tongue licked my lips lightly, dipping between them, lingering, tasting with closed-eye rapture as though utterly overcome. And then, after a moment of sweet, laden hesitation, he pulled back. "Good evening, milady," he said, bowing to me in a nobleman's gesture of courtesy.

With a last glance, I turned from him and as I walked away, the lingering picture of his face as I took my leave stuck in my mind: he'd appeared younger than usual, bereft, his features touched once again by the sorrow that had all but left him by the shores of the moonlit loch.

CHAPTER SEVEN

I CONTINUED MY lessons in the morning, dedicating all my time and energy to preparing and teaching.

The children were improving at all their practices quickly. Edward was becoming proficient with the Latin verbs, and Greer had taken a renewed interest in calligraphy, now that she could decorate her writings with the pictures she was so very talented with. Her mother discouraged this unnecessary frivolity, but I assured Katriona that the drawings were harmless, that the lass would likely outgrow her imaginative fancies over time.

This was clearly untrue. The child possessed a gift I had never before witnessed in someone so young. Her drawings were uncannily true to life, her proportions of line and dimension astoundingly correct. And the artistic flair she gave the realism only added to the beauty. I planned to try to placate Katriona soon, just before I took my leave of Kinloch. I would make a genuine attempt to enlighten her to the extent of her daughter's talent. Whether or not she chose to listen was beyond my control.

Katriona had softened toward me somewhat. She could see that her children were progressing in their studies already. And she was appreciative of what I had so far done with them, I could see that. Still, there lingered a wariness in her that involved more than a hint of distrust.

I supposed I could hardly blame her. I was a stranger, with a wild, violent past and a waywardness that I could do little to tone down, even though I tried. My nephew also possessed this point of difference from his noble playmates. We worked on this. We discussed it in the evenings and we did our best to play our roles. For the most part, we succeeded.

I also did my best to avoid Laird Knox Mackenzie. In the light of day, I was as embarrassed by my euphoric responses to him as I was needy for more. He did not summon me to visit him again and I was grateful. We ate at the same table during two evening meals, but I made a point to sit as far from him as I could. I avoided eye contact even as he'd watched me throughout. Several times, I'd had to make a concerted effort not to sigh or flee or cry from the funneling heat of his subtle attention, which delivered a channel of sparks that he fired out of his eyes and directly into every erogenous zone I possessed. At the end of each meal, I took an early leave of the camaraderie, safely retreating to my private guest chambers, where I could predict my own actions and control my own mind. Knox Mackenzie had a powerful effect on me, aye, and one I was resolved not only to evade, but to conquer. And I was glad now that he had not given in to me. He had been right, of course. If he had relented to my wanton requests, I would now be not only a tainted woman—which was, if I was being honest to myself, hardly an issue with my unconventional background already coloring my reputation beyond all repair—but also bound to him in an irrevocable way.

It was best if I kept a very large, safe distance between myself and Knox Mackenzie until it was time for me to return to Edinburgh. And the date of my departure was growing closer. The money, I expected, would be paid to me soon and as soon as it was, I would steal away to the boathouse, down the river and into the night. I was almost glad of the distraction this provided. Plans and tactics allowed my mind a reprieve from the scorching memories of Knox's kisses. His hands. *His mouth.* These reminiscences were, at times and especially in his presence, extremely difficult to corral. I couldn't help replaying the tender beauty of his touch in my thoughts, over and over. And the memories, despite my attempt to put them out of my mind, seemed to infuse my body with a light, radiant awareness. Of itself, oddly. Of the soft smoothness of my own skin. Of the curl of my hair and the touch of the sun upon my face. Of my own pulse, which I felt not just in my heart but in the tips of my breasts and in my intimate, secret place.

It was disconcerting. I was existing in a state of elusive, understated arousal. I remembered every sensation. Every flutter. I was awake in a way I had never before experienced.

But I forced myself to forget.

I felt as though I was being haunted by a fiery ghost whose hair was as black as midnight and whose big, perfectly formed body was equal parts lure and liability. While my body was convinced, even as I fought against this base, burgeoning insight, that he was everything I had never known I'd wanted, delivered in one flashy-eyed, wide-shouldered, blue-blooded package, my mind knew better. *His* desire had been founded on a falsely given story. Everything about me was in fact a lie. We were not a match, and we never would be. This is what I concentrated on when I thought of Knox Mackenzie, as I worked and planned and avoided him as best I could.

It was Friday morning, and the Mackenzie clan was preparing for the arrival of their esteemed noble guests. Several members of the Munro clan would arrive this evening, as well as a number of Buchanans, Machardies, Macintoshes and Macallisters. Workers were busy preparing the grand hall with decorations and flower arrangements, and delicious scents from the kitchens hinted at the feast that would greet the visitors.

The children and I decided to hold our lessons at the far end of the orchards, where it was quieter, where we weren't in the way of the ranks of Mackenzie clan staff.

I had brought a simple picnic of bread and cheese

and dried meat, as the noonday meal would not be served today, so the grand hall could undergo its transformation for the festivities of the evening. The children, too, were excused of their afternoon tasks since even the soldiers and farmers were immersed not only in their regular work, but also in the art of presentation, it seemed. As I already knew, the Mackenzie clan conducted their everyday activities with precision and meticulous attention to detail, and appearances, to the eyes of guests, were also important. The keep was being cleaned, groomed and organized above and beyond even its usual splendor. Admirable, I thought.

The day was mild. I was practicing French conversation with Greer as Edward and Hamish solved several pages of written sums I had prepared for them. Both were seated at large, smooth stumps, which worked well as makeshift desks. And both finished their work as the sun was high overhead, an hour or two after noon, I guessed. I served them some of the food, then let them wander and play.

"Amuse yourselves as you wish while I check your work. Don't go too far, in case there are mistakes you need to fix." I let Greer draw while I perused the boys' arithmetic and I could hear their voices in the near distance. Greer wandered off to join them. After I had taken little notice of the three of them for some time, my attention was diverted by their raised voices.

An argument had broken out.

Edward was shouting and sounded agitated, almost in tears. I walked in their direction and could see them through the tree branches before they noticed me.

Pricks of panic pierced me as I saw what they were doing.

Not again. They were playing cards. Betting with money. Not only that, but with Edward's most prized possession: the finely made bone-handled knife that had once belonged to his father. It was laid on the grass in the betting pile, surrounded by silver coins and trinkets typically found in young boys' pockets. A fishing hook. A whittled stick. A small, perfectly rounded skipping stone.

"You cannot have it!" Edward shouted.

"You lost it fairly, Edward," Hamish explained. "I told you the rules. You understood the risk you were taking. There's nothing worse than a sore loser."

"You cheated!" Edward picked up the knife and held it against his chest. "I won't give it to you."

"You haven't *given* it to me. You've lost it in a fair game, Edward. There's every chance you could win it back. What else have you got to bet with? We'll play again."

It was then that I stepped in, desperately hoping that this damage wasn't irreparable. These tricks were too ingrained in Hamish, too much a part of his upbringing. He was having trouble recognizing what was acceptable in polite society. He had once again forgotten to play his fictional role.

This crime, I knew, was more severe than that with the dice. That had been forgiven as child's play, but this was organized, educated gambling. It could ruin everything. I had to *leave* Hamish with this clan. If they thought him a thief and a swindler, they might banish him from their keep. Thievery was not taken at all lightly. I had thought we had conquered our lapses and were past this life of dishonesty, but old habits, I knew, were difficult to break. Especially for a willful nine-year-old boy.

"Hamish," I said gently, forcing a calm tone. "Where did you learn to play that card game? Where did you get those cards? And where are your manners? You know we don't gamble."

"He knows how to play *many* card games," Edward insisted. "He's shown me. He pretended to be ignorant, but he's not. I know it. He's too skilled to be a beginner." Edward was an astute, clever boy who was not about to be told what to believe. He ran off, in the direction of the manor, no doubt to complain to his mother and his laird, and anyone else who would to listen. I could not blame him for this. To get nearly swindled out of one's dead father's hunting knife was no small thing for a boy like Edward, who spent much of his time lost in fantasies reliving the stories of glory, pining for his loss, and basking in the oft-given praise that he was the spitting image of his noble warrior father: a fine boy, with dark hair and green eyes, just like *his*.

"Edward!" I called. "Wait! I'm sure this can be

resolved easily. Of course your possessions will be returned to you!"

But he was gone.

"How do you know so many card games, Hamish?" asked Greer innocently. "And dice games, as well. Where did you put the snake eyes? Do doctors in Edinburgh gamble?"

"Of course not," I chuckled, doing my best to smooth this over. "Hamish had a friend in Edinburgh who had some shady associates, that's all. These things happen from time to time in the big city. 'Tis of no concern to us here, is it, Hamish? Give me those playing cards. We won't be needing those anymore." I knew for certain we hadn't brought playing cards with us. These had been fashioned. Out of parchment and ink. He'd made them.

I was irate, aye, but it was not the time or place for severe admonishment. That could be given once Hamish and I were alone. This would best be handled with earnest disbelief and light bemusement. I would need to be as shocked as everyone else at the playful experimentation of my nephew—nay, my *brother*— whose creativity had once again led him in directions that must be scolded and curbed. Laughingly, I would apologize sincerely, then quickly attempt to put the indiscretion behind us all. I could only hope that undue fuss would not be made. It would take skill to skirt this gracefully, I knew. Katriona would be even more suspicious of us than she already was.

She might not be so forgiving this time. I might lose my position of employment.

That, of course, hardly mattered. I would, very soon—perhaps even tomorrow—make my way south. Then again, if Hamish's crime was treated as such, to be punished with more severe consequences or even banishment, then we would be back to square one. I hoped it wouldn't come to that. And I was glad that the guests, who were due to arrive at any time, might distract Laird Mackenzie from making unnecessarily harsh decisions over the games of an innocent child.

I had become too relaxed, perhaps, in this idyllic place. I'd let the ease of Kinloch lull me into a false sense of security. For the past few days, I'd almost felt I'd *belonged* here, as a real teacher with real talent for it, fulfilling a real purpose beyond mere survival. I could see now that allowing myself these feelings of well-being had been foolish. I was playing a role, as was Hamish, and I had not reminded him adequately, nor stressed often enough how important our vigilance was.

Greer was climbing a tree nearby, an activity her mother would definitely not have approved of. I allowed it, so I could speak to Hamish without being overheard.

Hamish handed me the cards. His angelic face was the picture of remorse. He'd coveted the weapon owned by his new friend and had forgotten the rules. I took the cards, shoving them deep into my teaching bag, resolving to burn them at my very first opportunity.

"I'm *sorry,* Ami," he said. "I forgot. Again." Fat tears pooled in his eyes.

I kneeled down in front of him and cupped his face in my hands, wiping his tears with my fingers. "It's not your fault, Hamish," I whispered to him. "You should never have been exposed to any of it. You're a good lad. You're smart and brave and honorable. You are the best person I know. One day you'll be a great soldier. Don't you give another thought to any of this. I'll fix it."

"I won't do it again, Ami," he sniffled. "I promise I'll try harder. When can we see my mother?"

The tacked-on question hit me like a spear through the heart. God, how I missed her. Defensively, I'd all but blocked her out of my mind as I'd navigated the new and somewhat choppy waters of Kinloch. But now, in the face of Hamish's sorrow, my fear for her safety came flooding back to me in a torrent of anguish. Her sunny hair and her laughter. Her survive-at-all-costs outlook, which had given me much of my strength. Her sacrifice, in the hopes that she could right our sinking ship.

My own tears fell, but I brushed them away. "Soon. We'll see her soon." *Once I find her, and have faced the danger that might finish us both.* "We'll all be together again."

"I don't want to go back to Edinburgh," Hamish said. "I want to stay here."

"Aye. We'll stay here. When the time is right, we'll send word to her, and she'll come to Kinloch and live with us here. But we must be careful, and remember our story."

"Is my father dead?"

The question jarred me. It took me a few seconds to recover, and respond. "*Nay,* Hamish. Of course not."

His quivering lower lip and shining eyes nearly undid me. I smoothed away a fresh tear from his sun-kissed cheek. And I gave him my full honesty, as he deserved. "I don't know. I know he was expected back from his trip a week or more before we left. He might have run into some trouble along the way. I don't know. Your mother doesn't know. That is why she waits."

"I wish we didn't have to lie, Ami," Hamish said. "'Tis harder than I thought it would be."

I did, too. So very much. But wishes, I'd learned long ago, were like clouds in the sky. Untouchable, wispy and more often than not, a sign of stormy weather when you were hoping for sunny skies.

After wiping both our tears away and smoothing his hair, I squeezed Hamish's hand and called to Greer. "We'd best return to the manor," I said. "Gather all of Edward's belongings, Hamish. Every last one. To return to him at once." To Greer, I said, "And we can show your mother your calligraphy and the complicated sums of your brother, which were perfect." Already I'd improved his accuracy; at least maybe that counted for something. And today I'd encouraged Greer to do her drawings on a clean sheet of parchment, to leave her writing page unadorned, a detail that would please Katriona far more than the artistry, regrettably.

None of it, likely, would be enough. But problems were best faced head-on. And so we began our walk back to the manor.

As we emerged from the orchard, a large, fine carriage was being pulled down the lane by a team of black horses. These were flanked by a large number—ten or more—warriors on horseback. Both the men and the carriage were heavily decorated with a bright red tartan. I knew little of the clan tartans, but Hamish had been studying them and he anticipated my question. "Munro," he said.

We watched as the carriages pulled up in front of the manor. Footmen assisted several women who disembarked. Ailie, Christie and Laird Mackenzie were on hand to greet the visitors, and it was then, without being seen, that I led the children through the side door, to deliver Greer to her mother, deal with the situation at hand and retire to my room for the evening.

THE PROCEEDINGS DID not go especially well. While Edward and Hamish reconciled immediately after Edward's possessions had been returned to him, this was not before he had recounted Hamish's entire offence to his mother, in meticulous detail. Edward, while not a particularly outspoken boy, was, when pressed to do so, indeed fairly eloquent. And thorough. And Katriona was now convinced, as she had wanted to be all along, that our history was rife with the lies we had so carefully attempted to conceal.

"I knew it from the minute I saw the two of you," she proclaimed. "Something was remiss. First the dice and now this. You're hiding something, Amelia, and I want to hear of it. Now. How did Hamish learn his card skills? Edward said he could shuffle, and deal, and practically predict the next card to be dealt as though he'd been doing it all his life."

That's because he has.

"There was a small gang of misfits that lived around the corner from our house," I said, scrambling for anything that might sound believable. But I was tired. My lies didn't sound convincing, even to myself. "Sons of one of my father's patients. 'Twas all fairly harmless. Just a game. It won't happen again, I can assure you of that, Katriona."

"That's what you said last time."

Our eyes met. I wondered how I appeared to her. Still windblown. Still filling out my gown too snugly, despite Ailie's expertise; the food at Kinloch was beyond reproach and I had been eating well. Still creamy-skinned with a light dusting of freckles across my nose. It was true that Katriona had become less antagonistic during the week, as we had discussed the children's schedules and the small improvements they made in their lessons each day.

I had believed she was genuinely pleased with my work and I thought she might, under different circumstances, have liked me to continue. That now might have changed, however, depending on her decision regarding Hamish's second mistake.

And I wondered about her association with her laird. I remembered the discussion of the women in Lachlan's cabin. They'd insinuated a connection. An interest, at least on Katriona's part, and one that might not be returned by Knox himself. I wondered if this had caused her disappointment, and her crossness. And I wondered if she suspected *our* fragile yet fiery attraction. Jealousy could, to be sure, be coloring her opinion of me.

It didn't matter, either way. She could have him. She could comfort him once I was but a distant memory.

And so, after smoothing the situation as artfully as I could, I returned to my guest chambers. The matter would be discussed with Laird Mackenzie, Katriona pointed out, when he became available. Only then would a final verdict be given.

Hamish had gone to the boys' quarters, with Edward, where he now spent most of his nights.

I was glad for the quiet.

I spent some time writing a letter to Hamish that I'd been working on, to explain to him the reasons for my departure and to do my very best to convince him that he must, under no circumstances, follow me. He must wait for me here at Kinloch until I returned, which I promised I would do. It was more than possible I would not be able to keep this promise, but sometimes lies had to be spun to keep loved ones safe: this was hardly a newfound revelation.

Outside, the bustle and excitement of more arrivals could be heard. I went to the window and I could see the approach of two more carriages, of different clans clearly marked by their varying tartans. Already, the late afternoon was alive with music and conversation, and the frivolity of friends meeting again to talk, eat, drink and share the news of the Highlands.

Frivolity that I would take no part in.

I could admit that I wouldn't have *minded* a dose of fun and laughter. But it was best if I kept to myself. I had to consider the growing list of topics I needed to studiously avoid in the presence of various members of the Mackenzie clan, including the debacle of Hamish's card tricks and the infinitely more humiliating fiasco down by the loch's edge with the venerable, arrogant, devastatingly appealing laird. Even as my mind skimmed the memory, already I felt a light flush heat my face, and elsewhere, and a swooping flutter in my stomach.

Nay. I couldn't take part in any festivities where *he* would be present. I would be offered ale, most likely. I would be expected to introduce myself and tell my story, over and over, to the people I met. Questions would be asked. And all the while, he would be watching me. Those lightning-bright eyes would rove the curves of my body, lingering in indecent places that he had already touched. And *tasted*.

The flush heated further, to a soft, centered ache lightly pulsing with sweet, tantalizing need.

A knock at my door made me jump.

Two servants, wheeling a steaming tub full of bathwater. "Christie has sent a bath for you, milady," one of them said. I opened the door to let them in and the bath was wheeled into my chambers.

"And a dress prepared by Ailie," said the other, laying a cream-colored gown on the furs of my bed. "They request that you be ready in an hour to attend the gathering in the grand hall."

"I'm not attending the gathering," I said.

"Christie was quite insistent, milady," one of them said. "Would you like assistance with your bath?"

"Nay, I—"

"Very well, then. We'll be back to collect the tub when you're ready. Just hang this ribbon on the outside of your doorknob when you've finished." One of the young women handed me a looped blue ribbon. Yet another clever detail of the Mackenzie housekeeping. Before I could protest further, the women left, closing the door behind them.

The bath, in fact, looked exceptionally inviting. The water had been scented and the steam filled the room with a humid fragrance. I could bathe and then send a message to Christie and Ailie with the women when they came to fetch the tub. *I* could be quite insistent, too. And I simply could not attend the gathering. My urges were too unruly, my responses too unpredictable. I didn't trust myself in the company of Knox Mackenzie: it was as simple as that. My conversation with Hamish had invigorated my urgency to return to Cecelia. I decided that if Katriona didn't pay me tomorrow, I would just have to do without it. I would spend the next day avoiding him, being as unobtrusive as it was possible to be.

The hot water felt heavenly. I scrubbed my hair and my body with the small cakes of rose-scented soap that were perched on a fitted wooden shelf. I luxuriated until the water began to cool, and then I rinsed myself clean. Drying myself, I decided to just *try* the dress. Not that I'd be needing it tonight, but it was beautifully made, as all of Ailie's creations. The fabric was a thick satin. Fitted and soft, it clung to my plentiful curves like a second skin. Instead of buttons, it was designed to wrap and tie at the side of the waist, cinching a flattering shape. It was cut revealingly and designed to gently support, showcasing my breasts like a pillowy offering. The dress was beautiful, aye, but it was bordering on scandalous. It might not have appeared that way on a more slender figure, but on me, it was a dress that would no doubt get attention. Very *unwanted* attention.

No matter. I wouldn't be getting anyone's attention here, behind the closed doors of my private chambers. I left the silky-soft gown on, nevertheless, as I brushed my hair until it was wavy and glossy. I remembered to place the ribbon on the doorknob, and as I opened the door to hang it there, I saw Christie walking down the corridor toward my chambers. I nearly scurried back in and closed the door, hoping she hadn't yet seen me.

"Amelia!" she exclaimed. "I'm so pleased you've put it on. I specifically chose this one for you. Isn't it perfect? Let me see you."

I had no choice but to allow her to enter my chambers. She circled me, taking in the spectacle of me. "My brother," she said gleefully, "will simply not know what has struck him."

"Oh, nay," I countered. "I'm not going to the gathering, Christie. I've got some work to do." Of course, I couldn't reveal that I was writing a letter to Hamish. "Preparing the children's lessons for next week."

I wondered if she'd heard yet of Hamish's swindling, and was not surprised when she said, "Oh, you simply *must*. Don't worry about the child, Amelia. We all know there are many layered mysteries to the both of you. Personally, I think that's part of the appeal. I only wish *I* was so mysterious. Regrettably, everyone in this clan knows everything there is to know about me and every member of my family for generation upon generation. Where's the fun in that?" She chattered happily as she fingered a long curl of my hair. "Trust me when I say you simply will *not* want to miss this evening's revelries. I've got good reason to believe that something *very* exciting is about to happen. Involving my dear sister,

Ailie, and a certain impending heir to the lairdship of the Munro clan."

I remembered Knox speaking of him. "The one named Magnus?"

"Indeed it is. I'm sure…" She paused, appearing to exercise control of her pronouncement, which was clearly requiring effort on her part. Her blue eyes spangled. "Well, I shouldn't yet say exactly what will take place tonight, but I know it'll be worth your while. And Knox has asked me to summon you. He wants you to speak to Magnus, regarding your kin. I believe he's already received word from messengers he sent to several neighboring keeps in search of information."

I had been told this would be done and I had done nothing to stop it, but still, this information, so cheerfully delivered by Christie here and now, was somewhat distressing: that people were going out of their way to seek out my fictional family was shameful of me. I had instigated their search and I felt more than a pang of regret over my frivolous lies. I wished now that I had never had the need to deceive these kind, hardworking people. I silently cursed Sebastian Fawkes. It was *his* fault, all of it. All the fear and sadness and lies. The despair turned then, into something else. Anger. Resolve.

I remembered why the dishonesties had been necessary.

Hamish.

Keep him safe, Amelia. Please. I beg you. Do whatever it takes to keep him safe.

A light knock signaled the return of the young women who would remove the tub. As soon as the door opened, Christie grasped my hand and began pulling me down the hall in the direction of the grand hall, where the festivities were already underway.

THE GRAND HALL was crowded and colorful, populated by big, tartan-clad men and beautiful women. I was struck immediately by the vast difference between this gathering and the ones I was used to: a gambling den full of downtrodden scoundrels seeking luck in all the wrong places. These people, in contrast, were wealthy and noble and looked the part. They were at the height of their game, or, more accurately, they were the pinnacle of what every Scot aspired to be, even the city dwellers, in a roundabout way. Even if they weren't aware of the deficiencies in their cramped, crowded lifestyle, any urbanite would surely desire *this* kind of freedom, splendor and armed, guarded superiority if given half a choice. I know *I* did.

Alas, I was not being given half a choice, nor any choice at all.

I supposed, in fact, I was wrong about that. I *did* have choices. But I would not be able to live with myself if I abandoned my sister. Not knowing whether she was alive or dead, imprisoned or hungry, ill or alone, was not an option. Already I had taken longer than I would have chosen to secure Hamish's safety. I was becoming restless with thoughts of my impending journey, and my mind was only partially focused on this scene I found myself in, surrounded now by Highlanders of all descriptions. In general, they exuded an air of health and fitness, with their suntanned faces, their shiny weapons and strong-limbed deportment. The light of day was beginning to fade now and the room was festively lit with torches and candles. An inviting fire burned in the large fireplace even though the evening was mild. The crowd convened in convivial clusters, and the ale flowed. A long table along one side of the hall was being laid with plate upon plate of sumptuous food. The feast would soon begin.

Christie led me through the gathering, stopping to greet several people along the way.

And there he was.

He was standing in the corner of the room, talking with another man who was copper-haired and handsome and almost as tall as Knox Mackenzie himself. Ailie stood next to the man with the unusual dark, flame-hued hair, and he was holding her hand. Magnus Munro, I guessed. His mien was that of a Highlands poet, although I'm not sure what gave that impression. A romantic broodiness. Or a windswept, observant sophistication, as though he was composing études or stanzas as he took in the details of the crowd and the setting. And now he spoke to Knox, but it was Ailie who was the focus of his thoughts;

his gaze kept returning to her face. And Ailie's eyes were round and glimmering with happiness as she watched the men shake hands.

I slowed my pace as I watched them. This had been a mistake. Just the sight of Knox Mackenzie, dressed in his full regalia, his black hair shining with fire-flicked shards, was enough to unfurl every tendril of longing I'd hoped I'd conquered. I had admitted to myself that I was besotted with him, some time ago. Our searingly romantic interlude by the loch had only further ignited a roaring bonfire of desire for him within me. Days of smoldering avoidance had dampened the memory only slightly, yet the embers had continued to glow. And seeing him now in all his majestic glory, the flames of my lust leaped back to life again, hotter and more voracious than ever before.

It wasn't just the heat of desire that burned me. My peripheral desperation played a part, as well. My imminent departure. My perilous destination. This could very well be the last night I ever spent in Knox Mackenzie's company. Tomorrow, I would sneak away, borrow one of the Mackenzie boats and sail silently southward, to return to my former life, which was full of downtrodden debauchery and real, dreadful danger. It was this conflagration of every hardship and unfulfilled yearning of my past that fueled my emotion, which shone through my lust as a white-hot flare. Not only was Laird Mackenzie handsome and regal, but it was that element of sanctuary in him that drew me to him most of all. He embodied decency. Safety. And the combination was beyond irresistible.

I knew now that I could, at least by degrees, get past his stern facade. I could touch his inner sanctum, that part of him that had murmured sweet words against my bare skin. *You're driving me to the brink of madness. You're so lovely. Too lovely. I want you more than I can bear... Perhaps I could show you....*

The realization flamed in a stunned, revelatory moment: *I loved him.* I loved what he represented. I loved how he looked. I loved who he was. God, how I wanted him, all of him, for my very own.

At that moment, his head turned, and he saw me. I could hardly breathe. My heart might have stopped completely for a moment or two before recommencing at a rapid, uptempo beat that I felt everywhere. His eyes widened, and his gaze dragged down my body, taking in every nuance of my fitted, pearl-colored gown. It was as though he could see right through it, burning me, stoking my fire ever higher. I remembered then that, in my haste, I wore nothing underneath the dress. All that separated us was the sultry air and the thin silk of my clothing. I thought of his hands, his touch. And I drifted closer, pulled gently by Christie's guiding arm.

I didn't know if he could read my thoughts across the crowded expanse of the hall. All I *did* know was that his eyes were locked upon me and the tenuous bond felt so real and so connective I felt almost faint with the intensity. I couldn't seem to breathe in enough air.

And then we were there, next to them. Magnus Munro was speaking to Knox, but Knox didn't seem to hear him; he was too focused on me.

There was laughter then, amused banter. I realized, just as Knox did, that our small assembly was commenting on the rapt obliviousness of our shared link.

Two more men stepped into our circle. Both had red hair and were wearing the now-familiar Munro tartan. "Who's this that holds Laird Mackenzie's spellbound attention?" asked one of them, clear delight in his voice.

"This is Amelia Taylor," said Christie. "She's a guest. Amelia, meet Tadgh Munro, Tosh Munro, and *this* is the admired Laird Magnus Munro."

"Where is Amelia Taylor visiting from?" said the one named Tadgh. He was a tease. The good-natured lilt in his tone was mischievous and laced with dark, playful intention. "And how is it that you Mackenzies have the good fortune of hosting all these ravishing young lasses you just happen to come across? Do they wander across the Highlands in search of Mackenzie blood? Or does Kinloch have some sort of beacon for lost maidens?" To Laird Munro, he said, "Why do *we* not possess one of these beacons?"

Magnus ignored him completely. "A pleasure to meet you," he said politely, to me. But he seemed distracted, almost annoyed at the interruption. To

Knox, he said, "Will *you* make the announcement, Knox, or shall *I?*"

Knox appeared to snap out of a lingering pensiveness. "Of course," he said. "I'll do it now. We have much to celebrate. 'Tis time to get started."

In the sort of gatherings I was accustomed to, those who wished to gain the attention of a wider audience might have clanged a chunky spoon against a mottled glass goblet, hooting for silence. Knox Mackenzie had no need for such banal tools. As soon as he began to speak, not loudly but with all that ingrained authority slicing through the crowd with soft-spoken command, the clanspeople immediately quieted.

"I bid a heartfelt welcome to all our guests. It is always a pleasure to host our allies from near and far. Munros, Buchanans, Macintoshes, Macallisters— we value, as always, your loyalty and your friendship and we are honored that you will share in our auspicious news this evening. Without further ado, I believe my soon-to-be brother has a few words he would like to say."

Murmurs rippled through the crowd. Christie clutched my hand and whispered, "This is it. He's going to do it."

Ailie looked on the verge of either crying or smiling, her face pale and perfect. Laird Munro still held her hand. He turned to face her and bent down on one knee. People gasped with excitement.

"Ailie Mackenzie," Magnus Munro said. "I cannot

imagine a more graceful, elegant, beautiful woman exists in all the Highlands. I have admired you from afar for as long as I can remember. I beg you to do me the honor of becoming my wife so that I may cherish you as long as we both shall live." His pause was filled with dramatic, adoring flair and sincere emotion. "Ailie, will you marry me?"

The grand hall was entirely silent, awaiting her answer.

Ailie's voice was barely above a whisper. "Aye," she said. "I will."

Magnus slipped a ring on her finger; then he stood. He took her face carefully between his hands before kissing her. Cheers broke out, the musicians began to play and the festivities began in earnest. When the newly betrothed couple finally broke their kiss, Ailie's cheeks were flagged with bright splashes of pink.

Knox kissed Ailie's cheek and Christie embraced her sister in an ecstatic hug. Magnus's kin slapped him amiably on the back.

The happiness surrounded Knox Mackenzie and me, fringing the edges of our invisible almost-delicious tension. I wasn't sure why I savored the spark. He was deeply incensed about something and I felt drawn to his ire as much as anything else about him. I knew that it was this ire that would unhinge his control, perhaps. And I, for better or for worse, held the key.

The focus was all about the wedding-to-be, and

we took our opportunity. Knox leaned against the stone wall. Behind him, the lively torchlight granted him a vibrant outline, shadowing his face. I stood near him, making no attempt at conversation. A server approached us, carrying a tray of clinking goblets filled with ale. I took one and Knox took another, placing his empty cup on the tray before the server moved on.

We were removed enough so that our voices would not be overheard.

"You are well?" he said. A prosaic pleasantry that was unnecessary. Yet he sounded sincere, as though he was actually curious about my well-being.

"Aye. You?"

To this he smiled faintly. "Not entirely, if I were being truthful."

I wasn't sure how I might have replied to this, so I chose not to.

"Your teaching appears to be progressing nicely," he commented. I looked at his face, attempting to read his meaning. Aye, it had been going well. Until the slipup with the playing cards. Did he know of this? His expression was carefully masked, but then I saw the flicker of irony. Of course he knew of it. And everything else. Very softly, without breaking his penetrative appraisal, he said, "Or at least it *was* progressing nicely."

Why hadn't I stood my ground and insisted on hiding away in my chambers? I should have known this was coming. I *did* know this was coming. Yet a part of me was too enchanted by the broad expanse of his shoulders, and the way the beautifully made white cotton of his shirt tightened over his muscled arms as he folded them against his chest. He could scold me, but he was equally mesmerized. He was having difficulty keeping his rebuke focused. His gaze kept sliding. To the wrap of my dress and the revealing cut of my neckline.

He realized his own captivation. He caught himself, mildly annoyed, and his comment was tinged with a lash of spite, as though to make amends for his uncontrolled drift of attraction.

"I have spoken with Magnus," Knox began, taking a swig of his ale.

I had a feeling I knew what this was leading up to but I feigned innocence. "Oh?"

Knox Mackenzie did not mince words, but leaped into the topic at hand with straightforward candor. "He, his brothers, his cousins and his officers—all of whom are exceptionally widely traveled and well connected—have looked into the mystery of your kin, at my request. They have extensive knowledge of the settlers, farmers and clans not only throughout the Highlands but across the lowlands, as well. There's one family named Taylor in the southern hills, but they have no apparent links to Edinburgh, nor do they have a family member named Michael who recently died in Edinburgh."

I paused, taken aback by his direct bluntness. "I'm

sorry you had to trouble your neighbors on my behalf. I—"

"Are you sure his name is Taylor?"

"I— Of course. I mean, unless—"

"Are you sure *your* name is Taylor?" he added
laconically. "Is your name even Amelia? Are you
actually from Edinburgh?"

So this was how it was going to be. Our last night
together would be spent exchanging cutting remarks
and prickly suspicions.

When I didn't indulge him with a response, he
said, "I consider myself to be somewhat gifted in the
art of reading people. 'Tis a skill I've had need to
hone over the years, and my intuition serves me well
on most occasions." Knox Mackenzie might have
been mesmerized, driven to the brink of madness
and suffering from loss of sleep over his attraction to
me. But he was also upset and mildly disappointed.
He had not only guessed but confirmed that I was
not being honest with him, and his patience, by this
point, had been sorely tested. It was understandable,
I supposed, considering his position and the trouble
he had gone through not only to help me but to harbor me.

A scurrying flush had already begun to creep
across my skin, and my blood felt as if it had turned
to lochwater: cold and swimming with silver-edged
minnows.

"I want the truth from you," he said, his voice
steely. "You owe me that."

I don't owe you anything, I wanted to shout at him, childishly. I could feel my face forming a huffy glower, which I made a concerted effort to smooth.

Of course I owed him that. He had taken us in, fed us, sheltered us, armed us, protected us and clothed us. Furthermore, unbeknownst to him, I was intending to leave my heart and soul in the form of my small nephew in his everlasting care. I felt a light sting prickling behind my eyes. But I took a drink of ale and held myself steady. He was waiting for an answer and I gave him one. A pleasingly noncommittal one. "I have given you the truth, Laird Mackenzie."

His head tilted and he surveyed me, a volatile flash lurking behind his expression. I watched him as he took another sip of his ale, sipping his drink as though searching for calm somewhere in its malty depths. He was wise to my avoidance techniques and he countered them with a gentle but very direct ultimatum.

"Amelia. If you refuse to give the truth of your history, I'll be forced to use the extensive resources at my disposal to uncover it. I would prefer not to do this, for two reasons. First, I would like to spare all of us the trouble. And second, I would hope that you might see me, in light of certain revelations, as someone to be trusted."

I might have told him that, already, I trusted him more than anyone I had ever known, save the closest members of my own family. I could have said that, aye, I not only trusted him, but loved him, desired him and wished that he would take me to bed immediately and ravage me beyond all limits until I'd all but forgotten my past, my duty and my name.

"Might you have mistaken the information you gave me, perhaps in a fit of grief?" he continued, relentless. "Or maybe as a result of your recent trials, which we all know have been significant."

Oh, but he was arrogant! And the uprooted sadness in me seemed to inspire more of a ruffling effect than a quieting one. I met his gaze defiantly. Why did he have to meddle in my business? Why did he have to be so maddeningly pedantic?

And he was undeterred. "We have scheduled messenger parties who travel regularly to Edinburgh for—"

"All right."

His eyes narrowed. "All right?"

"Aye. All right. I'll tell you everything."

My plan was crumbling ruinously around me with every stab of his painful insistence. If his soldiers asked questions throughout the streets of Edinburgh, one man in particular would hear of it. He would figure out where we had fled to. The information would reach him, and inform him. *Highlands warriors on horseback, you say? Clan Mackenzie tartan? Aye, Mr. Fawkes. They picked up a lass and a boy whose descriptions leave little doubt as to their identity. We have discovered where they are hiding.*

What would I do with Hamish? How would I save Cecelia?

I felt, in that moment, very tired. Not physically tired, but spiritually. I realized I could have left earlier. Quite easily. In fact, the longer I stalled, the more difficult my escape would be. I knew by now that Hamish would not only survive but thrive with these people and in these surroundings. And so would I. He had been accepted by the other children easily because he was an exceedingly likable boy who endeared himself to everyone he met. That, too, had me hanging on to this fantasy. I didn't want to leave him no matter how badly I was needed elsewhere. The time to do exactly that, however, was nigh. I must reacclimatize to the downtrodden and the tarnished. I must once again face the reality of who I was.

"Tomorrow."

He glared at me coolly. "Nay, Amelia. Not tomorrow. *Now.*"

"I didn't get much sleep last night, you see," I said, backing away from him.

He reached to clasp my fingers, gently but with strength, holding me in place. "One of the messenger parties I was telling you about will depart on the morrow and—"

"*Please,* Laird Mackenzie!" I pleaded in hushed tones. "I'm really not feeling well. If you'll excuse me, I must return to my chambers to take some rest. I—"

His hand slid up my arm, where his clasp was firm, almost painfully so. "I must *insist,* Amelia," he said quietly but with firm, unquestionable authority, "that you accompany me to my den. You may take a rest there, while we discuss this new information— or, more aptly, this new *lack* of information that has come to light."

"Take your hands off me," I whispered, fuming and quietly frantic.

"Gladly," he said. "If you would agree to speak with me where we might not be overheard or inter- rupted. I will have the truth from you."

I looked around me. I could try to break free and flee, but such an act would be idiotic at best. Where would I flee *to?* I could continue to lie, to grasp at fibs that we both knew were ridiculously untrue.

My humiliation was somewhat indescribable. I felt more than defeated, more than defiant; I felt wild. Manically so. I wished I'd... Oh, my thoughts were muddled and anxious. Tendrils of genuine fear at my predicament skulked through my body.

Knox Mackenzie touched his fingers to my chin, tilting my face up to look at him. "Amelia," he said, his voice so deep and reassuring I was taken wholly off guard by him, not only by the sound of him but by the vision. "You're safe. I'm not angry with you. I'm not going to hurt you or cast you out. Nor Hamish. I just want the truth."

I stared up at him, and I was ashamed by the tears that welled in my eyes. It almost seemed wasteful, that his beauty had become blurred like that.

How I wished that his words were true. How I wished that I *was* safe. I brushed the tears away.

"You're going to walk out that side door just behind you," he murmured, "and follow the corridor to the left. It will take you to my private meeting room, where we can talk. I will use the other entrance. There's no need for us to call undue attention to our meeting."

Knox watched me consider this. The thoughts churned, to be sure. This was my chance to flee the disgrace of my trial and my exposure. Hamish would be forgiven; he was only a child. He would find my nearly finished letter, in my belongings, which I would leave behind. Could I somehow grab a fur wrap as I fled? I was hardly wearing traveling garb, just a thin film of cream-colored satin. I could run to the boathouse. I could travel tonight.

One of Knox Mackenzie's eyebrows rose as he watched me consider my options. He appeared mildly amused by my labored deliberation, entertained by my false perception that I had options. This irked me. "There's a guard standing just outside that door," he said. "He will escort you where you need to go."

He had already anticipated my desertion and *preempted* it? *Bastard!* How could any man possess this much self-possession, this much practical confidence? He'd been thinking about this, plotting and planning to trap me and force me to confess my long list of sins! And I hated him for it!

The paradox was not lost on me. Not five minutes ago I'd been swooning over the arrogant beast, floating in some sort of love-struck haze and picturing his thorough ravishing. What infuriated me most of all was that the residue of that haze still clung to my new, vehement resentment. He was—irritatingly— just as beautiful as he had been five minutes ago, still touching his thumb to my jawbone, drawing attention to our hushed conversation even as he avowed not to.

"I *said* all right," I said churlishly. "I'll come with you. I'll speak with you."

To this he did smile—almost. "Good lass. That's my sweet Amelia. I will see you shortly." And with that, he walked away, disappearing into the crowd and through a far door.

And I, damn it all, was pathetically swooning in the aftermath of his flattery. *That's my sweet Amelia.*

Equally irate at my own delight over his possessive endearment and delirious for the very same reason, I headed toward the opposite door, as he had directed me to do. As promised, a beefy guard was waiting for me. After furrowing his brow for a brief, disarmed moment as he studied me, the guard began walking down the corridor, watching me to make sure I would follow.

I did.

And I soon found myself being ushered through the door of Knox Mackenzie's private den, illuminated only by a number of candles; these seemed to offer only meager circles of cast light, leaving much of the room shrouded and eclipsed. The door closed behind me and I was once again alone with this infuriating, beautiful man, who was leaning, shadowed and patient, against one of the wide windowsills, backlit by moonlight.

Already, the intensity of this encounter did not bode well.

CHAPTER EIGHT

I NEARLY FELT AFRAID. Not of Knox Mackenzie himself but of what might happen. What *could* happen. What very likely *would* happen.

The icy flare of his eyes offered their odd, contrasting gleam. Luminous, light-flicked opalescent gray rimmed with circles of darkest black. There was no indecision in him, just a patient sureness, like a player who holds an unbeatable hand. And under it was a new presence that I had not noticed before. A new thread to his personality that, in a sense, I recognized. A little devil of his own, but one that was not small at all but quietly monstrous, imposing and alluring, lurking behind his expression and the soft clench of his fist.

I leaned my back up against the solid plane of the wooden door, adjusting to the silent wisps of abandon that coiled throughout my body like ethereal whispers.

Knox Mackenzie walked over to the fireplace, where a fire burned low. He added several logs to it distractedly, which caused sparks to jump and the flames to lick higher. "Come," he said. "Stand by the fire. The night is cool."

When I didn't move, he stepped away to allow me some space. I didn't want to get too close to him and he sensed this. He half sat against a sturdy wooden desk and folded his arms across his chest, watching me. Once I judged him to be at a safe distance, I followed his command.

Walking to the fire, I held my hands close to it to warm myself and to calm myself. I succeeded only in the former. The heat of the fire chased away a chill and I shivered as the warmth settled in a simmering glow.

"Your hair is as colorful as the flames," he commented, his voice raspy. "More so, in fact. A thousand shades of red, copper and gold. And the very tips—the end coils of the longest strands—are nearly blond."

I looked at him, watching him revel somehow at the sight of me. Some detail of the look of me pleased him and intrigued him: I could clearly detect this. And I took comfort from the connectivity of his appreciation; it was as warming as the fire, steeping my body in a tranquil, prolific awareness.

His hair was also richly colored, I could have said. Aye, the colors of him were distinctive. The black and the gray. The dark blues and greens of his tartan kilt, the threads of red. The white of his shirt. Earthy leather straps and spare, metallic weapons. All those shades were but a canvas for the fiery play of light that seemed to illuminate him, always.

He was radiant, even in the dimness.

"Whenever you're ready to begin," he said.

"What was it you wanted to know, exactly?" I asked, staring into the red heat of the embers.

"What is your name?"

"Amelia Isobel Abbott Taylor."

"Where are you from?"

"Edinburgh."

"And what was your father's profession?" he asked. "If he has in fact passed."

"Aye. He was a doctor."

Knox looked into the fire. His expression took on a stymied, exasperated scowl. His fists were white-knuckling on the wooden rim of the table he was leaning against. It was crystal clear from his posture and the look on his face that he thought my claims to be false, again.

Was it *that* difficult to believe that I was the daughter of a skilled, cultured professional? "'Tis true!" I protested. "He was a doctor!"

He launched directly into the next question. "And are you a trained teacher?"

I faltered at this one, but Knox was tired of waiting.

"Katriona has said that you are talented," he said. "Yet your methods are highly…unorthodox. She has asked that you provide proof of your qualifications. After a mishap, so it seems, in the apple orchard. An incident, I believe, concerning a sword and a game of cards, as described in detail by both the boy Edward and his mother." He paused briefly to assess my reaction to this. I gave none, but my knees felt decidedly weak. "Edward's father, you should know, was one of the most loyal and excellent soldiers I've ever had the honor to lead. I must take their concerns to heart. Katriona has requested that, if you are to continue teaching her children, either you offer more information about yourself or we gather it through our own means."

I was a chaotic mess of too many tempestuous emotions to name. One I could identify, however, was a tiny yet billowing fury. The mention of Katriona, perhaps, was the worst thing about his dictatorial tirade, or the cutting distinction between "yourself" and "we." Us and them. He and Katriona occupied their idyllic, virtuous realm and I existed separately in my own domain: one that was shameless and base, worlds away from their shared utopia. *That,* more than anything else that he had ever said to me, infuriated me beyond control or compunction.

"Well, by all means, *Laird* Mackenzie," I seethed. "Do Katriona's bidding, each and every one. She's right about me, I'm sure. Has she mentioned to you that I'm the wickedest, most terrible deviant you've likely ever come across? I've lied to you, aye! I've told you half-truths, for no reason other than to bask in the glow of your complete ignorance."

There was a crease between the dark stripes of his eyebrows as he contemplated me with something akin to confusion. "I—"

"I'll tell you everything there is to know, and

more," I interrupted, an act of insubordination that was somehow immensely satisfying. I wondered if anyone had ever interrupted the venerable Laird Mackenzie before. I hoped I was the first. I wanted to undermine his steely authority in every way I could think of. Just the thought of doing so was having an odd, heady effect on me. Distinct points on my body felt humid and riled, as though I was channeling my agitation physically, and in a *very* intimate way. The soft satin of my gown felt suddenly confining and excessively tight. "But first, let me ask you one tiny, trivial, innocuous little question. *If* you don't mind."

"Go right ahead," he offered, intrigued. Slowly, he stood. He walked closer to where I was standing and he sat on a tall, sturdy-looking armless chair that was mere feet from me.

The very first time I had met Knox Mackenzie, one of my initial thoughts had been this: *he doesn't know what to make of you.* I felt that now, more than ever before. He didn't know how to read me. And there was more to his manner than that: he *wanted* to know. Very much so.

"You and Katriona are…acquainted?" I dared to ask.

He hesitated, and a near smile played at the corner of his mouth, as though my jealousy was agreeable to him. "Acquainted, aye. I know her as the widow of an officer."

"She…" I faltered. It was too personal a subject to discuss with him. Yet I wanted to know. We were alone in a secluded, candlelit room. We had shared an unspeakably intimate moment, and the memory of it was recurring to me in devastating detail each time I happened to allow myself to look briefly in his direction. And it was a memory that promised— perhaps—to be not only repeated but also surpassed. I felt the beginning of my descent, the slippery slope. The astounding draw of him was enveloping me, causing my nipples to tighten and the fluttery, hot cove between my legs to swell and to yearn. The sensation was distractingly voracious, greedy, as though my own inner sprite had transformed into a shameless, lustful siren who was not only adamant but *voracious*.

I wanted to ask this question of him because I felt entitled to, in light of what I was intending to do. He had admitted to me in our private moment by the loch that he was not inclined to promiscuity. He'd defined himself as, if I recalled correctly: *a very faithful, particular, singularly devoted romantic*. One overcome moment, or two, could hardly be considered promiscuous, or unusual. I wanted to know, either way. "She hoped to acquaint herself with you in other ways, too. Was she able to…in any way…to *get* acquainted with you?"

Knox rubbed his jaw, where the stubble was faintly sparkled in the firelight. The thought of that rough bristle touching me, rubbing against me as it had done once before… *Oh, damn it all to hell!* My intimate flesh grew soft and wet, throbbing with a rhythmic, succulent ache.

His gaze speared me but his voice was gentle, almost indulgent. "Where did you hear of this?"

"I have my own sources," I said.

"Which sources are these?" he prodded patiently.

"The ladies in Lachlan's home. The weavers. They discussed it at some length." *I don't blame her for trying,* one of them had said. *I just don't think it's a good match. He needs a woman who can pull him out of his mood, not mire him deeper into it.*

He placed his hands on his knees, which were apart and draped only partially by the cloth of his kilt. "They did, did they?"

"Aye. They did. And I wondered if—"

"Let me lay your concerns to rest, then. To answer your question, nay. At the time, I was still mourning my wife. And I was not inclined, at all, to yet follow my brothers' advice." I remembered: *'Tis time to move on.*

My eyes stole to the collar of his shirt, which was open at the top to reveal the bronzed hue of his throat, the light dusting of hair at the top of his chest—and the absence of his gold chain.

"Where is it?" I said. I looked up at his face, shadowed in the textured darkness. "Where's the chain?" I asked. "And her ring?"

"I put it in a very safe place."

'Tis time to move on. And so, it seemed, he was. He had mourned for his wife and child for more than

*two years. It gave me a great sense of joy to realize
that he was beginning to move on, and I might have
been the one who inspired it.*

"What was she like?" I whispered to him, almost
regretting the impulse but too curious to withhold
my question.

He was quiet for a moment. And the response he
gave was surprisingly matter-of-fact. "She was beautiful. Quiet. Gentle. Gracious. A sensitive soul. She
was small, very slim. Too slim. She wasn't strong
enough."

She wasn't strong enough to bear his child.

All the reasons behind his long-held sorrow might
have speared the moment with regret and distance.
Oddly, they did neither. There was an insinuation
here, one that was flicked with sadness but also with
an outlying, unexpected revival. I couldn't be sure
about what he was thinking, but with his eyes on all
the plentiful curves of my body, I guessed at a small
part of this attraction. *I* wasn't small, nor slim. My
soul had never been referred to as sensitive. Not once
had I ever been described as quiet.

Nor was I refined or noble.

No doubt about it, I was a complete departure in
every way from his lost wife. And I had a feeling that
we were both glad of this. There could be no com-
parisons. Neither were there guarantees or promises.
Just a mutual attraction that was divinely, wickedly
potent. His wife was lost to him. But *I* was here.

'Tis time to move on.

I dared to whisper my next question. "And now?"

He contemplated me lazily, his mouth forming that tempting pout that drove me mad. "And now?" he repeated.

I did not speak, waiting for his answer.

After an excruciating pause, he gave it. "So it seems," he said darkly. "I am now…very much, so inclined. Much more than I can begin to express."

This admission ignited a spark of hope in me that I could not name, but before I could bask in any promise it might have offered, he promptly extinguished it.

"Either way," he said. "I did not bring you here to my private chambers tonight to indulge any inclinations beyond those of seeking the truth from you."

This irked me, and in no small measure. He had not brought me here to seduce me, but to scold me. And to bully me into revealing all my dark, horrible secrets and my true identity as an expert gambler, a seedy cardshark, a wayward waif, all rolled up into one wild, wanton, misfit package.

Because that's how I felt: wild and wanton. Desperate. Alone. And ridiculously, almost uncomfortably aroused. It was this heavy lust that provoked me most of all. I willed myself to maintain control, but I could feel it slipping.

"I'm only asking you to confirm the truth, Amelia. I just want to know who you are," he said gently, reading my agitation, I hoped, and not my desperation. "Begin at the beginning, and tell me everything. I can tell you that your carriage was searched for, yet nothing was found. No murdered driver, nor gang of black-clad bandits. So I will ask you, why did you flee Edinburgh? What are you looking for here in the Highlands?"

His eyes wandered from my face to my body. In my impassioned outburst, the tie of my dress had loosened, causing the neckline to gape just a little lower, revealing a fraction more of the rounded curves of my young, full breasts. My nipples poked against the filmy fabric. But I was too mired in the topic at hand to immediately address this.

It was time. He was waiting for my explanation. Here was the moment I had done my very best to avoid. I had lost this crucial round. Laird Knox Mackenzie would have his way. In all his absolute power and his unwavering authority, he would win *every* round, I now realized. I could no longer fool myself into thinking I had ever had the advantage against a man such as this. The social divide between us might have been a vast continent instead of a distance so small I could have reached to touch the flicked strands of his midnight hair with my craving fingers. Instead, I fingered a strand of my own hair, twisting it around my finger as I began to speak. There was no point in lying any longer and the sudden, stark realization that I was no better than the devious thieves I struggled to avoid sent a lunging pang of sadness through my heart. I could have given in to the tears that threatened to spill, but I held them back, choosing instead to look him in the eye and give him every honesty. There was sadness in my voice, but also a lingering defiance.

"My name *is* Amelia Taylor. Hamish is not my brother but my nephew. He's not to blame for any of this. I asked him to lie, to hide our true identities because I feared you would not offer us refuge if you knew the truth. We played on your sympathies so you would harbor us, and feed us. My father's name was Dr. Robert Taylor. He died ten years ago, as did my mother. My sister, Cecelia, married a business owner named James Scott."

I paused to allow my intrinsic panic to quiet. Knox's expression was smooth, unreadable. He waited for me to continue, which I did, slowly.

"She married him to keep us off the streets after the death of our parents. There was no money left after the debts were paid. We moved into an acceptable house not far from our parents' home, but the business was not as prosperous as we might have hoped. James ran a gaming club, and after only a few months of marriage, he was forced to sell the house to fund the struggling business. We had no alternative but to take up residence in the club. Among the gamblers and the reprobates. I could not continue to go to school. I was needed as a worker at the club. As a dealer. I showed promise. I learned quickly."

I faltered again, but there was no point prolonging the agony. I continued, laying it all on the table, coiling the curl of my hair tighter, keeping my voice as light as I could, but I could hear the resignation there, the return of my impudent survivalist guise. "In actual fact, I'm a prodigy with a deck of cards, Laird Mackenzie. I almost single-handedly kept the business afloat for the past five years, swindling drunken louts out of their money by counting the cards and sometimes by stacking the decks. I've been known to slip coins out of men's pockets and to skim the winnings from a lucky hand. My livelihood is to lie, to cheat and to steal and I have a remarkable talent for all three. I had thought to attempt to reform my ways, but it's no use, I'm afraid. I am what I am."

"So you *did* lie to me." I was almost surprised by the roughness of his rebuke.

"Out of necessity, aye. I—I'm sorry."

Knox rose from his chair and began to pace broodily. His silence unnerved me. I could see that he was angry. Hurt, even. I could hardly blame him, but I would have preferred a livid tirade to this cold, impenetrable ire. "Would you have taken me in," I said, "and Hamish, if you knew we had run from the halls of a gaming den? Or would you have turned us away?"

"I would have tried to help you as best I could."

"Out of pity," I said, "as you and your clan looked down on us like a couple of street urchins in need of charity." I didn't bother adding, *because that is what we are.* And for once, it had felt so damnably good to be free of our downtrodden reality, to play the ruse of what we might have been, if our lives hadn't become debauched and dominated, steeped in fear of poverty and violence. It felt so good to be free.

He flicked me a surly glance, but he did not stop pacing. I wished he would. "Why, then, did you flee?"

I wanted to be honest with Knox Mackenzie, because I respected him and because he had changed my outlook. The pure honor that shone out of his approach was inviting in its sureness; he never had any need to lie, nor cheat. That must have been an immensely satisfying way to live one's life, I thought. But I couldn't bring myself to say it: *A very wealthy, nasty, horrible man was coming after me. He was going to rape me and I was very, very afraid. If I didn't comply, he threatened to hurt Hamish, just so he could demean me, ruin me and own me.* I would be honest, but my answer was spoken with my most important priority in mind: keeping Hamish safe. "Some trouble was brewing at the club. It was no longer safe for Hamish. Nor myself. We fled to escape that trouble."

This information piqued Knox's interest sharply. He stopped pacing. "Is there any chance that the trouble you speak of might…follow you here?"

"Nay. I—"

"How can you be sure?"

"That…trouble…doesn't know where we fled to."

"If perchance that trouble happened to *find out* where you had fled to, would that trouble seek you out? *That* is what I'm asking." His deep, imperious voice filled the room like a military hymn.

Damn my own weaknesses! My eyes had begun to leak again, from shame, from fear, from knowing that eviction from heaven and straight into hell was imminent.

"It is possible, aye." *More than possible. Guaranteed.*

Laird Mackenzie was getting more irate with each word I spoke. He was not a man to yell or even to raise his voice, but his formal, steady reproach was in some ways far worse than an emotional rant might have been. "So you not only *lie* to me but you neglect to share *critical information* that could put *my clan and my family in danger,* if this *trouble* were to find its way to you?"

My heart felt broken. The periphery of my vision already felt darker, as though the city shadows were reaching out to me, calling me back. I could feel it: the possibility of salvation slipping away. The taint of my dishonesty coloring everything, dulling the vibrancy of the room and the fire-touched night. But not him. He was his own entity, separate from my scandals and my confessions. Untouchable, as ever.

I raised my chin and looked him in the eye. "Aye. You're right. My actions are unforgivable. I never, ever meant to bring my kind of trouble to your family. 'Tis time for me to be on my way. To go back to where I came from." To face the hand I'd been dealt, whether I liked it or not.

His expression changed almost imperceptibly.

My hands clasped in front of my chest in a prayer-like grip. "You'll be rid of me as soon as I can pack my bag, Laird Mackenzie. But this trouble has nothing to do with Hamish. He's only a child. A beautiful, innocent child. I beg that you'll allow him to stay. Please. He'll be very useful to you, I'm certain of it. He'll learn quickly, and he'll work willingly. One day he'll make a very fine soldier. He should be given a second chance." My voice sounded hollow when I repeated, "He's only a child."

"You're not to go anywhere," he said, his eyebrows furrowing with his stern command. If I wasn't mistaken, a note of alarm clung to his words. He reached out to grasp my hand in an almost trance-like reflex, as though his response was beyond his own control. He uncoiled my pleading clasp. But I slid my hand away, and withdrew from him.

Yet I needed his assurance before I took my leave. "You'd allow Hamish to remain with your clan, then?"

"Hamish has already proven himself useful." Knox's temper had taken a turn. His fury over my lies and my omissions hung on, yet there was a yielding thread to his curtness that I couldn't define. As a stubborn, detached tenacity, perhaps, as though his anger was not only pointed at me but further afield. A lesser man might have clung to his rage, but Knox Mackenzie was a born diplomat and a trained leader; it was his way to remain calm and make peace. Or at least attempt to. "He's clearly at home in the barracks."

At home. Aye, he was. "I can't repay you, I'm afraid. He'll do that himself, I'm sure. By proving himself, in time, to be among the finest of your recruits."

I looked at the timeless flames of the fire, feeling utterly drained. If I was even allowed to bid him farewell, I knew it was likely that I wouldn't see my nephew again for many years. Maybe one day he would seek us out, when he was a fully grown man. Maybe he would remember our long-ago life in the dirty alleys, where he'd never wanted to be. Or maybe he would choose to forget. He'd yearned for green spaces, even before he knew what green spaces were. He'd coveted his sword before he knew its purpose. Now he would fulfill all the abundant potential he possessed and I was glad of that.

I turned to face Knox Mackenzie. He had taken a seat once again on the tall, sturdy chair near the fire. His expression was no less stern, but behind the aggression lurked a concentration. An intensity, as though he was conflicted in new, unfamiliar ways. I was standing almost between his spread knees, which were as tanned as the skin of his throat. Something about his princely manner and his garb, the tall boots and the tartan kilt, the finely made leather belt and the golden ornamentation made him appear as though he'd stepped out of another time and place altogether, like a Roman god or an Egyptian pharaoh.

I'd spent many an hour lost in the pages of books and my own imagination, aye; the beauty and perfection of him seemed more like those of a fictional character than a real, live man.

Of course, I knew I could have asked him for help. He had a large, formidable army at his disposal, after all, which could possibly have stormed all of Edinburgh and wiped Sebastian Fawkes off the face of Scotland with relative ease. His brothers led armies of their own, too, which could also be summoned if the need arose. Not that such a thing would be necessary, but the point was there were at least three armies—or possibly four, if the Munros were also petitioned—at Knox Mackenzie's beck and call. If there was an injustice that needed to be forcibly addressed, and if I had the compunction to call upon him to do so, well, then I had certainly chosen my host well.

Aye, I considered it.

Even as I debated the matter in my head, I already knew I would not ask for Knox Mackenzie's assistance. And as I made the decision almost before the deliberation had fully formed, I wondered at my own sacrifice. I simply was not willing to put him in harm's way, even if doing so would make my task easier. It was, quite possibly, a foolish decision. The logical part of my brain assured me that my problems could be easily solved if only I were truthful with him. He might—and very likely *would*—offer to help me.

Yet as I rehearsed my unspoken plea, I knew that it was one I would never make: *Oh, Knox, I'm in trouble. My sister waits alone for a husband who has committed countless crimes and who may or may not be alive. She is at the mercy of a sinister man who may have imprisoned her, or worse, to lure me to him. I knew this would be his reaction, yet I left her, anyway. And when I attempt to find Cecelia and ensure her safety, he will be waiting for me. He will have set an elaborate trap. Once he catches me, he will force me to submit to him. I'm afraid. I know him to be wicked. Greedy. His appetites will be laced with revenge. He will take great pleasure in my torture. It might placate you, after the exquisite moments we've shared, to assure you that he may touch my body but he will never touch my soul, not as you did. 'Tis one of the reasons I wanted you so much. So I could know and remember tenderness, real passion, love. And now I beg you to put your perfection at the mercy of these scoundrels in the hope that you may infiltrate their elaborate, entrenched underground web of criminal activity. I ask that you take your valued officers, like Lachlan, to Edinburgh, leaving behind their pretty wives and tiny, beautiful children. Sacrifice young warriors like Hamish will soon become, too, who are loyal and good. I want you to put these honorable soldiers at risk of death by men who kill solely for the thrill of it, for the power it grants them, for the game it represents. They have guns and knives and*

every advantage in the familiarity of their murky al-
leys. They would not hesitate to stab you in the back
at their very first opportunity. I ask that you do this
for me, because you are an honorable, charitable
man. A beautiful, perfect, glorious masterpiece of
masculine magnificence, whose—

I needed to concentrate.

Regrettably, I had spent many years in the company of underhanded men. I understood them all too
well. I understood lying, cheating, stealing and all
the layered deceit they were capable of. I felt certain that, whether one army or four was summoned,
whether a small war party was assembled or whether
one lone stubborn, beautiful laird took matters into
his own hands, there would be casualties. No matter how well trained and well armed the Mackenzie soldiers happened to be, I had a strong feeling
they would not walk away unscathed. And I simply
could not allow Knox, or Lachlan, or anyone else to
be harmed. This was not their war.

It was mine.

"Good night, Laird Mackenzie," I said. "And
goodbye. Fare thee well."

"Wait," he said, grabbing my wrist.

I tried to pull away, but he wouldn't allow it. "Let
me go. I will take my leave of Kinloch at once."

"Nay. You will give me all the information I ask
of you. Then I will decide the best course of action."

"I already know what the best course of action

is. Unhand me, Laird Mackenzie, and allow me to take my leave."

"*I* will decide what the best course of action is," he growled, pulling me closer as his grip tightened. His breath was uneven, and heavy. "I *demand* that you do as I ask. *You will answer me and you will obey me!*"

I returned his obstinate glare, where we remained locked in a glowering, heavy-breathed standoff. "I already told you, Laird Mackenzie—I am *not* one of your loyal subjects. You cannot *force* me with your haughty commands. Now unhand me!"

I struggled against him to no avail. My turmoil and my struggles had caused the neckline of my gown to open farther. Ailie's design was a stunning one, but I might have suggested to her that a satin dress needed more to fasten it than a flimsy satin belt that happened to slip when one became agitated.

Then, Knox did unhand me.

And then, as he looked into my eyes, he grasped the edge of the bow that held my gown in place. Slowly, he pulled it.

I made a small gasp as the tie loosened completely, allowing the fabric of my gown to list open, revealing my pale curves, the bountiful mounds of my breasts. My pinkened nipples tightened under his gaze. My own near nakedness, rather than making me feel vulnerable, achieved quite the opposite effect. I felt empowered, as though I'd been reborn as a loch nymph who had no inhibitions and existed wholly in a lusty, sensual realm that allowed no regrets or hesitations. Knox made a low, savage sound when he saw I wore nothing underneath.

It was going to happen. It was happening. The air was heavy, almost bruised with anticipation; whatever anger or resentment or indignation that resided along with it was overcome by this current of desire that hypnotized us both. We drew closer. He bowed his head slightly, until his hair touched my cheek.

"I can't sleep," he whispered, as though this troubled him greatly. "I can hardly eat."

"Poor Laird Mackenzie," I replied softly, barely sardonic. The mysteries of his body, which he had not yet allowed me to explore, were within my grasp. I let my hands rove. To the wool of his kilt.

He kissed me.

As soon as his mouth touched mine, my lips parted. I licked his lips with inviting, tender supplication. He groaned. His tongue sank into my mouth, filling my entire being with want. I sucked on his tongue, gently greedy, desperate to take more of any part of his body into any part of mine.

"Amelia," he gasped. His voice was rasped with lust and…not indecision, but turmoil over a decision already made. "The taste of you is more than I can take."

"You can take it," I whispered, kissing his perfect lips.

I wanted more from this towering monarch than I had ever before imagined, ruled entirely by the pull of his intention and the promise of his touch. I had never done anything like this before—except once, nearly, by the shores of his loch—but I knew exactly what to do. My instincts were suddenly highly attuned, understanding this connection, knowing entirely how to play my role. And I wouldn't take nay for an answer this time. I had a feeling, too, that nay wouldn't be the answer he would be giving. My breasts were close to his mouth and felt sensually full and appealing. I touched myself, playing with my nipples, pinching them. "Taste more of me," I said. I offered myself to him, equal parts innocence and impulse. He took my breasts in his big, warm hands, plumping them to his mouth, taking a nipple in ravenous, lust-driven pulls. One, then the other. I moaned with the billowing sensation he inspired.

And it wasn't enough. Each tug sent a flood of liquid feeling to my softening core that was profound and ripe and nearly unbearable.

My hands were on his impossibly solid thighs, wandering farther until I felt the miraculous hard, hot length of his manhood. *"Oh, holy God,"* I whispered, to which he made no response. He was silken and dusky and immense. I lifted his kilt away, entranced. I had no basis for comparison, but he was clearly laird of lairds in every possible measurement. I thought he might protest, but he was unusually acquiescent as I took him in my hands and caressed the long, rigid length of him, touching him tenderly with both hands, feathering my fingertips everywhere. This inquisitive, tactile exploration caused him to gasp in a low growl. A string of oaths, if I heard him correctly, that would have rivaled any in the backstreets or gaming halls. Both the sound and the sensation stoked my longing, bathing my body in a humid, wanting flush.

And we weren't close enough.

We'd stepped across some invisible threshold of need. He was as frantic as I was. He lifted me and I willingly climbed onto him, straddling his hips as he slid farther back in the chair. His strength was brutal, his grasp almost painful, and this only fueled my lust. His hands were wrapped around my thighs. Gently yet forcefully, he pulled me closer, and closer, until the intimacy was almost too much to bear. My moist, delicate flesh touched him, rubbing along his length, wetting him with the slickness of my desire. The hot bulk of his shaft pressed against me, kneading the soft furls of my sex, pressing against the tiny nub, causing piercing shards of astounding pleasure to build and to hold. His thumb circled my dewy folds, centering. With the squeeze of his fingers, he pulled softly on that little erect bud, igniting a potent bloom that almost undid me.

Blind with need, I guided the broad tip of his cock to my snug, slippery entrance. He swore under his breath, the sound agonized. Wild and more uncontrolled than I'd ever seen him, he bucked upward, at the same time grasping my hips in his secure grip, thrusting into me, once, and again. I had expected pain but the brief pang was swathed in an aching sweetness. The tight constriction of my body hindered him, yet his insistent, thrusting drives forced his thick shaft deeper. He lifted me slightly, moving my hips in a careful swivel, allowing my arousal to moisten him, to ease his passage. My body began to open to his lusty invasion. As he sank deeper with each drive, the sensation built with feverish momentum. He said my name. Each thrust stoked the unfurling rapture, until I was fully impaled and riding a wave of pleasure that promised to rise and break at an astoundingly intense summit. Adjusting, I clenched my soft core invitingly around the huge length of him as I moved with him, arching my back and pivoting my hips to take him deeper. I was aware of nothing but the harmony and the rising pleasure of our joined bodies, the bliss overflowing with heartbreaking effect. The ecstasy began inside me where I gripped him, erupting into a million pinpoints of blind rapture. I lost myself, engulfed by a release so powerful that my body writhed with the overload. My inner muscles drew so forcefully around him that he groaned as if in pain. He was saying something but I could barely comprehend. *Wait. I can't hold on.* But my body was too slippery, too overcome and too possessive. I was still riding, still pulling him deeply, again and again. *"Christ,"* he groaned, and his voice was rasped and euphoric: "God Almighty." I thought he might be praying. I felt the flooding wetness, the violent pulse deep inside me. The silky beat of his climax rubbed sensually against a miraculous catalyst, causing another wash of spiraling waves that milked him softly until I had collapsed on top of him, wrapped naked around his big, hard, sweat-dampened body.

We sat that way for some time, rocked by the intensity of our passion. My head rested on his chest, and his arms were around me. I could hear his heart racing. After what might have been several minutes, the pace of his heart began to slow.

I could have felt remorseful for the brazen totality of our actions. In fact, I felt a million miles removed from remorse. What I felt was joy and a permeating peace. It was true that consequences of what I—what *we*—had just done could be far-reaching. Whatever ensued from this intense, beautiful bond would bring me more comfort than temperance and distance ever would: of this I felt certain. I was warm, and serenely elated, cocooned in a guarded haven far from the merciless city, wrapped in the arms of my peerless prince and still wetly connected to him. I didn't want to move. I savored the lingering bliss, the recalcitrant pleasure that, even now, held on.

Knox held my head against his chest with his hand, caressing my hair. He held me that way for a minute or more, and it was the right kind of comfort. Our actions had been rash, to say the least, but there was no turning back. We were bound now, already and tightly; it was the way of it. We allowed that truth to settle into our minds as it had done so eagerly into our bodies.

It was the most perfect, complete happiness I had ever known.

"Amelia?" he said.

"Aye."

"Are you all right, lass?"

"Aye," I replied, and it was true. There was something so *right* about this tempestuous link that I could only wonder at the beauty of the moment and how good it had felt, how good it *still* felt, with his body wedged inside mine, his strong arms secure around me. My body felt more sated and more alive than it had ever been, but already I could feel my spirit disengaging. I knew I had to leave him. I looked into his unusual, sparking, black-rimmed eyes. "Knox."

"Aye, lass."

"I want to tell you something."

He waited and I cupped his jaw in my hands, tracing the lines of his cheekbones, feathering down to his mouth and his chin. In another time and place I might have held back; I might have kept my emotions to myself, to be confessed at a later time, when this bond was better forged, safer, without risk. I might have waited until I was absolutely certain that the sentiment was mutual, to save face or to spare myself from heartache if his attraction was merely physical, and limited. Such a time would very likely never come. I wanted to say it, and to leave this piece of myself behind.

"I love you," I whispered. "I felt it when I saw you that very first time. I knew I wanted you even then.

Even if I couldn't have you. I've loved everything about you from that first moment I saw you in the apple orchard. You were framed with sunlight. And you were the most perfect vision I had ever seen." I touched his hair. "I love your hair. And your eyes. I love how decent you are, and kind. You make me feel safe." I kissed his lips. "I love your mouth. Your face. Your hands. I treasure every moment I've spent in your company. You have touched my heart. I would like a thousand more nights with you, just like this."

There was an unmistakable anguish in his eyes. He started to open his mouth and I put my fingers across his lips to silence him.

I wanted him to remember these words and be re-assured by them, in whatever way they might reassure, after I was gone, but I didn't want him to feel obliged to return the sentiment, when there was no need to do so. "I will cherish this night as long as I live," I said. "I feel you inside me, inside the very heart of me, and this is how I'll remember you for-evermore."

Holding his face in my hands, I kissed him. His closed eyes, his mouth. I nipped at his lips, parting them to my supple appreciation. I touched the tip of my tongue to his.

I could feel him hardening again, growing inside me. There was a quiet ferocity in him that was freer, and looser, than I had yet witnessed. The barrier of his restraint was gone, and his lust was tempered by vast hidden oceans of emotion. His manhood had revived. Sitting astride him as I was, he felt immense, rearing deep into my body. The liquid of his release made my own tightness slippery. The sensation, of his thick possession eased and entranced by the silky embrace, was riveting, vivid with beauty. I tilted my hips against him, working him, squeezing, drawing him deeper and then retreating in an undulating enticement. Each time I drew toward him, taking him, he lunged with subtle, perceptive force. Without disengaging or breaking this rhythm, he picked me up as though I weighed no more than a feather. I was reminded again of his brute strength, his height, his utter splendor. I wrapped my legs around his hips and he carried me to the large couch. He lay on top of me, thrusting deeply into me, where he held me as he gazed into my eyes. The beginnings of the succulent tremors teased me. The welcoming constriction of my tight, wet core gripped him mercilessly. I could have summoned the ecstatic spasms with only the slightest movement. I sensed his own precipice was equally tantalizing. Yet we lay motionless save the sweet, cadenced clasp of my intimate invitation.

I might have preferred, if I'd thought about this beforehand, that he not return my immoderate endearments. I don't know why I almost flinched at his reply, even as he thrust again and so exquisitely that my innermost muscles began a sensual, gripping dance that threw me into irrepressible throes of euphoria. I would have silenced him, but I was too overcome. Even as my body sang with the worship of his skewering aggression, my soul shrank back from his words.

"Amelia," he groaned as his shaft leaped inside me, gushing out its warm life in surging bursts. His litany spewed out along with his pleasure, spooling and uncontrolled. "I cannot sleep without dreaming of your hair and your womanly body and your soft, willful mouth. You are milk and honey and innocence and lust. You are agony and pure, pure ecstasy. So sweet, so sweet, I want you. *I love you.*"

So Knox Mackenzie *was* a romantic, not only virile beyond comparison but highly eloquent at that. Damn him. And *I* was a lost cause. So in love my heart felt heavy and constrained by its physical inadequacy, as though it was but a small earthly vessel that couldn't contain the heavenly potency of what had just taken place.

I have to leave him.

It couldn't be. This—us—*we* couldn't be. We couldn't be star-crossed lovers or destined soul mates. We were strangers, temporary acquaintances, two ships that pass in a star-studded night: *that* was our destiny.

Not *this*.

Not this complete, symmetrical perfection of body and soul.

My mind grappled with the unexpected as my joyful sex continued to flutter tightly around his softening manhood in beatific, luscious ripples.

I existed wholly in this moment. Tomorrow's landscape would be vastly different from tonight's. But I was here now. This nirvana was mine.

We whispered the words again and again. We couldn't get close enough. We kissed endlessly, wrapped tightly around each other, connected in every way it was possible to be.

And it was this way we remained until long into the night. Each of us was reluctant to disengage. We were each mesmerized by the eyes and face and mouth of the other, the textures and the warmth. In time and at the encouragement of my intimate caresses, he rose again. He spilled his seed inside me several more times. After his first release, which could have been considered a mistake or an act of desperation, it hardly seemed to matter if the abandon was compounded or prolonged; this abandon was simply too sweet to refuse. He made no move to retreat and I didn't ask him to. Instead, our bodies remained moistly locked in greedy harmony until, much later, we drifted into an enchanted sleep.

I awoke to the light of early morning. A single candle burned low, flickering out.

I was curled up next to Knox's big, warm body. He had draped a fur over us. Under it, I was entirely naked. And so was he. Knox was still asleep, his face peaceful, his black hair in wild disarray.

Very carefully, I climbed over his sleeping form, taking care not to wake him. I was sore, my thighs stained by traces of my virginal blood. A trickle of milky liquid seeped from my body as I stood, reminding me of the magnitude of all that had taken place during the dreamlike night. My virtue had been not only compromised but practically obliterated by Knox Mackenzie's thorough possession, and his seed even now warmed me from within.

I regretted nothing, but I felt different. I was changed, not just in a physical sense but a spiritual one. Emotionally, I knew I had been profoundly altered by Knox Mackenzie's lovemaking in all its spectacular fervor, but on this I did not dwell. An unfamiliar tightness in my chest accompanied that thought process, and for this reason I chose to avoid it altogether. I had known how this relationship would play out. It had begun as a finite phenomenon, and so it would remain.

It was time to go.

I found my dress and wrapped it around me. I put on my shoes. I could see through the window that the hour was just past dawn. Indigo skies were tainted with a dusky lavender glow at the base of the distant horizon line, which was jagged and curved to the shape of the mountains, veiled by a gauzy layer of misty drizzle. The clouds were thick. It looked to be another stormy day.

A sharp knock rapped on the door.

And another.

"Laird Mackenzie," someone was calling, their voice impatient.

Knox woke instantly, sitting up. It took him a few seconds to fully comprehend the situation. He looked thoroughly disheveled, his hair tangled and shambolic. The departure from his usual sleek composure was so endearing I felt the urge to disrobe and slide back under the furs with him. To run my hands through his hair. *To kiss him and to sit astride him. As his thick, glorious manhood filled me deliciously, slippery and colossal and oh, so inspiring. He's so unfairly resplendent he stuns my senses. I want to touch him again. I want to taste him, and kiss him, and feel his hands on my drugged, lust-soaked naked body. I love the way he moves. His scowling face. I want to turn that expression, to inspire his smile or even better, his rapture. I could. I have every power to drive him to the deepest throes of ecstasy. I know what he looks like when his bliss overcomes him.*

"All *right*," he yelled at whoever it was that was so insistent at his door. "I'm coming."

His dark eyebrows furrowed when he noticed I was fully dressed. He rose, displacing the furs as he reached for his kilt, providing a glimpse of the glorious manhood I'd just been casually recollecting. This did not help my concentration, nor did it tone down my restless cravings.

Knox strode toward the door, clad only in his kilt.

"Knox," I said. "I'm…here. Shouldn't I perhaps… *leave?* Before I'm discovered? With you?"

"You're here, lass, because I want you here." *My, but it must have been grand to be so sure of your own superiority that there was never any need to question it.*

"Will people not, perhaps, *gossip* on the subject?"

He appeared to consider this. Very briefly. "Not for long," he said, and I couldn't be sure of his meaning. "If you'd prefer, there's a small alcove behind that curtain. Wait in there, if you're inclined, while I attend to this. It won't take a minute, whatever it is."

I did feel inclined to keep this...*love affair* private. Technically, I had disgraced myself beyond all hope of redemption. But, God help me, it had been more than worth it. I hid, shielding myself behind a thick red velvet curtain in what revealed itself to be a storage space. There were shelves piled high with rolled-up scrolls of all sizes. I wished I had the time and the light to unroll one or two, and read them. Another secret library, of a different description. His drawings and plans. His maps, letters and tactics. I was mildly enchanted.

Several women's voices could be heard. I recognized them. Katriona and Christie. Katriona sounded upset about something. I peeled back the curtain an inch so I could hear more clearly.

"I tried to find you last night, but you'd left. 'Tis an urgent matter, Laird Mackenzie, that I knew you'd want to hear of urgently. I waited till the morn because I knew you wouldn't want to carry out a banishment in the middle of the night, but—"

"What is it?" Knox was short with her, forcing patience. It was clear by his question that he believed whatever that matter at hand was, it could have waited.

"Well, you know I always had my suspicions. Even at the very beginning of her appointment. Since we first saw them in that tavern in fact, and—"

"Does this concern Amelia?" Knox asked.

"We just can't decipher what it might mean." Christie's voice. "'Tis most unusual. We knew you'd want to know of it. In case it's a threat to her."

"Or to *us*," Katriona insisted.

"What threat?" Knox said. "What is it? Show it to me."

All were silent for a few minutes. I thought I heard the crinkle of parchment.

"Where did you get this?" Knox snapped.

"Well," Katriona began, somewhat nervously if I was judging correctly. "As I said, I had my suspicions. One of the messenger parties was departing. It was just a day or two after they arrived at Kinloch—*after* she'd been appointed to teach my children, mind you—and I asked them to make a few inquiries. At the teaching college."

My heart was in my throat, and my consciousness spun.

"The *teaching* college gave you this?" Knox asked. "What does it mean?"

"Nay," Katriona answered. "They had no records of Amelia there. But there was a sentinel of some description, Balfour said, who had heard of her. Who was in fact looking for her, as well."

Christie had clearly been told the entire story before she'd arrived at Knox's chambers. "Balfour said the sentinel wouldn't tell him what it meant. But he said that Amelia would understand it."

"'Tis a message," said Katriona. "For Amelia."

"Have you seen her, Knox?" asked Christie. "We can't find her anywhere."

I stepped out from behind the curtain.

The women were entirely agog at the sight of me, but I walked over to them, undeterred. In his hand, Knox held the piece of parchment that had been inked with three scrawled lines. I took it from him.

The king is dead, the knave is spared.
The queen of spades feels the knife.

The queen of hearts holds the deck.

I felt myself pale. I understood instantly what the message conveyed.

"Is it a riddle, Amelia?" Christie said. "What does it mean?"

"Who is it from?" Katriona asked.

I feigned lightheartedness, which took a great deal of effort. "Oh, it's nothing. Nothing at all. Just a message from a…an associate of mine. In Edinburgh. 'Tis a greeting of sorts. Well-wishes, about our quest."

"But *who?*" Katriona insisted. "It doesn't *look* like a greeting. What does it *mean?* It has something to do with those playing cards Hamish was using, doesn't it? Edward spoke of them. I'm sure I recognize the names."

I glanced at Katriona, once again fighting an impulse to react to her in a way that was not only inappropriate but bordering on violent. But that infernally logical side of my mind knew that she had every right to question me, to research me, to find out the details of the person who was appointed to spend time with and educate her children. I had always taken an avid interest in those who shaped Hamish's upbringing and she was entitled to do the same.

Still, I fought to keep the vitriol from my body language. *Say something convincing. Lie, cheat, steal, do whatever it takes to get back to Cecelia, before his blade makes its final cut.* He had her. He was using her as bait, as I'd known all along he would. *The queen of spades feels the knife. The queen of heart holds the deck.*

Come back, or I will kill her.

That was the message.

I was almost breathlessly grateful when another knock shattered the expectant, waiting silence. This time, a group of officers strode into the room through the now-open door. They glanced curiously at our little assembly before one of them stated, "The Machardies have arrived, Laird Mackenzie. They traveled through the night and they await you in the hall."

Knox ran his hand across his jaw and turned his head, glancing once at me. He sighed and nodded, and attempted to smooth his hair, unsuccessfully.

"Ladies," he said, putting on his shirt. In the company of his guards and officers, his authority returned to him in full, pompous force. "I will greet our guests. Amelia, my guard will escort you to your guest chambers, where I will meet with you shortly. Gunn," he said to one of his officers. "Escort Amelia to her rooms immediately. Guard her door so she is not disturbed. Katriona, Christie, I thank you for bringing this matter to my attention, and for delivering this message to Amelia. I will take full responsibility for getting to the bottom of the riddle when Amelia gives me a full explanation later today. That is all."

I followed Gunn, as I'd been ordered to do, more willingly, to be sure, than I'd ever followed an order in my life. He led me through the quiet, empty corridors of the manor. He did not speak, nor did I.

When we reached my chambers, Gunn took up his post beside my door. I closed the door firmly, locking it.

I didn't waste time. I took the sheets off the bed and ripped each of them into four strips, carrying out my task as quietly as I could. I tied the strips together tightly, creating a long, thin, reasonably strong rope. I knew how to do this; I'd done it before. I tied one end of the rope to the bed, then opened the window, looking down. Not overly far. And I could see no one about. It was still early. I tossed the sheet-rope over the edge of the windowsill. The end of it didn't quite reach the ground, but it would do.

My mind worked on several levels.

Let him help you. He told you he loved you. In the throes of passion, aye. That's all that had been. Lust. And the louder, chanting, challenging litany echoed: *keep him safe, keep him safe, keep him safe. His clan needs him. Do not put him in harm's way. He'll fight for you if he learns of your plight. You know he will. And he might lose.* I knew I would rather wage my war alone than risk his life. I would rather live out my days imprisoned in Edinburgh than watch Knox Mackenzie die at the hands of the men I had led him to. It seemed almost perverse, this sense of protection I felt for him, of *preservation.* I had never seen beauty and morality so condensed in one person before. I couldn't bear the thought of all that perfection being harmed in any way whatsoever.

I held the note I had written to Hamish. I kissed the folded parchment, and placed it on the bedside table behind the oil lamp, where it was inconspicuous enough yet could still be easily found if anyone were looking.

I quickly changed into my traveling garb, packed my few belongings and climbed down the rope into a cold, blustery, overcast day.

CHAPTER NINE

WALKING QUICKLY, I descended the slope of the hill
to the loch. A rising layer of mist hovered over the
smooth expanse of the loch and I was glad of this; it
would afford me an element of cover.

The boathouse was eerie in the early morning light. The water lapped against the rocks with
cool, gloomy regularity. There were several boats
to choose from and I had no preference. My only
requirement was that it float. Giving a cursory appraisal, I chose the smallest. It would be easier to
launch, I reasoned. It was a good choice. The vessel was far heavier than I expected it to be and took
all my strength to lug off its rack and down to the
water. I retrieved two oars. Then I pushed the boat
clear of the rocks, wetting my shoes in the process.
The water was icy.

My boat sailed through a small passage of the
high, stone bridge, the one that linked the encircling
walls of Kinloch. The passage was so small I had
to lean low in the boat in order to fit through it, and
the tunnel itself was dark and unnervingly confined.

Once clear of the tunnel, I began to row. I had
never steered or rowed a boat before. I was grate-

ful that the current of the small river was strong enough to propel me without much expertise on my part. Without *any* expertise, more accurately. I had never captained a boat before. Finding an awkward rhythm, I was able to guide the boat so that the front was facing more or less forward.

The mist was thick and soupy, almost completely obscuring the view in any direction. But there was only one way to go. Downstream.

I floated without much difficulty for a time, pleased enough with my escape. I willed myself not to think of Hamish apart from the fortunateness of his new home. Knox would find me gone. He would be angry, at first. But he was already angry. For the lies. For the trouble that could be inflicted on his clan because of me, if I were to stay longer at his keep. I hoped he would feel relieved to be rid of me: a pest, a vagrant, a hussy. He might think of me now and again, when he had the occasional lurid thought, or when he ate an apple.

I entertained myself for some time recounting my memories of Kinloch. A mythical Eden, to be sure. And one that would remain as such, in my fading recollections. As I sailed and found comfort in my revelries, I thought an hour might have passed since I launched my boat. Maybe several.

A thudding noise brought me back to the present. Behind me. A bump. A splash. My eyes had adjusted to the murky mist and I could detect a shadow. Moving closer.

Terror surged through my chest.

Someone was following me.

I WAS AS frightened as I had ever been in my life, but also oddly prepared for the fear. I had known to expect dangers.

And here one was.

Was it Fawkes's men? Had they tracked my trail north, now that they knew of my whereabouts? Had they waited outside the walls for their opportunity? This seemed unlikely. They would have been spotted, hanging around like that. The environs of the Kinloch keep, outside the walls, had been cleared of trees for a mile in all directions, I had heard it said. For that very reason: so intruders would be easy to spot. I had also heard, from Hamish, that the Mackenzie guards were especially vigilant. There had been an unexpected invasion of some sort a year or two ago and the army had vowed that it would never happen again. But I was no longer within the confines of Mackenzie land. Far from it. I paddled faster, remembering only then that I had forgotten to ask for—or borrow, as it were—a weapon. I silently cursed myself for such a glaring oversight. Maybe I wasn't cut out for this life on the run, after all.

My pursuer was gaining on me.

The river was getting wider, and swifter.

My senses took on a peculiar, sparky sentience. In my mind I had prepared myself for peril, even death. To face such things is a very different experience than preparing for them from afar and from a safe vantage point.

Whoever he was, he was strong. Trained and able. He was able to steer and accelerate. The gap between his boat and mine was shrinking.

It was the glint of gold in his black hair that triggered my recognition.

"Amelia!" he shouted.

None other than Knox Mackenzie.

The nature of my fear took a turn. I no longer feared for myself. I feared for *him*. "Go back!" I shouted at him. "Don't follow me!"

He ignored this completely, pulling his boat up next to mine. I took my oar and pushed at the edge of his boat with it. The shove was enough to propel his boat away, but he jumped, lunging.

With the swift currents guiding the boats erratically, he almost missed. He was half in the water, his arms wrapped over the edge of my boat, tilting it severely. I was nearly thrown overboard by his heavy impact, and his efforts splashed water over me in a shocking torrent.

"Let go! You'll sink us!" But I grabbed his arm. *Damn this man! He might get swept away by the strengthening current, pulled under, drowned, killed!*

"These boats are designed not to sink when a man climbs aboard," he gasped, pulling himself up. I clung to him as he dripped all over me. "We've tested them and developed the shape to make them virtually unsinkable."

I paused, finding this somewhat interesting. Then I resumed my outburst. "You shouldn't be here," I accused. "I don't need you to save me!"

He climbed into the boat, his big body rocking the small craft as he levered himself into it. Soaked and stunning, he said, "I know. I'm the one that needs saving."

The blunt confession struck me for its honesty. Knox Mackenzie, with all his considerable powers and potencies, was not, as I knew him, prone to admit such things.

Even so, now that he was safely in the boat, I released the full force of my fury. "Knox Mackenzie, I don't want your help! I want you to stay at Kinloch, to safely tend to your clan and fulfill your regal purpose. I forbid you to chase after me. You're not my keeper!"

He eased the oars out of my hands and sat on the supported seat at the middle of the boat. He began to steer us, through undulating rapids that were gaining momentum. The boat was tossed in a lurching roll. I had no choice but to sit next to him and hang on for dear life.

"Did you hear me?" I said.

"Aye. I heard you."

"Will you go back?"

"Nay."

"*Nay?* Why not?"

His eyes were flashing and his face bore an expression of severity. Errant strands of his black hair ruffled in the wind. I was barely able to comprehend through the radiating prisms of his glory that he did not look at all pleased. "I'm going to help you do whatever it is you need to do. I always protect what's mine."

I always protect what's mine. I let it echo, but I refused to let it permeate me.

Knox continued to focus on the task at hand—steering the boat—which, admittedly, did look as though it required some element of concentration. He did not appear at all fazed by my rage. In fact, he seemed to barely notice it. Once he had steadied us, he said, "My darling Amelia. There is a question I need to ask you. I didn't get a chance to before you fashioned a rope with my sheets, climbed out the window and stole down to the boathouse to borrow one of my boats."

"What question?"

His silver eyes appeared liquid in their volatility. He pulled on the oars in a heaving stroke. The boat tossed in the waves and I was forced to wrap my arms more tightly around him for fearing of falling overboard. He had to speak loudly over the roll of the river water. "In light of what happened last night, there is only one thing to be done. It is only right that you should agree to… Well, that we should—"

He paused to navigate around a rock.

A fleeting jab of panic was laced with curiosity. "We should what?"

He looked down at me and I could see the circle

of a muted sun glowing above the thick fog behind him, like a halo. "Amelia, marry me."

At first I thought I'd misheard him. But the words hung there in the ensuing river-silence like white windblown moths in a dark night, collecting light, dancing and taunting yet utterly blind.

My response bubbled out of me before I could stop it. I laughed. "Don't be daft. I can't marry *you*."

"Of course you can. And you must."

"I—" I brushed a strand of hair that had blown over my eyes. And I thought of my sister. I imagined the cold prison in which *he* held her, with damp stone walls and iron bars at the tiny windows. My fate was decided, and it was far removed from the splendor of Kinloch and the fantasy of Knox Mackenzie. "Nay. I'm sorry. I cannot marry you."

He stopped rowing and looked down at me. There was incredulity in him. Confounded, brewing indignation. Rage, even.

When the boat began to drift and swivel, he turned his attention momentarily back to righting our course and once again we glided through relative calm.

"I realize," I said, "that you might feel obliged to approach me with this proposal, but truly, it isn't necessary." A particularly intimate detail of last night's revelries crept into my thoughts. "Aye, we've shared a moment. A very beautiful moment. I'll always treasure the memory of you, and of us. But you'll be far better suited to one of your noble Highlands ladies. And I, well, I must—"

"Amelia," he said. "There is no question about this. You *must* marry me. The marriage is already all but sealed. All we need is the blessing of the minister to make it official." Even as he prepared to say it, I could sense that he was questioning his own tactics. He knew me well enough by now. "It *will* be done."

"I'm sorry but I cannot agree to—"

"I am laird of this keep," he thundered, looking around at the foggy expanse into what would have been, if we could see clearly, non-Mackenzie land. "I am laird of *my* keep, and it is my—"

"Aye, I am well aware of that. You are very lairdly and important. Yet we are no longer in your keep. And, as much as I'd like to, I am not returning to your keep any time soon. Furthermore, as I've mentioned to you upon, oh, three or four occasions, I do not abide orders. Not yours or anyone else's!" *Unless they threaten me or mine with a slow, torturous death, that is.*

Knox was staring at me with a mixture of fury and exasperation. He took several deep breaths, clearly attempting to calm his own temper. He spoke slowly, as though to a child who was having difficulty understanding his dictates. "You are already mine, Amelia. We have known each other in a biblical sense, which means that we are bound in body and soul. In life. I am a devout man, and a powerful one. With great influence. Mock me if you will, but

I do not take these things lightly, as I have already explained to you."

I wasn't sure if he had intended to ask me—or order me—to marry him before we had succumbed to our baser urges last night, or if he had decided somewhere between then and now. I suspected—and this occurred to me only at this very moment—that he had decided that I would become his new wife long ago, maybe on the night we had shared by the loch, under a crescent moon and a million stars. Or perhaps as long ago as the afternoon in the apple orchard, at our very first meeting—although this seemed incredible, almost absurd. Who decides such things in a fleeting moment? Who believes in love at first sight? I was seeped in cynicism, until I remembered that *I* had already admitted to *him* that I had loved him that very first day, from that moment he had appeared to me as a sun-touched vision. And I had meant it.

I believed in love at first sight. I had well and truly experienced it. *Deeply. Madly.*

Yet I felt almost as though I wasn't entitled to indulge such a luxurious fantasy. I couldn't allow my whims to interfere with my mission. Perhaps, if I was successful—which, I knew, was a long shot— I could mull over the idea of accepting this fairy-tale ending to my debauched, very un-fairy-tale life thus far. What he was offering me was the type of happiness I had never, ever envisioned for myself, even as I had once sketched pictures and scrawled poems about green hills and peaceful meadows in my little red book as I skulked in the corner of the small, underused library of the gaming club, hiding from amorous wanderers and overzealous drunkards.

Curse these inconsistencies and confusions he seemed to incessantly introduce!

Annoyed by my silence, he continued, spelling the situation out with even more clarity. "There may be a…child to consider, and protect. A very important one. The heir of Kinloch."

This startled me. I hadn't thought of that. Clearly I should have, but my impulses had guided me and I knew in my heart that such a consideration would not have changed my decision. It was true that I'd acted without thinking of much at all, aside from Knox Mackenzie's superb physical attributes and endowments.

"I…I don't think you should worry about that," I mumbled.

"Why not?"

I had read enough of my father's books on the human body to understand the intricacies of the matter. I thought it too early in the month. Not that, if truth be told, I had counted especially carefully before now. "The timing would make that unlikely," I said. I sounded, I thought, somewhat convincing.

But he was not appeased. "Either way, even if the slightest possibility exists, which it does, then such a thing must be prepared for. Celebrated."

His demeanor changed then, quite suddenly. He

looked tired. He made some adjustments to our direction using the oars. Then he rested the oars on his knees and ran a hand through his thick hair. I understood this change in him. Of course, the possibility of a child would be immense, in his mind. He had lost a son, and a wife. And here was I, the chosen one. I could fill his void. I could overflow his void with life and love. I remembered the words he had whispered in the heat of an unequalled moment. *I can't breathe when I can't see you. You are milk and honey and innocence and lust. You are agony and pure, pure ecstasy. I want you. I love you.*

I felt heartless, in that moment, and so very torn. I felt my eyes burn, but I held back the tears.

Knox then took a very different approach. He smoothed my hair with his hand. "Amelia. I know I have acted rashly. Irresponsibly, even. Something I have never done. I was blinded by my desire for you, and for that I refuse to feel regret or remorse. I love you. I do. I don't care about your upbringing, or your past, whatever it involves. I don't care that I've known you for only weeks. I don't care that you lied to me."

"I'm sorry I lied to you," I said. "I—"

"I understand why you did it," he said. "I thought about it this morning. As I was climbing down your homemade rope, as it happened. You cheated in order to help feed your family, is it not so?"

I stared at his extraordinary face, framed as it was by the shock of his rich black hair. "Aye," I said.

"I've killed men to protect my family and I would do it again without hesitation. I would steal, cheat and certainly lie if it meant keeping any one member of my family or clan out of harm's way. There's no shame in that."

Much of my association with Knox Mackenzie had been all about my futile grasp to be on equal footing with him. He was a laird and a leader, born and bred to not only act on but embody the complex intricacies and high expectations of his role. His lairdship was not only his job but his entirety. It clung to him and emanated from the set of his shoulders. It was written in his posture and sculpted into his form. It shone out of his eyes.

And here, after all my frustrations in the face of his overblown power, was a new discovery. He was informed and experienced. He was philosophically in tune with struggle and survival. And he was using all of this vast wisdom to *comfort* me. Not to disparage me. To guide me and help me.

"You've grown up in the backstreets through no fault of your own. You feel this way of life has become your identity. But it has not. I can see your worth, lass. You're clever, as sharp as a knife blade. You were born to teach. And you have spirit. I have no doubt that whatever you aim to pursue in life will become yours for the taking, once you get your bearings."

My perceptions felt shady, unreliable. After all the angst I had learned to bear over my upbringing and my circumstance, here he was, sweeping away the river of despair with a single empathetic exoneration. I was shocked by this. And indescribably heartened.

He understood me. And he forgave me.

"Not only that," he continued, and his voice was roughened from some emotion I couldn't define. "Every time I look at you, I think for a moment you might be a mirage, a fabrication of my own mind. Your fiery spark and your lively beauty surpass anything I might ever have imagined."

"My beauty is *nothing* compared to yours," I heard myself say.

"Then again, if I were to fabricate the ideal woman," he mused huskily, "I might have made her just a touch less argumentative."

I was quite literally speechless, from all that he had confessed, and all that he was offering.

"I felt myself come alive again when you walked into my life, lass. *Alive,* as I've never, ever felt alive. I want more of it. I want more of you. I want you to be my wife. This lonely wretch asks for your hand. Please. Please marry me."

This was more than I could bear, truly. I felt my entire outlook shift. Powerfully.

Misconstruing my silence for doubt, he continued. With each word I fell deeper and more irrevocably in love with the man, until my heart might have seeped out of me and into a puddle on the already wet floor of the boat. "I love your smile," he said, his voice rasped with emotion. "It lights up my world.

I want you with me each day because you make me happier than I ever thought I could possibly be. I'll take such good care of you. I promise to. I'll cherish you, and love you as you deserve to be loved. You'll have everything you could wish for. You'll want for nothing, ever. I'll move heaven and earth to make all your dreams come true. I'll use all the resources within my grasp—which are considerable—to ensure that you are inundated with lavish finery of every description under the sun."

By this time, the tears were trickling in warm lines down my face. I was holding tightly on to him, even though the waves had calmed. I didn't care about *this* vulnerability. His beauty, of heart and soul, was opening me, changing me. "You don't need to do that last one," I whispered. "I have simple tastes."

A little furrow appeared between his eyebrows, the one that creased there when I confused him. But then he smiled. *That* smile. The one that broke my heart every time he granted it. I wanted to keep it, keep him, just like that.

"My tastes are basic and somewhat lewd, in fact, I'm afraid," I added, to ease any and every anguish he possessed.

He laughed lightly, the sound laced with relief. He held my hand to his cheek. "Aye," he said. "I know of your lewd tastes. Shocking, you are."

"Lurid, even, from time to time."

He looked down at me and his eyes were glittering. "Does this mean aye?" he asked.

How to handle this? How to keep him and keep him *safe* while I attempted to find my sister and fight off Sebastian Fawkes? I felt a boiling anger at the thought, more than ever before. Very suddenly, there was much more at stake than just my own happiness, which had always felt small and unimportant before. Not that I had minded that. It was how things were, and what I was used to. I found joy along the way, in unexpected places and in small threads of each day, where I could. The look on Hamish's face when I read his stories to him. The successful swindle of a hapless cad out of some of his money. The jingle of the coins in my pocket as I walked. The feel of a book as I leafed through its pages. There was happiness to be found between the lines when you looked closely enough.

But *this*.

This was bigger than me. This was a chance to live a life that was good and decent, built on love. This was a chance to embrace happiness on a scale that I had never before imagined. Not just for me. For Knox. For his clan and a hopeful future. It seemed wasteful not to at least fight for the possibility with everything I had.

My arms curled around his neck and I gently pulled his head down to me. "Aye," I said, kissing him. "Aye. I'll marry you. I'll marry you."

His strong arms folded around me, crushing me

to his great, hard form as his mouth took mine in an aggressive, erotic, brain-demolishing kiss. He was whispering love words in that eloquent, unreserved way he had that was such a departure from the staunch, authoritative shell of his public persona. "You are luscious and sweet and irresistible." His hands roved over the bodice of my dress, fondling and gripping. "You are a sunny day and a moonlit night. A perfect flower." So intimate, it was, and so endearing. *Mine,* I thought, loving him all the more for giving this part of himself to me, for letting his guard down. *This part of him is mine.*

AND SO IT WAS. I was now Knox Mackenzie's betrothed who could be carrying his child—a child that would inherit the title of Laird or Lady of Kinloch and the leadership of the entire Mackenzie clan as well as all of its resources.

I supposed it was understandable, his imposed watchfulness, his guardianship. Possibly.

I might have *allowed* myself to be guarded except for the fact that Knox's guardianship was in fact drawing him into my downward, possibly lethal spiral, which I desperately wanted to toss him back out of, before it was too late. I had to think of some way to protect him.

We were floating down a smooth, open stretch. Along the banks of the river, shadowy trees glided past, indistinct and shrouded in the lingering fog. I eyed Knox's weapons belt, which holstered his gargantuan sword as well as several knives. If I could take one of them, I could use it when it was least expected of me. When the time came. When the queen of hearts played her final hand.

"Knox?"

"Aye, lass."

"I have a request that I would like you to grant me, even though you won't want to. Especially now."

"What request is this?"

I knew it wouldn't wash before I spoke it, but I wanted to say the words nonetheless, so he'd know why I left him, at my very first opportunity. I was more resolved than ever before that I would have my victory, that I would end this dreadful conquest once and for all. That I would gain my freedom and return to Kinloch, to Knox and Hamish, and live out my life. *I could do it.* It wouldn't be easy. It would be terrifying. But it could be done. "I can't allow you to accompany me to Edinburgh. I request sincerely that you allow me to go alone. I beg you to return to Kinloch at your first opportunity. I'm perfectly capable of doing what needs to be done without your assistance." This was a matter up for debate, but I wasn't about to let him know that.

He didn't even hesitate to consider it. "You might be capable. You could very well be capable. Nevertheless, I'm afraid that is one request I will not be able to grant you."

I had expected this response, yet I tried again. "You *must* grant it to me."

"Nay, lass. I don't. And I won't."

Knox Mackenzie was more self-important than any human being I had ever known, and that was saying something. He had an overbearing way of speaking to me at times as though I were a child or a simpleton. I returned the favor now, embracing his technique. "The business that requires *my* assistance does not require *your* assistance. And I would prefer to conduct it alone. Do you understand this?"

"Oh, I understand it. I will not, however, agree to it. It simply is not going to happen that way."

"Then I regret that I will have to take my leave of you when you sleep—and you will have to sleep eventually."

Our eyes remained locked in a dueling challenge of wills.

"Why won't you let me help you?" he asked. The tiniest trace of pained affront clung to his subdued indignation and his muted outrage.

"I don't need your help."

"I don't believe that. There's more to your story than you're telling me. As usual. What little I do know allowed me to figure out your riddled message. It wasn't difficult to decipher, not at all. The knave is not only spared but well protected, which can comfort us both. Your brother-in-law—regrettably—seems to have met an untimely end. Your sister is in danger and the 'trouble' you referred to is waiting for you—to return to Edinburgh under the threat of her murder with the blade of his knife. Am I getting all that right? And I'm not letting you wander off into the night without protection, unless you assure me beyond a shadow of a doubt that where you're going is safe. Which, quite clearly, is not the case. Therefore, I'm afraid, you're stuck with me."

With that, he took some sort of device out of the pocket of the coat he was wearing. I saw the glint of metal in the flickery darkness, and before I could object or even react, I felt the cold clasp of a metallic ring click into place around my wrist. There were two rings, I could see. Adjoined by a short chain. I heard a second click as Knox secured the second ring around his own wrist.

He had locked us together.

It took me a moment to grasp the audacity of his high-handedness. "What do you think you're doing?" I asked him. I could feel the heat of my outrage burning my cheeks.

"I'm ensuring that you don't take your leave of me when I sleep—and I will have to sleep eventually."

I tugged at the constraints, fingering the cool silver cuff to search for a release of some sort. "You are the most incorrigible bully of a man I've ever met! Release me at once!"

"I'm afraid that is something I cannot do."

"You can!"

"All right, then, I can. But I won't."

"Give me the key. Give it to me!"

He reached into his pocket again, extricating a thin, looped leather cord. A small silver key hung from it. I grabbed for it, but he held it out of reach, dangling it from the end of his very long arm as though this were some sort of game. I thought I detected a quirk at the corner of his mouth.

I crawled onto him, straddling him and grappling for the key roughly. He didn't fight me, but the fury of our little altercation caused us both to topple backward off the seat and onto the wet floor of the boat. He landed with a thud onto his back and I lay on top of him. I clawed for the key, but he grabbed my wrist in a viselike grip. As furious as I was, the hard bulk of his big, masculine form under mine inspired a raft of impassioned memories. My body echoed with the astounding pleasure he had inspired. I arched against him and felt the stirrings of a deep, visceral warmth.

"Damn, you little heathen," he growled. "Calm down."

"I will not *calm down!* Now give me the key."

But Knox Mackenzie was far stronger than I might have given him credit for. He lifted me in all my writhing indignation easily, setting me back on the seat as he slipped the looped cord over his neck, tucking the key inside the layers of his shirt and his coat. At the same time the boat lurched abruptly as we struck the sand of the river's edge. Only then did I realize he had steered us ashore. We were beached in a small cove. Knox jumped overboard, wetting his boots. The link of our cuffed bonds pulled me along with him, causing me to nearly topple out of the lurching rowboat. He pulled the boat with a muscular one-armed heave onto the shore, securing it. Then he reached in and scooped me into his arms. The man was as strong as an ox, and equally as bullheaded.

"Let go of me, you brute!" I said. "I'm getting back into the boat."

"Not if you want to live, you're not," he said through clenched teeth. "There's a waterfall just around that next bend that will smash that boat to splinters, and grind you to a bloody pulp. And *that* would be a damn shame."

This rendered me temporarily silent. *Overbearing bastard.* Among all his other kingly attributes, we could now add to the list that he had saved my life. I could admit the information quieted me somewhat. He was carrying me across a meadow that was dotted with large haystacks and a few small trees. "Where are you taking me?"

"We'll rest here for a time, to dry our clothes. The wind has picked up and you might catch a chill."

He set me aside a haystack that was as tall as I was, looming large like a hulking, mounded sentinel. The fog had cleared with the breeze, but the sky was thick with dark clouds.

"Do you have a woolen blanket in that bag?" he asked.

"You mean you don't *know?*" I said, petulant. "You didn't have your guards rifle through my belongings to scour for clues and incriminations?"

"Actually, I did. I *do* know you have a woolen blanket in that bag. That and your wrap will keep us warm as our wet clothes dry in the wind. We're both soaked to the skin. We'll hang our clothes on the branches of this tree."

Silver eyes challenged me to protest, which I promptly did. "Oh, you'd like that, wouldn't you? You'd *love* me to strip naked right here in the middle of this field and hang my clothes on that damn tree."

"As a matter of fact, I would," he replied, and I detected his brazen superiority was mildly ruffled by the very thought, and also faintly amused. "I *will* enjoy watching you remove your wet clothing as you hang it on that damn tree. I'll also enjoy the fact that you will most probably survive the night if you're dry and warm. The cold and the damp have a way of taking their toll on a blustery night. Such a chill can be deadly. So, if you value your life and your health, you'll follow my orders."

I stared at him warily. It was true I had little experience with such things. I'd spent most of my life indoors. I knew enough about cold, but had never spent a night out-of-doors in the wind or the rain. The scenario had once been one of my deepest silent fears.

Sensing my doubt, he said, "I'll not take nay for an answer, and you can test me all you like. I'll undress you myself if you refuse. Take your time," he added generously.

I accepted, not without a degree of rancor, that he was probably right. "I can't undress while I'm chained to you."

He contemplated me evenly. Then he reached to

pull the key from inside his clothing. "I'll warn you now. I'm faster than I look."

"It would hardly be in my best interests to bolt across this field into the unknown without a stitch of clothing on, now, would it, Laird Mackenzie?"

His eyes flashed with my impertinence, but he unlocked my cuff, then his own. He put the contraption back into his pocket. The key, he looped back around his neck. Then he removed his saturated coat and hung it on a low-hanging branch. In silence, we undressed. It was true the air had a frigid bite to it. My skin was cool and dimpled with the chill.

But with each item of clothing I removed, the center of me grew warmer. I was cold and damp in the breeze, and I found I was not averse to feeling the broiling heat of his body against mine. I reminded myself that this was all about survival.

"Can I keep my shift on, at least? 'Tis hardly wet."

"Nay," was the soft reply. "'Tis warmest skin to skin."

Skin to skin. Aye, we had lain skin to skin last night, but that romp had come about with fervor, and abandon. Disrobing in this deliberate, teasing way was a wholly different experience. I found my pulse quickening, not only in my chest but in the heated tenderness within me. I removed my shift with not an entirely unintentional flair, revealing all the abundance of my eggshell-white curves, which fairly glowed in the muted afternoon light.

He came to me, holding up the woolen blanket

he had retrieved from my bag. It was impossible not to notice the significant protrusion of his massive arousal, which slid against my stomach as he wrapped the soft wool around us. "Pay no attention to it," he said.

"How could I possibly do *that?* It's enormous, and as hot as a newly forged sword."

"I'll thank you for the resounding adulation, milady," he said. "Now come. We'll rest here until our clothing has dried."

Keeping the blanket wrapped around us, and holding my woolen wrap, which was nearly dry from the wind, he maneuvred us onto the haystack. He placed his weapons belt next to us within easy reach. Under our weight, the hay compacted, molding around the shape of us. It was in fact quite comfortable. We lay back into our pleasantly soft bed, and Knox draped the fur cape over our wrapped bodies, which were pressed together. Side by side. Skin to skin.

Above us, the dome of the dark sky was strewn with pillowy clouds that rolled and blustered across the heavens.

I was very aware of Knox's hot flesh insinuated tightly between us. The velvet-hard texture of him against the skin of my stomach was having a potent effect on the already softening, delicate throb between my legs. He made no move to touch me in any other way.

After a few minutes, I felt mildly disappointed by this.

Not that we'd planned this outcome, but now that we were *in* this situation, it hardly seemed realistic to expect that something intimate wouldn't come of it. Yet he lay still, his eyes closed, almost as if he were actually attempting to go to sleep. "You're not going to chain me up with the cuffs?" I whispered.

"I'm a light sleeper and, entwined as we are, I think you'd wake me."

I fingered the thin leather cord around his neck. I wanted to rile him. "Let me have the key."

"Nay. Go to sleep."

I wasn't fooled by his complacency. His eyes were closed but it was obvious he was rampantly lusty. I crawled up his body, half climbing onto him as I attempted to slip the cord around his neck. He caught my hand, squeezing tightly. "Drop it," he murmured.

I obeyed, only because his grip was ridiculously powerful. But I had other ideas. Easing myself down his body, I found what I was seeking, without difficulty. I wrapped my fingers around the rigid length of his engorged shaft. With my other hand, I cupped him from below, quite snugly, too.

He uttered the filthiest oath I'd ever heard.

"Laird Mackenzie," I scolded, tightening my hold. "'Tis hardly the way to speak around a lady. Especially one so delicate and meek as myself."

He began some response that wasn't entirely flattering, so I increased the pressure mildly and he reconsidered, offering only a muffled curse.

I let my fist slide along his massive silken length.

Up and down, I caressed with his pleasure in mind but firmly enough to let him know I was very much in control.

"Please," he wheezed.

"Nay," I said, enjoying myself. Without releasing my hold, I slid farther down his torso. My bare breasts skimmed across the hair-roughened surface of his chest and I gasped lightly at the tickling, pleasure-laden sensation. I drew lower, until my breasts touched the scorching hardness I held in my hands. A drop of liquid had seeped from him, and the discovery emboldened me further. I kissed him, licking lightly, tasting his essence, playing the beauty. With my hands, I continued to explore an undulant coercion.

"Jesus Christ Almighty," he groaned.

"May I *please* have the key to your metal manacles?"

His oath was pained, his answer unclear. And I was not satisfied.

So I continued. I licked the broad tip, moving my tongue indecently. His incessant moaning and cursing was somewhat removed from my scope at this point. I was quite fascinated by the taste of him, and the textures. And his responses to my exploratory touch. I was very aware that he was entirely at my mercy, that every held breath and broken exhale took place at the direct consequence of my exploits.

Opening my mouth, I took him deeper. I experimented with the suction, the depth. And the continued pressure of my squeezing, wandering hands. Very, very gently, I touched my teeth to him.

He flinched but didn't dare move too abruptly. I did feel, however, the leather cord being placed on my hair. *"Here,"* he groaned again, more clearly this time, but no less aggrieved. "Here, have it. Have everything. Anything you want."

I gentled my hold, and I sucked him tenderly now, which only caused him to groan as though his very heart was breaking. I eased him out of my mouth, removing my touch altogether to pull the leather cord around my neck, where I intended it to stay.

As soon as I loosened my hold, he grabbed me in a sudden, clinching movement, turning us, drawing me up to him as he bore me down, pinning me to our makeshift bed. He held my wrists now in the manacles of his own fists. I could smell the river water and the travel dust on his warm skin; that, and the musky sheen of his rage-edged passion. He spread my legs forcefully with his thigh. His hair tickled my face and his manhood pressed strongly into my belly.

I waited for his possession, simultaneously bracing myself and going exquisitely wet with anticipation. His utter forcefulness was arousing me beyond belief. I liked him rugged and riled.

He was still but for the rise of his chest and the beat of his heart. I could sense that this domination was equally as affecting to him, yet he wouldn't take me by force. There was a note of uncertainty in him: he was unsure if I was entirely willing. I wasn't exactly sure *how* he could be unsure at this point, but I remembered he had taken a somewhat extended hiatus from intimacy of this persuasion. His instincts might have suffered from the lack of womanly contact.

The longer he waited, second after second, the more provoked I became.

I lifted my head and I could get close enough to graze his lips with my own, but he pulled back, staring down at me with an expression of more supercilious superiority than ever. Lord, but the man was a high and mighty handful! I'd met my match in every way with this brute, but I was determined to get my way.

"Kiss me," I said. I would *show* him how willing I was. "Give me your mouth."

It was almost surprising to me when he obeyed. His parted lips eased over mine and I opened to him. I touched the tip of my tongue to his, enticing him, drawing him into me, suckling and inviting.

"I can't…be gentle about it, lass," he rasped. "Do you want me?"

I was splayed and fastened, unable to move. "Aye, you beast. I want you. All of you."

After a moment of searching intimacy, he sheathed himself to the hilt in a single thrust. I cried out from the immensity of the invasion. I was expecting pain, but there was none, just a sweet totality. He thrust again, pushing himself even deeper. "You're mine, Amelia." His invading drives were intensely possessive, pounding deep into my body with the aggression of his need. "How *dare* you run off like that and put yourself in harm's way? *How dare you?* You are mine to protect, lass. You are *never, ever again* to allow your safety to be risked in this way, do you understand? *Never.*"

Knox's aggression barely calmed, tempering into an avid adulation. His movements were greedy, filling me entirely with each covetous drive. He released my wrists, and his hands moved down my body, exploring the curves of my breasts, my waist, my hips. As inexperienced as I was, I could detect that the man was carnally *famished.* His rapacious desire seemed to almost hum from his touch.

I wrapped my arms around him. My fingertips glided over his skin as I marveled at the sculpted, muscular perfection of him.

"You're too important," he said. "Too beautiful. I can't lose you. I love you, lass, I love you. With everything I have. All of me. Everything. I love you as I love sunlight and air. You are happiness incarnate. My new lifeblood. I can't breathe when I can't see you."

The words echoed within me, fired and forged with his love and his rage. I understood that this onslaught was all about his fear, that vulnerability in him that I had not only touched but taken ownership of. Whatever glory and sovereignty he embodied, *I* was his true salvation, the one remedy to the unbearable loss he had endured. I could feel this in the grip of his fingers and the completeness of his conquest.

And his thrusting drives continued, thickly impaling; a solid, inexorable grinding that reached my womb with each stroke. His hands cupped my backside, his fingers gripping into my flesh, ensuring that his occupation was absolute. The fullness was overwhelming. The sensual, accumulating friction filled me with star-studded sensation. Each drive forced the aching beauty deeper, higher. I had no choice but to surrender entirely to the building convulsive glow. I was moaning and quivering, my flesh clenching in spasms around his invading, vigorous presence.

"Aye, lass," he murmured into my ear. "Give in to me. Let me own your body and your soul, as you own mine. *Feel* my devotion and my obsession. You're mine as I'm yours. Give in. Give me everything. Let go."

I was melting, perched on the edge of some looming physical abyss from which I might never recover. My legs wrapped tightly around him, to contain the sensation, to hold him and aspire to the promise of a cataclysmic release. His punishing grip was bruising me, marking my flesh with painful force that only compounded the rising pleasure as his plunging drives went on and on. I bit his lip and tasted blood. My fingernails dug into his skin, scratching and clawing as I attempted to pull him closer, to become one with this rise. I arched up to him, meeting him stroke for stroke, consumed by his sublime, perfect assault.

I felt his teeth then, on my neck. The spear of pain provoked a spark deep within me where his pummeling aggression launched a spiraling pleasure so intense I cried his name.

"Knox, oh, Knox. Oh, God, you beauty, please don't stop."

And there it was, a bursting peak of rapture that cascaded in jolting rushes through the entirety of my being. The fury of my bliss grasped him, savagely tugging him deeper into my body. I could feel the gushing warmth of his own release mingling with my surging, gripping pleasure. We were lost in this eruptive bond, fierce and entangled, wholly immersed in a lingering moment of completion.

I AWOKE TO the sound of birdsong. In the distance, the hushed, broad lull of the river rolled in its endlessness. We had slept through the night. I was curled on my side, drowsed with warmth and sleep, entirely encompassed by Knox's protective embrace. He was kissing my shoulder lazily. His arm, which had been wrapped around me, fondled my breast. He teased my soft nipple between two fingers, rolling gently until it hardened into a tight little bud. Then he moved to the other breast, doing the same, touching them both with the scan of his fingers, playing with sensual tenderness. His hand roved to my hip, caressing lower, to the back of my thigh, which he eased higher, positioning me. I felt the head of his scorching manhood against my backside, rubbing between. His fingers found the moist petals of my sex, opening me. He guided himself into me, just barely entering me from behind.

I was sore and I moaned as he pressed into raw, sensitive tissues. I gripped his wrist in a reflexive plead. My whole body felt bruised and battered.

"I'll be so gentle with you," he whispered. And he was. He stroked and touched my breasts unhurriedly. With his other hand, he fingered the tiny delicate nub between my legs, caressing with languid deliberation until my core became slick. He pushed his thickness deeper, pulling out before parting me again, gaining depth gradually, and only as my body welcomed him. The slight pain of his advance was sparked with a light, sweet throb. He pulled back again, his passage silky now. And as he entered me once more, I arched back against him, taking him deeper, little by little, until he was fully inside me. Like this, we lay still, as he allowed my youthful body to adjust to his magnitude. He was exceedingly patient this time, waiting for me to nudge back against him before giving me any movement at all. The leisure of it was delicious. Knowing that he would only react to my lightly squeezing muscles, or the gentle persuasion of my body pressed against his, was divinely enticing. This peaceful allowance fortified my desire.

"Are you trying to make amends?" I said softly, teasing him.

He pulled me even closer, causing his immense shaft to press deeper into me. I gasped as the throb escalated.

"Maybe. It seems I cannot possess you without losing myself completely. Even now, I feel as if any moment could be the complete undoing of me. My release is my surrender and my vow. My body is my oath. I love you, my sweet Amelia. I am yours."

His words, accompanied as they were by the thick, impaling, pain-flecked pleasure and the skate of his fingers across the astoundingly sensitive nerve center of my body, ignited me. The pulsing glow bloomed in a sudden swell. Just the clench of my ecstatic inner muscles was enough to spur his own upheaval, which spilled into me in torrid, pulsing bursts.

I was beyond replete. My heart beat in a languorous cadence, as though slowed by satiation of body and soul.

THE SUN CREPT over the horizon, lighting the sky with a hazy yellow brilliance. Knox lifted me, carrying me to the tree where our clothing was hanging, now dry from the wind. With an element of care that was almost foreign to me, he placed me on my feet. Every muscle was sore, yet my naked body felt sated, beatifically used. And I could only stare at the magnificence of my lover. His mussed-up coal-black hair gleamed with early morning sunlight. His swarthy face, darkened by the gold-glinted stubble of his beard, made him look like a pirate who'd discovered vast treasures. Most of all, the fervent ardor in his light gray eyes seeped into my beating heart.

He touched his fingers to my neck. A mark. One of many on my body. He kissed the light bruise. "I'd apologize," he murmured against my skin, nipping softly. "But you're not the only one who got bit."

I smiled, but something occurred to me. "Knox?"

"Aye."

"Did you tell your clan where you were going?"

"Nay, lass. As soon as I realized you'd fled, I ran after you. I knew I needed to catch up to you. That was my only concern."

This admission infused me with some strangely provocative emotion that might have been—actually, there was no doubt in my mind what it was: love. In vast, profuse quantities. He stood there in his finely made fur-trimmed leather coat, looking like something you'd want to paint for posterity, just to remember how stunning he was, with his tawny, rugged handsomeness and his gold-flicked coloring. To think of him dashing heroically after me in a fit of protective concern, without even telling his clan, his family or the army that would go to any and every length to protect him: I was overcome. At his beauty. And his impulsive desire to keep me safe. "They'll be worried about you."

"Aye, they will. But they will have seen the sheets, and the note you left. They'll have noticed the missing boats and they'll follow our path down the river. They'll know that you fled and they will deduce from that detail that I've followed you. They know how much I care for you."

"They do? How?"

"I told them, of course. If you recall, half my officers were there when you were in my den, in the early morning, while I was half-clad. It wasn't difficult to figure out. They know me very well. They know of my…principles. All the clan, by now, will be buzzing with the news of our impending nuptials, lass. Good news has a way of traveling fast."

"Oh." This unsettled me slightly. I didn't want any of the Mackenzie clan involved in my mission, and least of all their laird. I was afraid of what might become of them, if they happened to find themselves in the wrong place at the wrong time. And all because of me.

"Several of my officers are gifted trackers. They'll have no trouble following our path. They'll be searching for us, and they'll likely find us before we get to the tavern. If not, we'll wait for them there, and I'll send word to Kinloch of our whereabouts."

I was not surprised by this information. My eyes scanned the horizon. I thought of trying to break away from him somehow, to run and hide in order to keep him safe. But it would never work. I couldn't outrun him. Nor would I be able to hide from his army. I knew for a fact that I wouldn't succeed in any attempts to dodge him. And truth be told, I didn't *want* to run from him anymore. The previous night had bonded us irrevocably.

The realization was somewhat daunting but also awe-inspiring. It seemed I wouldn't be facing Sebastian Fawkes on my own, to sacrifice myself in whatever way I had to do to save my sister's life. Instead, I would be confronting Sebastian Fawkes with the support of one of northern Scotland's most prominent Highlands armies.

"Does this sinister foe have a name?"

I didn't answer immediately. We'd been walking for a short time, in the direction of the tavern. He waited patiently and after a moment I said, "Aye. He has a name."

"What name?" I didn't want to tell him, not yet. Oddly, I didn't want to dirty the air that he breathed with a name like that. He watched my face, understanding that I was choosing to refrain. "Tell it to me."

"You might go looking for him without me."

His eyebrows rose slightly as he considered this and he made a face that suggested approval of some sort. "I hadn't intended it, but aye, I suppose I could. It isn't at all a bad idea." He was holding my hand as we walked and it seemed an almost comically tender gesture for such a manly, battle-honed warrior such as himself. He looked down at me from under his long eyelashes, almost imploring.

"You don't know these foes like I do," I said. "City foes. Ones without scruples. Ones who would stab you in the back when you least expected it."

"What makes you think city foes are different from the foes we fight here in the Highlands? Why do you assume that a Highlands foe wouldn't stab you in the back?"

My gaze traversed the plains and the foothills beyond. "I don't see any foes here at all. Where are all these sinister foes you speak of?"

"They've all been bested. For now. You'd be a fool to think their ghosts and their bones aren't scattered about, and those of their fathers and grandfathers before them. Another enemy might rise from the ashes of our battles any day, at any time. We train for war every waking hour of our lives and remain ever vigilant for that very reason."

I hadn't thought of this place in those terms. It seemed so peaceful, so undisturbed.

"You'd be surprised," he continued, "by how often small skirmishes do arise. Which is why we took your bandit story so seriously, at first."

I felt foolish about it now, for telling lies and even more, for thinking that they might be believed. "I'm sorry about that."

"I forgave you for that long ago," he said, his eyes full of kindness.

"I don't want to put your life at risk," I said. "I think *these* particular foes are more underhanded than most. I think they might trick you, or surprise you, mainly because you're an honorable man. I think their methods might thwart your strategies, because what I know of you and your men—like

Lachlan, with his pretty wife and innocent children. I know that you expect people to behave like you do. With honor and courage and all those Highlands values you like to spout on about."

He smiled at this, but I continued.

"You're used to beauty and compassion," I said. "Not ruthless malevolence. Your home is tranquil and protected. Untouchable. I don't want to upset that. I don't want to ruin or damage or even *touch* that perfection with my sordid past. *That's* why I don't want you to come with me. I *expect* people to behave badly. I'm prepared for it. Which is why I think I'm better equipped to handle this fight than you are. I'm ready to walk into my trap, to fight, to kill, to get my sister and return to my new home."

This statement triggered a barely detectable yet deep-seated reaction in him. His expression changed to one of checked ferocity, reminding me that he wasn't only a passionate lover and benevolent protector. He was a war-hardened soldier and a trained, experienced leader. Capable of killing men. "What is it this foe expects from you, Amelia? What does he want…" He seemed fairly pained by the follow-up. "From *you?*"

"Complete ownership. In every possible way." I knew this would infuriate him and I wanted it to. Something in me had turned. There was nothing I could do to dissuade Knox Mackenzie. If he was going to be involved in this, then I would tell him everything. And suddenly, I wanted to. I wanted his help. It was the kind of help that could save not only Cecelia's life and my own, but also the life of *this,* of us and our future together.

"Well, he cannot have it," he growled.

I got the feeling he was taking a moment to allow his fury to dissipate before he spoke again.

"You seem to think me some sort of puppet that sits on his throne all day to be admired and protected," he said, his rage only barely edged with compassion. "I can assure you that is not the case. Kinloch has been fought for, died for and achieved over many lifetimes of struggle. My clan has fought scores of ruthless, sinister, underhanded men. Only through work and solidarity have we been able to build and foster the peace we hang on to precariously, at best. There is no such thing as untouchable. And just because Lachlan has a pretty wife does not mean he cannot be as ruthless as any man. It is *because* he has a pretty wife and innocent children that he's capable of ruthlessness, in whatever way it's required to protect them."

I wiped my tears and he continued.

"You're wrong about us," he said. "We value honor, aye, but we are not above taking whatever means necessary to secure the safety of our own. *You* are my own, lass. Don't you see? *You* are what I want. If I have to stab an evil crook in the back to rescue your sister and convince you of that, then so be it. My honor will have no issue with that whatsoever."

"But—" I sniffled. "Are you sure?"

He surprised me by scooping me into his arms and lifting me, hugging me close. "We'll need my officers and we'll need a plan. Tell me what to do to attend to this matter so I can take you home and marry you."

"His name is Sebastian Fawkes," I began, letting the truth—at last—spill out. It felt immensely cathartic to finally share this burden with someone who might actually be able to help me. And help us. My voice was rasped with the heavy weight of my memories. "The debts were always accumulating. 'Tis all I've known for a very long time. Crippling, constant debt. James was a spendthrift and a gambler." I had never revealed that to anyone before. "He skimmed the earnings. He would deny it, and promise to mend his ways. But he couldn't do it. Cecelia never knew. I never told her. For all his faults, she loved him. Or at least she *convinced* herself that she loved him. She tried so hard to be the person she thought she should be. The honorable wife. Because that's what a wife is supposed to do with a husband. Love and honor and obey. 'Tis what our mother did, until her dying day. 'Tis what she believed in and how she lived her life. And it's what my sister aspired to.

"James got involved in riskier schemes. He became indebted to the wrong kind of people. Smuggling rings and black markets. The ganglords began to target him because he owed them money. His deals never worked out the way he planned. In the end, we were forced to sell him the controlling shares of the business. To a man who…didn't like my attitude. A man who expected obedience from everyone he met. At first he was amused by me. But then he started coming to our club more often. Watching me. Noticing things about me that…frightened me. He was very observant. Very threatening. He sat at my table, always, and he wanted me to serve his drinks. He…well, he propositioned me. I refused. He became angry. I was a society lowlife, he said, compared to him. He could elevate my status and alleviate our debts. If only I would agree to perform my role as he described. *Exactly* as he wanted. That was a condition of his demands.

"I couldn't do it," I whispered as the line of a tear wet my face. "I just couldn't do it. It felt like selling my soul. And it wasn't worth the price he was offering. Despite everything."

"Of course it wasn't," Knox murmured, wiping my tears with his fingers. I'd never been prone to excessive crying in my life, but in the past few days I'd made up for ten years of dry eyes and survivalist grit. "You're all right now, lass."

"He might own everything by now, I don't know. I don't care. I just want to find my sister."

I was almost startled by how intimidating Knox's expression had become as I told him the story. He wanted the truth. Well, here it was. In all its gory detail. "Cecelia feared for my life, and Hamish's. Fawkes threatened to harm him if I didn't agree to his demands. I almost did. But my sister begged me to flee and to find a safe haven, far away from Fawkes and his men. She would cover our tracks somehow. She would buy us some time, she hoped, as she waited for James to return. So Hamish and I traveled north. To the Highlands. And now I've brought the danger upon you, as well. I never meant to."

"Danger is what I've trained my entire life to confront," Knox said. "You're not alone anymore, lass. I'm here to help you. And your family. We're together now."

At first I thought the thundering sound was some sort of heavenly response to the emotional rush of the resurrection I was experiencing.

But as it grew louder, I realized what it was. They appeared to us: a clustered line of galloping horses in the green distance, the dusty cloud of their wake rising behind. Upward of twenty-five of them, in full war regalia, with swords and flags raised.

Knox Mackenzie's men.

CHAPTER TEN

THEY SWARMED AROUND us, curious, fierce and much relieved to see their laird and commander. Those that had not met me before eyed me and I remembered what Knox had told me: that his men would have figured out his decision by now, that the news of our engagement might have circulated. I almost regretted that I was so windblown and wild from the ride and the travel and the repeated attentions of my husband-to-be. I could feel the color on my cheeks and the twinkle in my eye. I remembered, though, that Knox Mackenzie had had his choice of all the refined noble women of Scotland. I knew by now what effect my unreserved tendencies had on him. I no longer doubted my value to him, nor my worth. His sincerity and his devotion strengthened me along with the memory of his words. *My body is my oath. I love you. I am yours.*

Lachlan rode up to us. "I believe congratulations are in order, milady," he said to me.

"Thank you, Lachlan," I said, but my divided happiness was soon pierced by Knox's announcement to his men. "We travel directly to Edinburgh. The future Lady of Kinloch's life is under direct threat from a menacing ganglord by the name of Sebastian Fawkes. We believe he holds her sister captive as a ploy to lure Amelia into his clutches. The threat will be dealt with and the sister rescued. We will discuss tactics en route, but the sooner this devil is eradicated, the better. Onward!"

WE RODE SOUTH.

Two messengers had been sent to return to Kinloch with the news of Knox's plans and whereabouts. Knox's men had brought his horse, a mammoth called Seven, named for Laird Mackenzie's lucky number, I was told. I didn't mention it to Knox then, but seven was my own lucky number, and one which I often employed in my card tricks. A magic number, every time. I liked its oddness, and the fact that many people considered it an inauspicious number, thereby avoiding it; this detail gave the number a mystique and a perversity that I'd once thought fit pleasingly with my own. I didn't know why, but that inclination drew me even closer to Knox Mackenzie. I loved him with a ferocity that swelled in my heart as we drew closer and closer to the enemy who would determine our fate: a peaceful life of beauty and plenty, or a gory, unnecessary death at the hands of greedy men. I could only hope our lucky number would preserve us.

Knox held me close to him, and I leaned back against him.

We rode until the sun painted the clouds with bold, brilliant swirls of red and orange.

A sixth sense pinged at my awareness, provoking a strong urge to look behind us. I twisted to glance around the significant obstacle of Knox's body, from where I sat in front of him on his horse. Knox took no notice of me. He was used to my wriggling by now. Personally, I thought I was handling the travel exceedingly well, considering I'd never ridden astride a horse before in my life. He seemed to disagree. "Sit still," he muttered, holding me closer even as he scolded me.

The feeling grew. Someone was coming.

I took another look. At first I could see nothing. Just a panorama of heather-layered plains and the jutting, craggy peaks of the Highlands rising behind. But there, I was certain, was a tiny speck on the colorful horizon. A lone figure. Nay, a horse.

I watched this horse gallop closer and I could see that there *was* a rider.

A very small one.

A boy.

Oh, God, nay.

It was Hamish.

I slipped out of Knox's embrace and off his gigantic horse, my mind a flurry of white-hot concern that was so consuming I barely noticed the jarring contact I made with the ground.

"Amelia?" I heard Knox's question fade out as he

might have noticed the reason I was now walking in the direction from which we'd come.

Hamish was riding at a hell-bent pace. How did he even know how to ride a horse like that? He might have sat on a carriage horse once or twice as a novelty, not as a mode of transportation. Either he'd been given lessons by a dedicated expert during his short time at Kinloch or the lad was a natural. Just another activity my clever nephew excelled at. My clever nephew whose neck I was about to wring.

His horse slowed as it neared me and he rode up next to me.

"Get off that horse right now," I told him, more irate than I'd ever been.

I wasn't sure if he would obey me, but he did. And he was in my arms before I could either scold him *or* wring his neck.

"Ami," he said, from somewhere in the depths of my crushing, heartbreaking embrace. I unclasped my hold on him and cupped his face. "You left without me."

I could barely get the words out. "Aye, Hamish. I'm sorry. I had to. I had to keep you safe. Why did you *follow* me? Didn't you get my note?"

"Aye, I got it. And I ripped it up! You said we'd stay together. No matter what."

"Aye, I did. And I meant it. But I couldn't bring you with me this time, Hamish. 'Tis too dangerous. You might get hurt. And I couldn't risk that. You're too important."

"*You're* too important to go alone!" he shouted. "You don't think I can handle danger! You don't trust me to help you!"

"I do!" Damn this new weeping tendency! "I just want you to be *safe,* Hamish!"

"And I want *you* to be safe, Ami. I want my mother to be safe. I saw *that* note, too. And I'm going to help you." He stood defiantly, with his hands on his hips.

"You saw that?"

"Aye. My father is dead. And my mother has a knife at her throat."

Oh, God! This wasn't fair. That this innocent boy understood all this. He was wise, as I'd taught him to be. I could only hope he wouldn't be scarred in some way, that his resilience wasn't forged only by the hardships he'd had to endure. I'd tried so hard to buffer him from all that. And from this. "I'm sorry about your father, Hamish."

"My father should not have done those things," Hamish said. His youthful voice was hard, but his eyes were shiny. "He took the wrong risks. He always played the wrong cards. Not like us, Ami."

Knox and Lachlan had dismounted and were walking over to us. I looked at them. "Make him go back," I said. "Someone take him back to Kinloch. *Please.* He's too young."

The two men exchanged glances. They were studying Hamish. I noticed only then that he wore not only the belt and small metal sword he'd been given, but another one: the finely made, glinting one he'd shown me that day in the arsenal. The one he'd yearned to use one day. "I hope you don't mind that I've borrowed this," Hamish said to Knox. "I'll return it when we get back to Kinloch."

"I followed my father into battle once when I was ten," Lachlan commented. "He wasn't pleased."

"Nay," I said. "He's only—"

"I'll be ten in one month and twenty-one days," Hamish offered spryly.

"I was eleven," said Knox. "My brother Wilkie first fought when he was nine. A skirmish with Clan Montgomery. My father always said a young soldier learns more in one day on the battlefield than in months of training in the barracks. And he was a wise man."

I couldn't believe what I was hearing.

"I'll keep him right next to me, Amelia," said Lachlan.

"That lad should be entitled to fight for his mother's life," Knox continued. "And yours."

"What kind of recruit would I be if I didn't step up, Ami?" Hamish insisted.

A safe one, I thought. But it was clear that my protests would not be given in to. Hamish was adamant. That he had the support of his idols only bolstered his determination. Lachlan was lifting Hamish back onto his horse. And Knox's hand was reaching for mine. "Let's get this over and done with so we can go home," he said.

"Guard him with your lives," I told them, the new accessory of my glimmering tears catching sunlight.

"As one of our own," Knox said, and I would take comfort from his words.

WE RODE FOR several days, across open plains, through small villages, along a rocky seashore. To the lowlands. Where the countryside grew more populous, less wide-open. Instead of feeling as if I was traveling home again, I felt as though I was distancing myself from the one place that had shown me true, unbound happiness.

At dusk on the evening of the third day, Knox decided we would camp for the night in a wooded valley. We would reach the city by the afternoon of the next day.

The men set up the camp, dividing into their campfire circles. I had learned that the army was organized into smaller regiments, groups of men that formed bonded teams, useful in battle and for hunting parties. These groups split off at night, sharing communal campfires and taking patrol shifts. Knox's group comprised his eight first officers, Lachlan among them. I had learned their names over the past few days and had found them to be good company.

There was Robb, a muscle-bound diplomat with a surprisingly gentle nature. He appeared to be the tactical expert and spent a good deal of his time drawing maps, plans and weapons in a small book he carried in a special compartment of his belt.

Gunn and Gow were brothers, huge men who spoke little but seemed to be Knox's key bodyguards. They would clearly sacrifice life and limb to keep their laird safe, and I pitied any man who had need to fight them. The sheer brawn of them seemed providential and I couldn't help thinking that the odds were in our favor with protectors like these.

Tavio was an inventor of sorts. I recognized him as the soldier who had been with Knox the day I was discovered by the weapons shed…wearing very little. If Tavio remembered the incident, he did not acknowledge it. I was grateful for that. He was tall and blond, and clearly possessing a keen intellect. He told long, involved stories about the contraptions he was designing to anyone willing to listen, Hamish and me included. His belts holstered not only knives and a single sword, but innovative devices and gadgets whose possible uses were a mystery to me.

Peyton, Kendrix and Alistair were weapons experts, trackers and gifted swordsmen, all of them big men, focused entirely on war and the task at hand.

And Lachlan was Knox's most trusted adviser, and also his closest friend. If Lachlan offered advice, Knox listened. I thought often of Lachlan's wife and children and wondered if these other men had families they had left behind. Of course, most of them would have. I hoped for the safety of these soldiers, who were putting their lives on the line for me. And I resolved to do everything in my power to keep them out of harm's way.

All in all, I couldn't have dreamed up a better group of warriors to storm the lair of Fawkes and his gang. Still, I worried. I worried about Cecelia. And about Hamish. And I wondered how the attack would play out.

We were seated around the fire, eating a meal of dried meat and bread. We hadn't discussed what might happen over the coming days, aside from general locations; these, Robb had mapped onto a drawing. Knox had asked Hamish, and me, for in-depth descriptions of the layout of our family's club, room by room. This information had been documented on paper, and studied.

It was time to discuss our plan of action.

"Do you expect Cecelia is being held at the gaming club?" Knox said. "Or somewhere else?"

"He'll have scouts at the club, waiting for me. He'll expect me there. Whether he's hidden her there, or somewhere else, I don't know."

"I can understand why Fawkes is hell-bent on capturing you," Tavio commented. He had a naturally flirtatious nature, even if he kept it almost wholly in check under the watchful eye of his laird. "The reason he wants you is obvious enough, but still, it seems he is taking excessive, almost irrational measures to lure you."

Knox's officers had so far treated me with utmost civility, out of respect for their laird, I suspected. It was true they seemed mildly fascinated by me, and by the marked difference between me and what they might have expected for Knox in a bride. I didn't get the sense they were disappointed by me, however. Quite the opposite.

"I've never known Sebastian Fawkes to be rational," I said. "He is a man of extremes. He likes to be noticed."

"He likes to get his way," Hamish said.

"Aye," I agreed. "Either through force or bribery."

"Or luck," said Hamish. "I used to think he could see right through the cards. Either that or he had spies in every corner."

"His luck has just run out," Knox muttered.

Just the thought of Fawkes's conquest, and facing it head-on, army or no army, caused the tiny hairs on my arms to rise. I knew for a fact that Sebastian Fawkes would not react well to the sight of Laird Knox Mackenzie, with or without his officers. Fawkes's power had been gained through force and founded on fear. Even the vilest soul would recognize the strength of conviction that radiated from Knox Mackenzie like an aura. I knew this detail would anger Fawkes to no end. He did not like to be upstaged or outclassed.

"If your sister is being held captive in the club," said Knox, "then the plan is straightforward enough. We storm the club and retrieve her, killing Fawkes or whoever guards her."

"Absolutely not," I said, which got the attention of everyone present. I supposed they weren't used to hearing their laird's dictates being refused. The laird himself, however, was getting used to it; he barely noticed. "I go alone, to begin with. If he feels threatened, he might kill Cecelia before we can reach her. I can't risk that possibility."

"There's—" Knox began.

"But if he thinks there's a chance that I'll do his bidding," I interrupted, "he's more likely to allow me to bargain with him. Once I've freed her—that's when I'll need you. Only then."

"There's no way in *hell,* lass," he growled, "that I'm letting you walk into that club alone."

"'Tis not a matter of you *letting* me do anything," I countered. Knox's men seemed entertained by the exchange and watched his reaction to my insolence with interest.

"Aye," he seethed. "It is."

My indignation at his incessant high-handedness was beginning, once again, to broil. "My sister's life is at stake, you brute! If she's even still alive, that is, after a whole month of my desertion! I *have* to go alone. And I *will* go alone. 'Tis the only way."

"Feisty, isn't she?" Tavio commented blithely.

"You have no idea," Knox replied.

"The lass is right, though," said Lachlan, the voice of reason. "'Tis what must happen. 'Tis essential he feels he has complete power, until the sister walks free. Then we can make our move."

"Too bloody dangerous." Knox was going to be difficult about this point. I'd known to expect that. He would exercise his power, for now, but in his voice I could hear the inflection of his realization. It *was* the best way. The only way.

Lachlan humored his commander as only a first officer and valuable friend might do. "We'll consider all other options first, of course. But say Amelia does make her presence known to him, at first, without us. He's not expecting her to arrive with a battalion in tow. It gives us the advantage of surprise. Amelia bargains with Fawkes, secures her sister's release, then relays a signal to us, at which time we storm the building."

"Too dangerous," Knox gruffed.

"We'd need a signal from you, Amelia," Lachlan continued lightly. "One that's sound. Completely watertight. Tavio, what have you got?"

Tavio surveyed his belt of contraptions. He fingered several before selecting a small tube-shaped piece of silver metal. This he unclasped from the belt and held up. It rattled as he moved it. At its end was a small hole below a narrowed mouthpiece. We watched as he raised the instrument to his mouth and blew into it. A high-pitched and very loud whistle pierced earsplittingly through the air, causing the men in the other distant circles to pause and look. "It can be heard across vast distances," he said. "And from within buildings."

"There's our signal," said Lachlan, looking at Knox.

Knox was silent. He was never going to like any plan that didn't involve him being chained to me with his manacles. But he had to grudgingly admit that it was the only plan that was likely to get us the results we were after, even if I was momentarily—as I would very likely be—alone with Sebastian Fawkes.

After several seconds, Knox said to Tavio, "Are you absolutely *certain* it can be heard from within closed buildings?"

"Aye," Tavio replied. "I tested it myself, in the barracks from fifty paces."

"What about upper floors or underground?" Knox questioned gruffly. "What about brick or stone as opposed to wood?"

"The barracks are constructed of stone, Knox," Tavio gently replied. "Well sealed. I was all the way up at the manor when I had Murtaugh blow it. *Behind* the manor, in fact. 'Tis a clear, far-traveling sound. It'll do the job without trouble."

"The gaming club is made of wood," I offered. "And the windows are open during the days, in summer. I think it'll be easily heard. I think this plan is a good one."

Tavio handed the whistle to me. I hung it around my neck, along with the small key to Knox's cuffs that still had not been removed by him. I looked at Knox and he was glaring at me.

I curled my fingers between his and held his hand with both my own. "You'd do it for your sisters, or your brothers," I whispered. "And you must let me do it for mine."

In his eyes I could read his anxiety, his sanction and most of all his love.

Our plan was in place.

THE HORSES WERE tied in a grassy, wooded area just out of town, and we made the last part of the journey on foot. Twenty-five Highlands warriors might get noticed, even when dispersed, and news of their presence would filter throughout the area over time. But the same number on horseback would be a trumpeted announcement throughout the city.

It was strange to walk through oily, gray streets of my city once again. The avenues and alleys felt unusually closed in. For the first time in my life, I had a sense of unease in the shadows of buildings. Already I craved the green of the trees. I'd never noticed before how dirty these alleys were, how heavily scented the air, with smoke, muck and desperation.

Knox drew me to him as we neared the club, just before we rounded the corner to its main entrance. He held me in his strong arms and he kissed me. "Amelia," he whispered.

"Aye."

"You're all right, lass." An echo to an earlier time and place. "I'm here with you and if I don't hear your signal soon, we come in after you. I won't let anything happen to you."

"Don't let anything happen to Hamish, either, I beg you. Have your men restrain him if need be. Whatever it takes."

"Aye, milady," he said. It wasn't difficult to detect his anguish, and his fear.

"I love you, Laird Mackenzie." I kissed him, but I didn't linger. It was time to find my sister. I could feel her memory now more than ever in these ancient, familiar streets. Even more so, I could feel her presence.

Letting my fingers slip through his, I walked around the corner and into the club.

After the splendor I'd become accustomed to, the blue velvet drapery and well-worn green felt of the gaming tables seemed overbright and gaudy. There was none of the subdued, tasteful wealth of the Kinloch manor.

I suppose I shouldn't have been surprised to find him there, waiting for me.

He was seated at one of the gaming tables, surrounded by a dozen men, who were well into both their game and their cups. There was a messiness to the scene that was pronounced. I'd known Sebastian Fawkes to be an intensely controlled, disciplined man. He looked different now. As though his control had frayed around the edges. His appearance was less meticulous than I remembered it, his posture looser. His hair still gleamed in the dull light, but it was longer than he'd formerly worn it, unusually disheveled. He held a glass of whiskey in one hand and his cards in the other. As soon as he saw me, he rose, and his glass tipped, spilling the contents over the pile of coins. "Amelia," he murmured.

Menace radiated from him in visceral waves.

It was a scene out of my nightmares, come to life. In my nightmares however, a very determined laird and his substantial troop of brawny warriors, all of whom were ready and waiting for my whistled signal, hadn't featured.

"You received my message?" he drawled. This looseness in him was disturbing.

"Aye. I knew you to be a tyrant, Fawkes, but to have James *killed?* You'll go to your death for this."

"I didn't kill James," he said. "James was caught at the border with his cargo. He fought the authorities and was hanged. His bad judgment caught up with him."

"You sent him."

"He was employed as a runner. He knew the risks and he chose to take them. He should have accepted prison, but he foolishly shot one of the British officers while attempting to escape. He died quickly, so I hear." Fawkes righted his glass and poured himself another drink. As he sipped, his eyes roved every inch of me. He smiled. "You look exceedingly well. Exile agrees with you, lass. You've never looked lovelier."

"Where's Cecelia? I want to see her."

He contemplated me with near-manic attachment. It seemed unlikely that my escape could have caused his apparent unraveling. Yet I suspected it had. My disregard and my refusals had wounded him in a way that seemed almost uncharacteristic of such a shady, unscrupulous man. I couldn't have known it for certain, but the looseness in him hinted at larger issues—maybe his clout had taken some other blow. This new shadow of volatility in him was even more frightening to me than his steely intimidation.

I feared his obsession, not only for myself, but for my sister. "Where is she?" I said. "Take me to her."

"Just as self-assured as always, I see." Fawkes smiled. "In that you have not changed, my dear Amelia." He paused, his eyes taking in every detail of my outfit, my windblown and healthful appearance. "You *have* changed, though. Where have you been hiding? With the heathens, I hear. Some Highlands backwater."

Aye. The most civilized place I'd ever been. "Tell me where she is."

"In a safe place."

I stepped closer to him, and his breathing caught. This gave me a degree of satisfaction, that I could affect him this way, that I could rattle him in any way whatsoever. "Where is she? Is she here? Take me to her."

His dark eyes were unsettling. A mad desire lurked there that cooled my confidence. "Seize her," he said. Several of his men jumped up, flanking me.

"Call off your thugs," I said, with an undue sense of calm. "I've come to you willingly. I will agree to your terms. All of them. On one condition."

"What condition?"

"She walks free. Immediately. Is she here in the club?"

He glanced at one of his men, then at the door, as though unsure whether to reveal the truth to me. "Aye," he finally said.

"Let her go."

"And in return?"

"I will give you whatever you ask."

"*Whatever* I ask?"

"*Anything,*" I emphasized, to which his eyes took on a glazed, hungry shine. "But you must take me to her now, and allow her to walk away at once. Never to be followed or approached or bullied ever again."

"I can agree to that, if you're exceedingly true to your word." He sipped again, draining his drink. "How true to your word do you intend to be?"

"I've already told you—anything. Your wish is my command."

He did not hesitate further. "Follow me." To his men, he said, "Allow Cecelia to take her leave when she appears. I am not to be interrupted. No matter what you hear."

This sounded distinctly ominous, and my heart leaped into a panicked beat. *Courage,* I thought, *please don't fail me now. Tavio, I hope your whistling contraption works. Hamish, be careful. Knox, I love you. Please come for me.*

I followed Fawkes up the staircase, to one of the many upper rooms that were used for night guests.

It vexed me that there were so many doors. So many places to search.

Fawkes walked to the very end of the corridor. "You took longer than we expected," he said to me, as though preparing me. "She refuses to eat."

He used a key to unlock the door. And there, curled up on the bed, was my sister. She opened her eyes and sat up when she heard us enter the room.

I hardly recognized her. She was heartbreakingly thin, her eyes like huge blue orbs in her pale, wan face. She was a shadow of the young woman who had once laughed easily and calmed all my fears. Here in her shadowed, sorrowful eyes were the ravages of all the sacrifices she'd made on my behalf. "Amelia," she gasped, her voice barely above a whisper. I walked to her and embraced her gently, afraid I might break her. "Where is he?" she sobbed. "Where is my son?" she sobbed.

"He's safe and well." *God willing.* "And so are you. I've come for you. No one can harm you now."

Her eyes searched mine imploringly. *How can you say that?* her expression conveyed. "You should not have come back," she said to me.

"What do you mean? You knew I would. As soon as I knew Hamish was safe, I came." At the mention of his name, fresh tears pooled in her eyes. I wanted to say more, to assure her that her son was not only safe but thriving—and *here*—but that was more than I could wisely reveal.

"James is dead, Amelia," she said. "He's gone."

"I know, Cecelia, I know." I held her close, comforting my thin, weeping sister as best I could. I had never wished my brother-in-law ill, not once. But secretly I wondered—nay, I *knew*—that my sister would be better off without him. His misfortune, in the end, had been beyond my control. I mourned his loss, but I did not feel guilt or regret as I looked forward to a new beginning. For all of us.

"Cecelia," I said, as steadily as I could. "I want you to walk down the stairs and out-of-doors. Can you manage it?" She nodded, but she looked so frail I feared she might not make it. "Trust me. Go now. Quickly."

"Nay, Amelia. I can't leave you."

Fawkes was growing impatient. "Do as your sister tells you, Cecelia. Take your leave while you have the opportunity. Or I'll get one of my guards to assist you."

I led Cecelia to the door. I hugged her close and whispered in her ear, "Trust me. I'm all right. Everything's all right. Please trust me. Please hurry." Then I added, even more quietly, because I knew she would listen to *this* reassurance: "Hamish is out-of-doors waiting for you. He wants to see you. Go to him now."

Fawkes closed the door behind her, locking it with his key, which he slipped into his pocket. "Now," he said. "'Tis time for you to fulfill your end of the bargain."

CHAPTER ELEVEN

I WAS HESITANT to blow the whistle until I was absolutely certain my sister was safely clear of the premises. She was frail and ill; she needed time. I could hear unusual clomping sounds from the roof and through the exterior walls, as though Knox's army not only had surrounded the building but was literally climbing its walls. I pictured Knox's sunlit silhouette as Fawkes drew closer to me, as though to somehow shield myself. *Hurry, Cecelia.* His ink-black hair. His tanned, rakish pirate's face. His lips.

Fawkes twirled a curl of my hair with his fingers, holding it to his lips. "I'll get you to tease me next time," he said softly, leaning close. "I'm keeping you all to myself. Locked away until you learn to obey and submit. I knew you'd come back to me. I knew you wanted me. Just like this." His feverish murmuring was revolting me more than it was frightening me. He was a delusional madman. I was disgusted, and infuriated. My family's hardships had begun long before this man had entered our lives, but he'd somehow managed to compound every injustice a thousandfold. The one concession I could grant him was that his actions forced me away from this hell-hole and into the arms of Knox Mackenzie. Arms I wanted to be held in *now*. Not here, by this violent, greedy reprobate. And his hands were sliding across my dress, to my breasts. He was becoming more insistent, his whispers more excited. "Just now, however, I'm not inclined to wait even a minute longer. My apologies, lass, but this will hurt just a little. Be as loud as you like. Scream all you want."

Fawkes pushed me back on the bed and laid himself over me. He thrust his knee between my thighs, groping to raise my skirts. With his other hand, he began to hastily unbutton the top of my gown. I made a sound when his thumb reached beneath my torn bodice to lightly skim my nipple. Distracted, he misinterpreted my distress.

"Aye," he murmured, squeezing my breast. "Moan for me, lass."

"I can do better than that," I said, reaching for the whistle and filling my lungs to give it the heartiest blow I had in me. The shrill signal filled the air with piercing, beautiful volume.

The response was almost instantaneous. Thumping, crashing noises erupted from outside the window and below the stairs. Fawkes froze, but his grip tightened and he slapped me across the face in a sudden realization. "What's this?" He ripped the whistle from around my neck. *Take it,* I thought. *It has served its purpose. But leave my key.* He paused to listen to the substantial commotion, which was only gaining momentum. "What *is* that?"

"You wouldn't believe me if I told you," I said. "You're about to be invaded by an army."

It all happened very quickly from there. A soldier smashed through the door, followed closely by a swarm of armed Mackenzies. "Here! She's here!" one of them bellowed. Lachlan ran into the room as Fawkes, stunned, finally began to react. Instead of drawing away, Fawkes pulled me closer, as though reading his own fate and scrambling to make the most of his last few seconds on earth. Lachlan pulled Fawkes off me at the same moment Knox burst through the door, his immense sword raised.

Damn, but the man was magnificence itself. His wrath only embellished his size and his strength. I could have sat motionless and rapt, just watching all that.

But I noticed Fawkes reaching for something, behind his back. A pistol had been tucked into an unnoticed holster at his hip. One that was now raised. And aimed.

At the doorway.

At the utterly determined small boy who struggled against Tavio's hold, wriggling, breaking free and running toward me. "Ami!" Hamish yelled, his new sword raised out in front of him, shining and eerily bright.

Time seemed to slow. Many things happened at once. I could see every one of them simultaneously and individually as though my senses were chronicling light and space with new superacuity. I screamed. Knox lunged for Hamish to block the bullet as Lachlan grabbed a handful of Hamish's tunic, pulling him back. At the same time, in an instinctive rush, I grabbed the barrel of the gun and tipped it upward, just as Fawkes pulled the trigger. The jolt of it jarred me, burning my hands. The noise was deafening.

My heart stopped.

The bullet struck. And a bell-toned note rang through the air. The bullet ricocheted off Hamish's sword, hitting the wooden floor with a small, rolling clack.

Knox pushed Hamish into Lachlan's arms and Lachlan held Hamish in a very secure grip, searching for injuries. Seeing that none were found, Knox turned and, without hesitation or ceremony, drove his sword into Sebastian Fawkes's chest, spearing him with the gargantuan steel weapon until it emerged from Fawkes's back, crimson and gruesome.

"You lived as a man without honor and now you die as one," Knox said, withdrawing the bloodstained weapon as Fawkes slumped wordlessly to the floor.

Knox fitted the weapon back into its sheath and stepped over Fawkes's lifeless form.

To Hamish he said, "You've enough courage for ten men, lad. Next we work on following orders."

Knox Mackenzie, laird of lairds, then gently scooped me into his arms. "Let's go home."

Fawkes's men were no match, especially surprised and drunken as they were, for the Mackenzie warriors. The few who fought were cut down. Most did not.

Knox carried me out-of-doors, back into the light. His men followed him.

He set me on my feet and wrapped his burly arm around my waist, pulling me against his big body. His voice lowered to a sultry growl, but his eyes were bright, and sure. "Amelia Isobel Abbott Taylor Mackenzie, you are milk and honey and innocence and lust. You're a sunny day and a moonlit night. I love you. And I now intend to make an honest woman of you once and for all."

And with that, the king of my kingdom kissed me. The kiss was fiery and passionate. Practically indecent, really. Downright *lewd,* in fact.

EPILOGUE

AS IT TURNED OUT, I *had* been carrying the heir of Kinloch, from that very first night. Nine months later, to the day, I gave birth to a son. Effie, the lead healer—one of an army of healers who attended to me, at my husband's lordish and understandably tense insistence—said it was the easiest birth she'd ever witnessed and that she'd witnessed too many to count.

Knox Mackenzie the younger has rich black hair that, in full sunlight, tints the slightest shade of red. He has jewel-blue eyes. He is strong and healthy and looks like a small replica of his noble father. His temperament, alas, skews rather more heavily toward that of his mother. He is, it must be said, rather headstrong and insists on the constant adoring attention of both his parents, which we are only too happy to give. Already, at the age of one year, the child seems to understand that he holds in his hand the key to an empire. He possesses the air of a thoughtful aristocrat: fearless, clever, spirited. With a marked trace of superiority, already; this I blame entirely on his father.

My son is happiest when we are with him, close

around him, and when he is holding his most coveted possessions: my small red notebook and his wooden sword, a gift from Hamish. He is, without a doubt, the most beautiful child I have ever seen. I admit I am somewhat biased on the subject, being his mother, but it is an oft-made comment of all who meet him.

Kinloch is a paradise. Each day I marvel at the paradise of my new home. The Highlands are a wild and stormy landscape, but here within the walls of our keep, all feels safe and lovely and untouchable. This idyll is achieved through the relentless hard work of the wider Mackenzie clan, but the work is carried out with obvious pleasure and skillful industry. My husband, as I continue to watch him and learn his ways, possesses all the best qualities of leadership. He is patient and knowledgeable and, most of all, kind. He has a moral center that grounds his clan and drives them to please him. They work with his approval in mind.

And so do I. Mostly.

I married Knox in the apple orchard. We took our vows under the tree where we'd first fallen in love, at that very first encounter, even if neither of us had admitted it to ourselves at the time. My husband has had no hesitations whatsoever, though, about confessing his love for me since then. Each day—each hour, in actual fact—he showers me with poetic litanies of his undying devotion, his rampant desire, his unequalled happiness. His romantic tendencies, already quite pronounced, have become more and more developed, so much so that I have become certain that I must be the luckiest woman who ever lived. I am regularly gifted with small treasures to remind me of his affection. This morning I woke with rose petals strewn across the fur covers of our bed. Yesterday I was delivered a bountiful breakfast with a single-stemmed thistle flower, stripped of every last thorn, and a poem. The night before, I was escorted under a full moon to our mossy terrace by the loch, where we go when the nights are quiet and warm. I was enlightened to yet another decadent detail on his secret list of lurid thoughts. It is a long and very thorough list.

My husband has yet to best me in a card game, although he continues to try with stubborn tenacity.

I have continued to teach Katriona's children, and many others, with successful results. But my husband prohibits me, as best he can, from working too hard. The work is a joy to me, even more so as I begin to teach my own son and also when I am able to spend time with Hamish, who has become a leader among his peers and a promising young soldier. Hamish has two swords now, and a hunting knife, and has taken an interest in weapons development. He has had several long discussions on the subject with Knox's brother Kade, who is somewhat of an expert, I believe.

Katriona and I have forged an amiable working relationship. She remains stoic and reserved, as I believe she must do to preserve her own sanity in the face of her substantial loss. She still pines for her husband, and I have gently prodded her to discuss his memory with me, over time. This she has become more and more willing to do, and I can see the change in her. We have forgiven each other for whatever wrongs we might have once begrudged, and have spoken of this at some length. Recently, a particular officer has made his presence known several times when I have been in her company. The map-writer Robb, who has dark hair and green eyes.

Edward has been appointed as a leading apprentice to oversee farming practices and continues his tutelage by the agricultural clan masters, who praise his intelligence and his knack for innovation. Greer excels at French and calligraphy and is still working on etiquette. Her mother has agreed to allow her to practice her drawings, which are gaining the attention of the clan artists and artisans. I sense that Katriona's attitude to her daughter's talent is changing; her disdain has largely been replaced by a quiet pride that I do my best to encourage.

My sister, Cecelia, continues to settle into her new life at Kinloch and I am grateful for her presence here. Her years of hardship are not cast off easily and she remains quiet and subdued much of the time. I see glimpses, though, of the vibrancy that dominated her character in her youth. She has spent time with the weavers and has struck up a friendship with Marin, the pretty young wife of Lachlan, and also Fionne, Marin's associate. Lately my sister has spent more and more time in their cottage workshop and has taken comfort from the bustle of activity of the clan women that gather there. Her health has returned to her over time, with sun and company and the absence of the constant stress her marriage was defined by. The fresh, plentiful food also helps, especially when delivered by a handsome, earthy, honest gardener whose name is Fyfe.

Our guests arrived late last night. I have met each member of my husband's family at least once before now, and the more I get to know each of them, the more I see in them their romantic natures. All of them possess it, this close-held philosophy that steadfastly revolves around love; it is as much an ideal they aspire to as it is a way of life.

My husband's brother Wilkie, his royal wife, Roses, their small daughter, Kenzie, and three-month-old son were escorted from their faraway home by a brigade of regal guards and greeted amid much excitement and commotion. Wilkie and Roses are striking-looking people whose bond to each other is immediately apparent. They are the sort of people that enter a room and hold the collective attention, seemingly giving off a linked aura that somehow holds the eye. What strikes me most about them is their awareness of each other. There's an anticipation in them, as though even when engaged with the wider crowd, they are already concentrating on their very next opportunity for contact.

Knox's second brother, Kade, also arrived yesterday, along with his wife, Stella, and their lively two-year-old twins, who have visited Kinloch regularly over past months. Their keep is only a day's ride from our own. I have grown close to Stella, whose soft-spoken manner is kind and comforting and quite the opposite to my own rather more unruly outlook. We are mutually fascinated by each other for our differences and have developed a sisterly bond. I am also fascinated by Kade's attention to his wife. Stella is a rare beauty, with unusual amber eyes and luminous skin. There's a vulnerability in her that I've yet to learn the intricacies of, but this timidity is offset by a sparked strength in her that is indefinable yet serves as perhaps her most engaging feature. Outwardly, Kade is the fiercest-looking of the three brothers—and in fact, of any warrior I have yet to see, with his abundant weaponry and rather abrupt manner. But each time his gaze lands on Stella, which it does often, his expression softens markedly. He becomes enchanted by the sight of her, smiling, laughing and altogether losing his pronounced ferocity. It is quite entertaining to watch. His children appear to idolize him and spend a good deal of their time vying for his attentions. He is so gentle and patient with them that the overall effect of the wild, intense first impression he gives is all but swept away.

Ailie and her new husband, Magnus Munro, are also in residence. Theirs was a long and somewhat tumultuous engagement, but they are so in love they are scarcely able to hold a conversation with anyone other than each other, which Ailie's siblings find endlessly amusing.

And a new player has recently entered the Mackenzie fray. Blake Macintosh, a topic of much discussion, has also been invited to the revelries, at the request of Christie. Knox has an inkling that another romance might be brewing. I am interested to meet Blake and learn his story. Any love interest of Christie's is bound to be intriguing.

It's time. Knox comes to me, holding my son who insists on squeezing me tight with his little cherub arms. But Knox will not allow me to carry him, considering my condition, which brings my husband equal amounts of elation and angst. I am still in the early stages of my second pregnancy, but this time I have suffered a mild case of morning sickness. I do my best to hide this from my husband; any sign of illness or distress on my part drives him almost mad with worry. He kisses me, his eyes searching mine. "I'm fine," I assure him. "More than fine, in fact. I'm happier than I've ever been and so besotted with my husband I can barely contain not only my glee but also my unbound lust."

He studies my face coolly, testing for mockery or sarcasm. Once I had perfected both of these arts, but I can unreservedly confirm that I have no need for either with him, ever. I kiss him. "I never mock my perfect husband," I whisper. "I love you with all my heart. You are the most beautiful man that has ever existed, inside and out. I cherish you every minute of the day and night. And tonight I'm going to cherish you until you weep or faint or see God, or possibly all three."

His slow smile breaks my heart. "I look forward to it." He kisses me tenderly but he says, "They wait for us below."

We have gathered here at Kinloch to celebrate our son's first birthday, the marriage of Magnus and Ailie, which took place privately at the Munro keep, and the birth of Wilkie and Rose's second child, whose name is William. We make our way belowstairs to the grand hall, which is as immaculately prepared as ever and full of the lively conversation of our extended family.

I have met Wilkie and Roses before, but I am struck again by Wilkie's resemblance to his oldest brother, although his manner is more carefree and verbose than Knox's. His hair is longer than my husband's and his garb more colorful; he wears the Stuart clan dark red tartan sash over a Mackenzie-tartaned kilt.

My husband's family appears amused by a change in him.

"I hardly recognize my elder brother without his stern glower," Wilkie teases him, but kindly.

Ailie smiles. "He laughs all the time now. And yesterday, I actually heard him whistling."

"Amelia, we have much to thank you for," says

Kade. "You have done a great service to the entire Mackenzie clan, near and far, by taking him on."

"Aye," agrees Wilkie, "'tis a brave lass indeed that would dare to tame such superiority."

"It hasn't been easy, I can assure you of that," I tease my husband, who smiles at me.

Kade's tone softens. He looks down at Stella, who is seated close to him. "We have some news to share." He leans to give his wife a rather scorching kiss on the lips, which makes her blush. To his assembled family, he says, "We're expecting another baby in the summer."

Knox stands, raising his glass. "That's good news, brother. Congratulations to you both." After a small pause, he says, "We also have news to share." And with a distinct shine in his eyes, he looks at me with more devotion than I had ever thought humanly possible; it warms me and fulfills me. "We are also expecting another baby in the summer."

After more congratulations have been exchanged, the focus of the assembly shifts to another figure, who stands behind Christie, somewhat removed from the gathering. He is tall, possessing what could be described as a lazy yet graceful athleticism, as though he is supremely comfortable in his own skin. This is understandable. His appearance is forcefully beautiful, in a much different way than that of the Mackenzies. His is a golden beauty. His hair is dark blond and reminds one of ancient treasure, glinting and gilded in the firelight. He leans against the stone wall with his thumb insouciantly hitched under his leather belt in a posture that suggests an unscrupulous nature.

This must be the famed Blake Macintosh, who has been the subject of much whispered attention in recent days. I know very little about him. I've heard fragments of various rumors to indicate that there has been some infighting among Clan Macintosh, regarding eligibility and suitability for the lairdship of the clan, but I do not know many details. I've overheard that both Blake and his half brother Thane, the man who visited the Mackenzie keep one night long ago, are in the running. I will make a point of asking Knox about it, and about Blake himself. He is an intriguing figure, with his golden, sparked, cavalier charm.

"Your Mackenzie clan is expanding at a prodigious rate," he says casually, and his glance slides to Christie. I cannot help noticing she looks somewhat upset, and nervous. This is highly uncharacteristic of my lively sister-in-law, whose outlook is unwavering in its sprightliness and vivacity. "'Tis a veritable bounty of fertility," Blake comments.

All eyes are on him and he does not shy away from the collective attention. I suspect he is used to attention, looking as he does, like a fallen angel up to no good. There is a pronounced thread of mischief in him, but a compelling one, as though whatever mischief he might be involved in would be highly engaging, irresistible even, and all because he was its instigator.

Blake Macintosh is working the silence, using it for effect. He is about to say something we all want to hear. We can sense this and we are riveted. He does not disappoint. "I'm pleased to say," he drawls, "that I have also made my contribution, as it were. And I would like to use this opportunity to humbly—and quite necessarily—ask for Christie's hand. We, too, you see, are expecting a baby in the summer."

The family gasps and erupts into chatter, but I feel the warmth of eyes upon me and turn to see who it is....

None other than Knox Mackenzie.

* * * * *

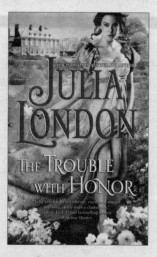

New York Times and *USA TODAY* bestselling author

LUCY KEVIN

brings you three stories about women who never expected to find their own "happily ever after" in this 3-in-1 collection.

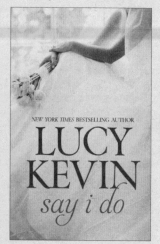

Working at The Rose Chalet—a gorgeous wedding venue set amid lush gardens overlooking the San Francisco Bay—is a dream. But while these three women are experts at putting together the perfect wedding, their own love lives are in the weeds. Dive into three fun, sweet and undeniably dreamy stories about women who get swept off their feet when they least expect it!

Available wherever books are sold!

Be sure to connect with us at:

Harlequin.com/Newsletters
Facebook.com/HarlequinBooks
Twitter.com/HarlequinBooks

www.Harlequin.com

PHLK901

REQUEST YOUR FREE BOOKS!

HARLEQUIN® HISTORICAL:
Where love is timeless

2 FREE NOVELS PLUS 2 **FREE GIFTS!**

YES! Please send me 2 FREE Harlequin® Historical novels and my 2 FREE gifts (gifts are worth about $10). After receiving them, if I don't wish to receive any more books, I can return the shipping statement marked "cancel." If I don't cancel, I will receive 6 brand-new novels every month and be billed just $5.44 per book in the U.S. or $5.74 per book in Canada. That's a savings of at least 16% off the cover price! It's quite a bargain! Shipping and handling is just 50¢ per book in the U.S. and 75¢ per book in Canada.* I understand that accepting the 2 free books and gifts places me under no obligation to buy anything. I can always return a shipment and cancel at any time. Even if I never buy another book, the two free books and gifts are mine to keep forever.

246/349 HDN F4ZY

Name	(PLEASE PRINT)

Address	Apt. #

City	State/Prov.	Zip/Postal Code

Signature (if under 18, a parent or guardian must sign)

Mail to the **Harlequin® Reader Service:**
IN U.S.A.: P.O. Box 1867, Buffalo, NY 14240-1867
IN CANADA: P.O. Box 609, Fort Erie, Ontario L2A 5X3

Want to try two free books from another line?
Call 1-800-873-8635 or visit www.ReaderService.com.

* Terms and prices subject to change without notice. Prices do not include applicable taxes. Sales tax applicable in N.Y. Canadian residents will be charged applicable taxes. Offer not valid in Quebec. This offer is limited to one order per household. Not valid for current subscribers to Harlequin Historical books. All orders subject to credit approval. Credit or debit balances in a customer's account(s) may be offset by any other outstanding balance owed by or to the customer. Please allow 4 to 6 weeks for delivery. Offer available while quantities last.

Your Privacy—The Harlequin® Reader Service is committed to protecting your privacy. Our Privacy Policy is available online at www.ReaderService.com or upon request from the Harlequin Reader Service.

We make a portion of our mailing list available to reputable third parties that offer products we believe may interest you. If you prefer that we not exchange your name with third parties, or if you wish to clarify or modify your communication preferences, please visit us at www.ReaderService.com/consumerschoice or write to us at Harlequin Reader Service Preference Service, P.O. Box 9062, Buffalo, NY 14269. Include your complete name and address.

HHI3R